Temptation
ISLAND

=== MURDER IN PARADISE SERIES ===

Temptation ISLAND

=== MURDER IN PARADISE SERIES ===

RACHEL WOODS

BONZAI
MOON

BonzaiMoon Books LLC
Houston, Texas
www.bonzaimoonbooks.com

Editing by Kelly Hartigan of Xterra Web
http://editing.xterraweb.com

Book cover designed by Deranged Doctor Design
http://www.derangeddoctordesign.com

ISBN 978-1-943685-05-9 (Print)

Thank you God for giving me creative ideas and the ability to write. Thank you to my family --- my extraordinary sister and my favorite mother!

Prologue

"Don't you wanna have some more fun, baby?" Henri asked.

My panic mutating into anger, I used the heel of my right foot to kick him in the shin. Yelping, Henri stumbled back. Encouraged by his pain, I turned, intent on kicking him in the balls, but he must have guessed what I had planned for him, because he slapped me—hard.

Crying out in pain and shock, I lurched away from him toward the galley kitchen. Frantic, I looked over my shoulder. Henri was walking toward me. Whipping my head back toward the kitchen, I scanned the area, looking for some sort of weapon.

There, in a plastic dish rack, I saw what I needed.

A large butcher's knife.

Without thinking, I rushed toward the sink, grabbed the knife, and turned.

An open hand cracked across my face so hard I saw lights popping and feared my jaw had been dislocated. Crying out, I stumbled back, the knife dropping from my grasp and clattering across the stained, sticky linoleum tile. Feeling nauseated from the sloshing in my head, I dropped to one knee, struggling to get my bearings.

"Get up, bitch!" Henri grabbed my arm and pulled me to my feet.

"Let go of me!" I screamed, trying to yank away from him.

"Shut up!" he said, and his hand came toward my face again, quick as a cobra's strike. I felt the stinging blow of his fist near my left temple. Desperate not to lose consciousness, I struggled to keep my eyes open as darkness converged, but it was no use.

The blackness pulled me into its boundless depths.

DAY ONE

Chapter One

Someone was trying to kill me.

They had already tried before—two times.

The first attempt had occurred following a break during a tense settlement negotiation. My clients, Kastor-Jones Pharmaceuticals were being sued for wrongful death, accused of paying kickbacks to doctors for aggressively promoting a top-selling prescription drug which they allegedly knew had fatal side effects. I had been going head to head with the plaintiff's attorney and was finally wearing him down from the multi-million-dollar settlement they were requesting. The pharmaceutical executives were pleased with my efforts, and as I washed my hands in the ladies' room, I thought I was sure I could get the plaintiffs to accept a settlement the company was more willing to pay.

A stall opened and through the mirror, I saw a woman step out. Dressed in black from head to tie, she wore an ironic smile and held a gun.

Shocked, I faced her, raising my dripping hands, ready to tell her she could have my purse, my cell phone, and whatever she wanted, and ready to beg for my life. Before I could open my mouth, a gunshot, as loud as a bomb in the small, tiled restroom, exploded. Seconds later, I felt something hit my chest and didn't need to look down to know I'd been shot.

I hadn't been killed, though. A janitor had come to my rescue, an ambulance had been called, and I was whisked away to the hospital where I underwent surgery to remove the bullet.

A month later, they'd made a second attempt, ambushing me in the parking garage connected to the office building where I worked. I'd been wrestling with a summary judgment motion all day. Close to midnight, I finally decided to leave work. My heels echoing on the concrete, I headed toward my car. Not paying attention, a purse on my shoulder, carrying a laptop bag, and staring at my cell phone, I scrolled through my contacts, looking for the phone number of an expert I wanted to testify on my client's behalf.

In the car, I turned the ignition and—

An eruption of glass exploded behind me, sending chunks and shards flying as white-hot pain seared into the back of my left shoulder. Screaming in shock, I caught an image of something in the rearview mirror and looked behind me. Pressing my hand against my throbbing shoulder, I saw someone standing a few feet from the trunk of my car.

A woman dressed in black, pointing a gun at me. The same woman who'd tried to kill me before.

Two more bullets had me scrambling to hide beneath the steering wheel. Another bullet slammed into the gear stick. One hit the sun visor on the passenger's side. The fifth bullet smashed into the center console. Terrified, I struggled to breathe.

Faintly, I heard sirens and then footsteps running away from the car. The cops had been alerted by the building security, and as the police officers questioned me, the paramedics tended to my injury. A flesh wound, the EMS worker told me. I'd been lucky. The bullet had only grazed my shoulder.

Hours later, lying in bed, still shell-shocked and unable to sleep, I tried to think of who might want me dead, and I wondered why they hadn't been able to kill me yet. Their first and second attempts to end my life had failed.

Hopefully, the third time would be the charm.

Because, honestly, I deserved to die for what I had done.

Exhaling, I squared my shoulders, shook the macabre thoughts away, and forced myself to focus on the task at hand, which wasn't as daunting as it was disappointing. Presently, I was in a courtroom, giving closing testimony to twelve jurors charged with the laborious task of weighing scientific evidence against compassion and sympathy for the plaintiffs, a group of seven individuals who had accused my client, Du Vert Industries, a billion-dollar pharmaceutical conglomerate, of committing consumer fraud by deceiving doctors about the health risks of a popular anti-depressant.

Standing before the jury box in my conservative yet classic navy Chanel suit and matching ballerina flats, with my hair pulled back in a smooth, neat bun, and wearing reading glasses I didn't really need, I implored the jury to reject the plaintiffs' claims of negligence and find in favor of my client.

"Ladies and gentlemen, the plaintiffs bear the burden of proof, and after weighing the evidence, if you cannot decide that something is more likely to be true than not true, you must conclude that the plaintiffs did not prove their claims against my client," I said. "You have a choice to examine and evaluate the scientific evidence, and I am confident that you are intelligent enough and capable enough to do so despite the enormous amount of scientific evidence presented to you throughout this trial. Ladies and gentlemen, it may be difficult to find against the plaintiffs, but your oath as jurors is not to be swayed by sympathy but to logically and rationally evaluate the evidence and come to the reasonable conclusion that my client, Du Vert Pharmaceuticals, should prevail in this cause of action. Ladies and gentlemen, I thank you once again very much for your time and your service."

Walking back to the defense table, I stopped in my tracks, paralyzed, horrified.

A woman dressed in black stood at the back of the courtroom, smiling, pointing a gun at me.

I opened my mouth to scream.

The bullet hit me in the chest.

Chaos broke out in the courtroom. Chairs overturned as my

support team and the opposing counsel jumped to their feet. The judge banged his gavel, but order would not be restored.

Dropping to the ground, I looked past the Du Vert executives, shocked, realizing I knew the woman with the smoking gun. The bitch who had shot me was—

"Miss, are you okay?"

Dizzy and disoriented, I blinked a few times, trying to remember where I was, trying to open my eyes. It took me a minute to realize someone was asking me a question and then another minute to respond. "Huh?"

"You were asleep, but then you screamed," said the woman, a slim, gorgeous *Sports Illustrated* babe. "I think maybe you had a nightmare."

"A nightmare," I whispered, groggy and confused.

"Want me to call the flight attendant?" the woman asked. "She could bring you some water."

"Oh, no, thank you," I said, embarrassed, slowly becoming aware of the attention from my fellow first-class passengers. Beneath their worry and concern, I noted traces of suspicion, imperceptible frowns, and slight narrowing of the eyes, non-verbal clues indicating doubt. Maybe. Maybe not. I wasn't quite sure.

Unbuckling my seat belt, I stood and made my way down the narrow aisle to the first-class lavatory.

In the tight, cramped space, I splashed cold water on my face, staring at my reflection. Surprisingly, I didn't look like a stark raving lunatic. Despite having just escaped a nightmare, I looked pretty good. I could be beautiful, when the situation called for it, but usually I was just pretty with dark brown hair styled in a sassy Tinker Bell pixie cut, delicate features, a heart-shaped face, and expressive eyes. People sometimes claimed I had a sultry sweetness. Or, was it a sweet sultriness.

Moments later, struggling to shift to a more comfortable position in the plush, leather first-class seat, I tried not to dwell on the nightmare I'd had, but I was worried. I was flying to paradise, the island of St. Mateo, specifically, which was supposed to be the cure for my paralyzing anxiety, so I couldn't understand why I'd had another nightmare.

The anxiety dream hadn't been invited to my tropical getaway. Why had it invaded my subconscious?

Sighing, I replayed the dream, trying to make sense of it, which would probably be a pointless endeavor.

Being shot to death during closing arguments was actually one of the many nightmares I'd been plagued by for the past five months. There was another one in which I exited the courtroom, triumphant and arrogant, having scored a victory for my client, a powerful pharmaceutical company, and was promptly shot by a woman in black. Despite being hit in the chest, the bullet didn't kill me. In my hospital bed, I stared at the morning news headlines on my iPad, one of which read, "*ATTORNEY SHOT IN COURTHOUSE EXPECTED TO RECOVER.*" And then, inexplicably, I was transported into the point of view of the woman who shot me, who was also reading the newspaper, pissed because she hadn't killed me, and thinking, *The bitch is still alive.*

The nightmares had become more prevalent and potent, robbing me of the ability to relax and disturbing my sleep. Though reoccurring, the dreams weren't exactly repetitive, but during my struggle to interpret the dreams, I realized they featured two disturbing similarities.

The lawyer who was shot in the dream was always me, Harlequin Miller, Esquire, senior associate at Ellison, Zupancic, and Cox, LLC, a premier full-service defense firm with offices around the globe, founded more than a century ago, focused on complex commercial litigation.

And the shooter was always me.

I'd been having anxiety dreams about killing myself. I should have been able to figure out the meaning of, and reasons for, my disturbing nightmares. What made me a hotshot litigation superstar— deductive reasoning and strategic thinking—was no match for these crazy dreams. Besides, my legal super skills actually weren't as effective as they had once been.

All the weapons in my arsenal were misfiring lately. My complex problem-solving skills, logical decision making, and discriminating judgment were also on the fritz. Everything that had made me the envy of the law firm was failing me for some reason I couldn't seem to figure out.

The plane shook. Worried, I clutched the armrests. Usually, I wasn't a nervous flyer, but just in case, I grabbed the seatbelt, trying to fasten it with trembling fingers. Shit. Why couldn't I fasten the seatbelt? What the hell had happened to my hand-eye coordination and fine motor skills? I needed to calm down, but I couldn't. Not only was I still dwelling on my nightmare, but now I was thinking about the so-called cure for my anxiousness, worrying about what would happen when I got to the island of St. Mateo.

Once the plane touched down, my fabulous fantasy getaway would begin, according to the letter I'd received from the hotel where I would be staying.

It had arrived yesterday afternoon while I was in the middle of my large hexagonal walk-in closet, surrounded by a sea of clothes, furiously trying to pull together a decent wardrobe for my trip to paradise.

Made of sheepskin, the envelope was pale aqua with an embossed heliconia flower on the front and sealed with an iridescent wax stamp. Inside, words in fancy, flowing calligraphy outlined what was in store for me, with enough detail to get me excited and a fair amount of mystery to leave me breathless with anticipation.

Thinking about the letter, tucked away in the Chanel bag under my seat, I was both jittery and terrified. But mostly terrified. Maybe this fantasy trip would end up being a huge mistake. I couldn't help but think of the old television show, *Fantasy Island*, where the guests would fly to a secluded island to have their wishes come true. But in the end, those fantasies sometimes became nightmares. Or, maybe not always nightmares, but definitely not what they'd thought they desired.

Still, part of me thought a fabulous, relaxing getaway might be just what I needed, a grand plan to get rid of my anxiety so I could get my mojo back. Said mojo being the most important weapons in my legal arsenal—critical thinking skills, discernment, deduction, and sound decision making.

Technically, a trip to paradise wasn't my idea. It had actually been orchestrated by my best friend, Lisa, who began designing it after I'd told her I couldn't sleep because I'd been having disturbing dreams about shooting myself for the past six months.

"Dreams are a way of dealing with problems or identifying problems that may need to be addressed," Lisa said.

Lisa was a therapist. A shrink. A neuropsychologist, actually. In her practice, she often encouraged patients to journal their dreams as a way to identify issues and concerns. So, she knew what the hell she was talking about. She wasn't giving me advice from a dream dictionary she'd picked up from the bargain book bin at Barnes & Noble.

"When did the dreams start?" Lisa asked, as we lounged on chaises by the pool in her backyard and sipped mojitos, basking in the warm sunshine on a lazy late afternoon in May.

"About five, maybe six, months ago."

"And what was going on in your life?"

"Nothing bad," I said. "Certainly nothing that would have given me anxiety."

Things had been going great six months ago, which was why the dreams made no sense.

"Well, if you want to skip the self-reflection and self-examination," said Lisa, in her "therapist" voice, a slightly condescending, dulcet tone, totally devoid of her urban twang, "then I could prescribe something for you."

"Something to stop the nightmares?" I asked, skeptical.

"Girl, please." Lisa dropped the "therapist" tone. "Something to put your ass to sleep so you can get some rest."

But, I didn't want any pills, especially any anti-anxiety medication. I knew all too well about the scary, adverse effects of mood-altering drugs. Didn't need my mind cluttered with rainbow-colored unicorns and psychotic thoughts. I'd made enough bad decisions.

"What are you anxious about?"

Shrugging, I said, "I don't know. Lots of things, I guess. Nothing really specific, I don't think."

"Anxiety is sometimes a tertiary emotion," Lisa said.

Lowering my sunglasses, I glanced at her. "A tertiary emotion?"

"It's an emotion that results from the primary emotion, which often hides behind the tertiary emotion, because often, the primary emotion is too difficult and painful to deal with," Lisa explained. "Once the primary emotion is exposed, it has to be validated and addressed. The tertiary emotion is usually easier to deal with, often with medication. But, the primary emotion may require psychoanalysis or more intense therapy, and most people are averse to that."

"So, my anxiety is hiding behind some primary emotion," I said, not sure I was on board with Lisa's theories, which were beginning to sound a bit like psychobabble.

"The primary emotion is probably fear," Lisa said, with an authoritative finality I found annoying and worrisome.

"Fear?"

"Fear can cause anxiety," Lisa said. "So, the question to ask yourself is, what are you afraid of?"

Lisa's question bothered me, and the defense attorney in me wanted to object. *Assumes facts not in evidence.* There was no proof my anxiety was based in fear. I suspected Lisa was right, though.

"Anxiety dreams are usually symbolic of some issue," Lisa went on.

"So, I'm not really suicidal?" I asked. "Even though, in all of the dreams, I end up shooting myself?"

"You might want to kill something that you don't like about yourself," Lisa deduced. "That's probably why you never die in the dream."

I sat up and stared at her. "But which part of myself do I want to kill?"

"Maybe a personality trait, or a certain belief," Lisa said. "Could be an attitude you secretly want to rid yourself of because you think it's holding you back or keeping you from recovering from something."

"Recovering from what?" I asked, my gaze drifting to the pool, where sunlight glinted on the surface like shimmering sparks.

Recovery implied that something had been damaged, broken, destroyed. Recovery implied some type of trauma had been sustained, either emotional or physical. But I wasn't broken or traumatized. Or maybe I was. Possibly. Or maybe not.

"You know what I think you need?" Lisa poured herself another glass of sangria from the pitcher on the little glass bistro table between our lounge chairs.

"No, but I'm sure you'll tell me."

"A good vacation."

"You think so?" I asked, not convinced.

Lisa was adamant, however, and according to my best friend, the best way to deal with my anxiety was to indulge in a nice, opulent solo vacation. And while on vacation, I needed to have sex.

"How is having sex going to help me get over this anxiety?"

"Dirty, mind-blowing sex with multiple nonstop orgasms is the best way to release tension and stop the anxiety dreams."

"Multiple nonstop orgasms? Not interested."

"And there is only one place where it can happen," she continued, again as though she was not listening to me. "There's only one place you can go."

"And where, pray tell, is that?" I asked, already feeling a bit worried by that mischievous gleam in her dark brown eyes. "Kalamazoo, Michigan? Djibouti, Africa?"

"St. Mateo."

Ah, St. Mateo. That was going to be my third guess. That wasn't true, though. I didn't even know where St. Mateo was. I'd never even heard of St. Mateo. But, after Lisa declared St. Mateo as *the* place to go for wild, mind-blowing sex, she began flooding my email inbox with all sorts of links to travel websites about the place. Eventually, I caved and did research on the island to get the basics. The Internet provided lots of glossy photos of a sun-splashed paradise with white sand beaches, tall, swaying palm trees, and clear turquoise water.

St. Mateo was part of the Leeward chain, about ten miles south-west of Montserrat, and with its four sister islands, St. Felipe, St. Cera, St. Basil, and St. Kilian, it formed what was called the Palmchat Islands. The island quintet was known for its breathtaking natural beauty and diverse culture, but the most interesting articles were about the fact that each island had its own separate and unique personality.

St. Mateo was the hedonistic party island, St. Felipe was the prettiest but poorest island with the least tourists, St. Cera was the island of saints, where lots of missionary work was done, St. Basil was the place to go for a quick, painless divorce, and St. Kilian was the place for lively nightlife.

A few days later while we were having lunch, enjoying grilled lobster tails and drinking too many screwdrivers, I told Lisa I was thinking of booking a suite at the Hibiscus Resort and Spa, the most exclusive hotel in St. Mateo.

"No, you can't do that," Lisa said.

"Why can't I go to the Hibiscus Resort and Spa?"

"Because you have to go to the Heliconia Hotel," she said.

"The Heliconia Hotel?"

Her smile sly, Lisa said, "It's the place where all of your fantasies will come true."

All of my fantasies? Each and every one of them? I'd wanted to scoff and toss her some sarcastic quip about how that was a tall order, one I didn't think some island hotel could fulfill, but the hint of mischief in her eyes intrigued me, made me want to know more about this Heliconia Hotel.

Later, despite my vodka-and-grapefruit-juice headache, I Googled the Heliconia Hotel, but nothing came up except informational links about the heliconia flower and about a bazillion links to various and sundry hotels. There were no hits for Heliconia Hotel.

"You won't find anything about this hotel on the Internet," Lisa said, being vague and mysterious when I called her the next morning. "They don't have a website. And they're not on Facebook, Twitter, Instagram, or Snapchat."

"What the heck kind of hotel doesn't have a website?" I'd asked, pissed by her evasiveness. "You know what, never mind. It doesn't matter. I don't even care because I'm not going."

"But you have to go," she insisted, as though the fate of the world depended on it. "You need some sexual healing to get rid of that anxiety."

"I don't have time for sex," I insisted, slightly less intense.

"I shouldn't tell you this," Lisa said, voice lowered. "But, last year, one of my patients, a high-powered female CEO, was desperate to get over a devastating divorce, and she told me that a friend of hers suggested that she take a sabbatical to recharge and refresh her mind, body, spirit, and soul."

"What does that have to do with anything?"

"Well, she was able to make peace with the divorce by getting in touch with her chi and her inner whatever the hell. But, she got more out of it than just deep contemplative mediation."

"Okay," I said, wishing Lisa would get on with it.

"She also got some damn good sex during her sabbatical," Lisa said, her voice low and conspiratorial. "Specifically, some damn good sex at the Heliconia Hotel."

"Wait, wait, wait," I stopped Lisa, holding up a hand. "The Heliconia is a sex hotel? You want me to get rid of my anxiety by going to a sex hotel?"

"It's not a sex hotel," Lisa chided. "It's a hotel where all your fantasies come true and fantasies usually involve sex, so—"

"Are you out of your mind?" I asked. "I am not going to a sex hotel."

"Will you just think about going?" Lisa asked. "From what my patient told me, you don't have to have sex, it's only an option. They also have lots of sensual pleasures that don't involve intercourse. The point is, you'll be pampered and catered to, and I think it will really help with your anxiety."

Sighing, I shook my head. "I don't know."

"Listen," Lisa said. "If you decide to go, I'll book everything for you, even the plane flight. All you'll have to do is fly to St. Mateo and get on with getting your mojo back."

Lisa had fulfilled her promise. She'd booked the entire trip— moments after I'd capitulated and agreed to go to the Heliconia to have all my fantasies come true. I wasn't so sure I could fulfill my end of our bargain. I was starting to think I should get off the plane, go to the reservations desk, and book an immediate departure flight back home.

Except I didn't really want to, and I suspected I knew why I was reluctant to go back home. *So, the question to ask yourself is, what are you afraid of?* The answer was simple though hard to admit. My career was in shambles, which was both an overestimation and an over simplification of the issue with my current employment. Suffice it to say, anyway I looked at it, and I had looked at it from all conceivable angles, things were not looking up for me at the firm.

Not anymore, anyway.

I'd gone from the top of the heap to the bottom of the pile in less than six months. After losing my last three cases, I'd suffered a long, heart-stopping fall to a hard, unforgiving landing. The most recent case I'd botched would be appealed, and I'd hoped to have the chance to redeem myself. I was desperate to convince the firm's founders, senior partners, and, most importantly, the partner steering committee responsible for recommending senior associates for partnership in the firm that they hadn't been wrong about me. I wasn't a fluke or a one-trick pony or a flash in the pan, which was what my colleagues said about me behind my back.

I could still be the rainmaking litigation superstar they expected me to be. I needed to prove I could be trusted to litigate for my clients and secure unimpeachable verdicts in their favor. Most of all, I had to get back on the track to partnership. At twenty-seven years old, I had been on the fast track to becoming the firm's youngest partner before being derailed by crucial verdicts against the clients I'd represented in three separate causes of action.

Last month, however, I'd been informed that the client had refused my continued representation of their company. Thus I would not be working on the appeal, which, thanks to my faulty decision making and negligent strategy, would most likely be eschewed in favor of secret settlement negotiations.

Three strikes and I appeared to be on the way out, much to the delight of a few fellow employees who'd joined the firm when I did but were still languishing at the junior associate level. Rumor was they were taking bets on how long I would last, though none of them were shedding any tears for me.

They figured I would end up back on my feet, walking right into a plum job at A.B. Miller & Associates, P.C., the premier powerhouse personal injury firm founded by my grandfather, Absalom Bartholomew "A.B." Miller, and currently managed by my dad, Absalom Bartholomew "A.B." Miller, Jr. However, the last thing I wanted was to be bailed out by my father. I didn't want to end up in a cushy corner office at my grandfather's firm trying to ignore the whispers of nepotism and wondering if people were only being nice to me because I was the boss's daughter.

After I passed the bar, Dad had been disappointed when I'd announced I was taking a position with Ellison, Zupancic, and Cox, LLC. My father had predicted I wouldn't last long at a firm specializing in "defending evil, greedy drug dealers" and prayed I would escape without having to sell my soul.

"Quinn, good lawyers don't belong at bad firms," Dad had said after I'd told him about the last case I'd screwed up, something he'd been telling me for the past five years. "Ellison, Zupancic, and Cox are the evil dead. Eventually, those vampires will demand blood, and once they've sucked the life from you, they'll leave your rotting corpse for the vultures."

Despite my dad's penchant for melodrama, he was sympathetic about my current professional dilemma. Though, I suspected he secretly hoped I would get fired. Then I would be free to work for him, which was what he'd assumed I would do upon my graduation from law school. I'd been able to resist my dad's wishes and had gone against his carefully constructed plans for my legal career. I wanted to control my own destiny and chart my own course.

For a while, it had been smooth sailing. Five years of spectacular, stunning victories, and then, six months ago, the first setback. A verdict against my client. The wrong expert had derailed the case. A month later, I didn't pick the right jury and lost again. Last month, I didn't employ the correct legal strategy. With my logical reasoning skills failing me, I made bad decisions, multi-million-dollar mistakes which could very well cost me the career I worked so hard to achieve. Pragmatism, intelligence, keen discernment, critical thinking, and rational judgment had guided me through all sorts of legal quagmires, successfully, efficiently and productively. With the recent failure of these skills, I felt unmoored and adrift in unfamiliar waters.

I had to get my career back on track, but I wasn't sure how. I wasn't sure I trusted myself to make logical, sound decisions. Case in point, the trip to paradise for no-strings sex. What the hell was I thinking? Did I really believe engaging in wanton escapades could get rid of my anxiety? How could that possibly make sense? The attorney in me wanted to argue it wasn't practical or rational, but the attorney in me had recently lost three cases, so what the hell did the attorney in me know?

The attorney in me could no longer be counted on to make the right decisions, I reminded myself.

As the plane glided over another air pocket, I grabbed my purse, opened it, and took out the envelope I'd received from the hotel. Removing the letter, I unfolded the fine, smooth paper and skimmed the words, focusing on the phrases that inspired trepidation and excitement.

Your fantasy awaits and will begin as soon as you arrive.

My gaze traveled to the second paragraph, below the welcome and introductory salutations.

We are delighted that you have chosen our deluxe luxury fantasy experience, which is the story of a woman, undervalued and unappreciated, who embarks on a journey to paradise and—

"Feeling better?" the supermodel lookalike asked, her gaze sympathetic.

"Hmmm? Oh, yes, I am," I answered, putting the letter away. "I'm fine now."

"Which island are you going to?"

"St. Mateo. What about you?"

"I'm taking a hopper to St. Marco," she said and then added, "Quickie divorce."

"Oh," I said, not sure how to respond, with sympathy or congratulations, because from her passive stare, I couldn't really tell if she was upset about the dissolution of her marriage or not.

"Well, hopefully, you'll have a better time than I will," she said. "I've heard St. Mateo is really fun."

"Hopefully," I agreed, though I wasn't convinced paradise could help me get my mojo back. I had to get over the crazy nightmares, relax, and restart my career. I had to become, once again, the smart, savvy, superstar litigator. Once my sabbatical was over, I had to go back to work, start winning cases, and then make partner.

If I couldn't, then my career was over and so was my life.

Chapter Two

As the United Airlines 757 floated over the island archipelago, I looked out the window, spellbound as the island came into view, gazing at the verdant tropical rainforest, ringed by brilliant, shimmering turquoise waters.

The plane banked left as the captain announced the beginning of our initial descent into the St. Mateo International Airport. Ten minutes later, we landed. After grabbing my purse and Louis Vuitton carry-on from the overhead bin, I followed my fellow passengers down the narrow aisle and eventually stepped over the threshold of the opened cabin door.

It was a gorgeous day in paradise. The sun was shining, the palm fronds were swaying lazily, and the breeze wafting across my flushed skin smelled slightly floral.

Stepping out onto a set of metal stairs, I walked down the steps to the tarmac. Heat rose from the concrete as I headed into the airport terminal, a low, squat, one-story building surrounded by towering palm trees.

Inside the airport, the mood was lively and festive, like a mini carnival. Making my way through security and then customs, I passed several groups of old men sitting on overturned crates. Some played steel drums, others beat bongos, and another quartet shook maracas and sang a rousing chorus of a salsa-inspired version of "The Girl From Ipanema." Despite my nervous trepidation, I found myself entranced by the festive island mood and swaying to the lively rhythms.

At the luggage carousel, I scanned the bags circling the conveyor belt for my suitcase. Minutes later, I realized there was no more luggage on the carousel, and the other passengers who'd been waiting with me had gotten their bags and dispersed.

Where the hell was my luggage, I wondered, my blood pressure spiking. Had it been stolen? Or, had the airline lost it? Maybe put it on a plane to St. Maarten instead of the plane to—

"Ms. Miller?" said a voice behind me, very deep and slightly gruff, the island accent prevalent.

Turning, I stared up into a pair of dreamy brown eyes, as potent as whiskey. The rest of the man was dreamy as well. He was tall, broad, and muscular in his chauffeur's uniform. And he was heartbreakingly handsome with a strong, square jaw, full lips, and a Roman nose. A ripple of excitement fluttered through parts of my body that hadn't fluttered in years as I remembered the letter from the hotel I'd read on the plane.

Your fantasy awaits and will begin as soon as you arrive.

"My name is Icarus."

"Icarus ..." I repeated, my voice a breathy whisper. The name was intriguing, and yet I was wary. In Greek mythology, Icarus was the boy who flew too close to the sun. His tale was cautionary, a warning against being too prideful or arrogantly trusting in your own abilities. Somehow, a handsome driver named Icarus seemed a bit too much like a harbinger of grim tidings.

Maybe I was making too much of things. Sometimes, a guy named Icarus was just a guy named Icarus. Maybe his mother thought the name was cool. Or, most likely, Icarus wasn't even his real name. The Heliconia Hotel was all about fantasy, I reminded myself. Mysterious aliases were probably *de rigueur*.

"On behalf of the Heliconia Hotel," he said, giving me a dazzling smile, "welcome to St. Mateo."

"Thank you. But, um, my bags," I said, remembering my missing luggage. "I think maybe—"

"I have your bags in the car."

"Oh, thank God," I said, relieved. "I thought they'd been stolen."

Icarus gave me a reassuring gaze. "This way," he said, placing a hand on my back and guiding me, gently but firmly, out of the airport and toward a limo parked at the curb. My heart slammed as we walked toward the car, and I couldn't help but feel self-conscious. Maybe I was paranoid, but I imagined the throng of tourists, milling about, waiting for taxis and shuttle buses, was watching me. I couldn't help thinking that they knew, somehow, I was one of those sex-starved, neglected women headed to the Heliconia to have her brains boffed out by a bunch of buff Island guys.

After opening the door and helping me inside the limo, Icarus got in behind me and closed the door.

Startled, and suddenly claustrophobic, I scooted across the bench seat. Trying my best to bury myself in the crook between the rear seat and the side sofa that ran the length of the limo, I noticed a bouquet of gorgeous red roses, a bucket of champagne on ice, and a crystal bowl piled high with fresh fruit cut in the shape of flowers. Nice but a little kitschy, although not entirely cheesy—the fruit hadn't been dipped in chocolate, thank goodness.

"So, here on the island of St. Mateo, much of our economy is dependent upon the crops we grow and sell to neighboring islands and a few countries in Europe," Icarus said. "Our island is known for its fruit, which is sweet and succulent, because of the intense concentration of minerals in the volcanic soil high in the mountains."

I nodded, not sure what to say.

"Would you like to try some mango or pineapple?" he asked, leaning a little too close, but he smelled good, a faint, intoxicating mix of sandalwood and something that was smoky and vaguely sweet, although not sugary.

Clearing my throat, I said, "Maybe later."

He nodded and then asked, "Champagne?"

"Yes, please," I said, hoping the Krug would calm my nerves. "Thank you."

He opened the champagne; the cork popped and foam erupted

from the opening, spilling down the side of the bottle. Icarus laughed as he grabbed a napkin. Nervous, I giggled and perched on the edge of the seat as the chauffeur poured bubbly into a flute and handed it to me.

He put the bottle back into the bucket and said, "Once again, welcome to St. Mateo. It is my pleasure to serve you so please let me know what I can do to make sure that you are satisfied."

It was one of those trite, stock "customer service 101" phrases, but considering the reason for my trip to St. Mateo, the words *pleasure* and *serve* and *satisfy* were practically dripping with sexual innuendo.

The generous sip of champagne I'd just indulged in nearly came spewing out of my mouth, and I had to force myself to swallow, which, of course, sent a bit of bubbly into my nose, and it was an effort to cough delicately and not hack like I longed to do.

"You okay?"

Taking a deep breath, I managed to nod and said, "Just too much in my mouth at once."

The slow lift of Icarus's brow was seductive, curious, and mischievous. Mortified at how my words could be misinterpreted, I coughed again, a bit less ladylike.

"Would you like some water?"

"I'm fine," I said, putting the flute on the wet bar.

"Okay, we'll get going now," he said. "Should take about an hour or so."

After he got out and closed the door, I winced, embarrassed by my behavior. Why was I acting like some silly, giddy teenager? Why was I giggling and behaving like this was the first time I'd ever had champagne? Why was I nervous and jumpy, as skittish as a filly? Maybe because Icarus was a dreamboat. *Dreamboat?* I shook my head at my choice of description as the limo's engine fired up and the wheels started to roll. *Who the hell says dreamboat? Well, I didn't actually say it out loud*, I thought, settling back on the leather sofa. I'd thought of Icarus as a dreamboat, and since no one could read my thoughts, I didn't care that it was a term from the 1950s.

Icarus was a dreamboat chauffeur.

He was tall and gorgeous, and he wanted to please me and make sure I was satisfied. But, no, not really, I reminded myself, reaching for the flute of champagne. The pleasure he wanted to provide me with had been bought and paid for; I couldn't forget that.

This was all fantasy. Nothing was real.

About ten minutes later, the intercom came on, and Icarus spoke through the system, informing me that he would point out a few sights along the way.

"But, if you would rather just have a relaxing ride without the narration, that's okay, too."

"No, that's fine," I said, looking toward the closed partition separating us. "I'd like the narration, please."

We headed away from the airport, down a wide avenue lined with palm trees, red hibiscus bushes and pink oleander trees, their leaves fluttering in the breeze.

Moments later, Icarus navigated the limo through the center of town, providing a bit of narration.

It was a thriving, bustling enclave of activity set amidst palm trees, plumeria, bird of paradise, oleander, and other flowering shrubs, all basking in the brilliant sunshine under a cloudless blue sky. Everywhere I looked, I saw a mix of St. Matean people and European tourists, going about their day, walking, talking, and shopping. We shared the narrow, paved road with taxies, cars, and small vans or jitneys.

The limo sailed along and we passed an open-air flea market where vendors sold everything from fresh fruit to hair extensions, hawking wares spread out on tables beneath blue tarps.

After some rather aggressive maneuvers through a busy traffic circle, we headed down a boulevard where there was a shopping plaza with various souvenir shops, a grocery store, and a few fast food restaurants.

We turned another corner, and Icarus pointed out the post office, the police station—a cute lavender building with a wide, wraparound veranda and tropical landscaping—the First Bank of St. Mateo, which had several branches throughout the Palmchat Islands, and several churches.

"We are all Catholic here," Icarus said. "And on Sunday, we all go to church, and the whole city pretty much shuts down, we don't work."

Leaving the city, the island's elevation increased, and I was able to look over the rainforest and down to the lovely white sand beaches, a small fishing village that fronted a bay where several boats bobbed in clear waters, and a banana plantation.

Silence ensued for about twenty minutes as the limo followed the winding road, ascending around the mountainous terrain. Icarus said, "In a moment, we'll stop so you can take a few photos at Plantain Pass. It is one of St. Mateo's most famous sites. Lots of tourists like to take a photo there because it is the only place where you can have our sister islands in the background of the picture."

As he promised, moments later, the limo angled left, slowly veering off the main road and onto a large gravelly shoulder. He parked the limo close to a low guardrail behind a shuttle bus whose passengers had already disembarked and were excitedly posing, positioning themselves for the perfect photo, which would feature the four islands in the background.

The limo door opened, and as I was about to get out, Icarus grabbed my hand. "Watch your head," he advised, and I was careful of the car's roof as he helped me out.

The balmy breeze carried a hint of the salty ocean as it propelled me toward the guardrail. The shoulder was a precipice overlooking several stories of rainforest, clusters of trees with large, dark green leaves.

"I'm afraid it might be awhile before we get a chance to take your photo," Icarus said, behind me, his deep voice close to my ear, the timbre brusque and yet tender, like a rough caress.

Nodding, I agreed. The shuttle passengers were hogging the scenery, crowded in clusters, jockeying for the best angles. "Maybe I could come back another time."

"Or, maybe you could have your picture taken somewhere else," he suggested. "A place that's much more beautiful than Plantain Pass."

Facing him, I had to step back to look up at him since he was so huge and imposing. And much too handsome. Entirely too sexy.

"There's a place just across the road," he said. "It's behind that little shack."

Hesitant, I turned and saw the shack, a small clapboard structure with peeling paint and boarded-up windows. Surrounded by a dense snarl of tropical trees, it seemed just about ready to collapse. Alarm bells went off within me, loud and blaring. Did he really think I was about to go behind that shack with him? He was handsome, absolutely. But not handsome enough to fool me into following him into the rainforest where he could do God only knew what to me.

"It looks a little dicey," he said, as though sensing my wariness. "But trust me, the photo you'll have will be worth it."

Glancing at the shuttle passengers, I silently cursed them for being inconsiderate tourists. I wanted them to hurry up and take their damn photos and then pile back into the shuttle so I could have my picture taken, but I wasn't holding my breath.

And Icarus was waiting for my acquiescence. I still wasn't sure about the photo opportunity behind the dilapidated shack, but something about those whiskey-colored eyes intoxicated me, and like someone under the influence, I stopped thinking clearly and said, "Okay, let's go."

He took my hand, and after several cars passed and the road was clear in both directions, we ran across the road. My heart slammed as we walked closer to the shack. Yards away, it was in worse shape than I thought, and I was half-convinced that Icarus planned to drag me into it and murder me.

"You okay?"

Taking a deep breath, I said, "Um, yeah, I just ..." I glanced back at the shuttle passengers, still striking poses and taking selfies. Would any of them even hear me if I screamed bloody murder?

"We don't have to go if you don't—"

"No, no," I heard myself say, even though everything within me was telling me not to go because I wouldn't return. My body would be found hacked to pieces. If it was found. And yet, some strange practical part of me rationalized that Icarus had to know he would be the prime suspect if anything happened to me. For one, the hotel had sent him to pick me up. And two, I was sure airport surveillance had us on camera. There was sure to be video of our brief conversation and of him getting into the limo with me.

"After you," I said.

Smiling, Icarus took my hand again and led me around to the back of the shack, where we were greeted by a cluster of elephant trees. Pushing back the broad leaves, he guided me into the tropical forest. Beneath the wide, green leaves of more elephant trees, we took a natural path between bamboo and banana, shrouded by flowers, cool and dim. The path seemed to descend and slope downward for the next few moments, and Icarus tightened his grip on my hand, making sure I didn't slip over any low-lying branches. Soon, we reached a clearing, and when I looked over my shoulder, all I could see was a tangle of trees and bushes. A wall of flora and fauna, impenetrable, I could never have found my way through if I needed to escape.

"You okay?" Icarus asked.

"Yeah, I just, um ..." Scratching my eyebrow and my heart slamming, I said, "I just wondered ... I mean, you do know how to get back to the car, right?"

"I know every inch of this island," he said, stepping closer to me, his voice low and deep, the timbre brushing over my skin like the whispery breeze floating through the trees.

Swallowing my fear, I nodded and we continued on. As we angled through more trees, the breeze seemed to pick up, tempering the humidity, and I heard a sound I wasn't really prepared for—waves crashing. Icarus pushed through another wall of huge, waxy elephant leaves. I hurried behind him, and moments later, I was walking on sugar-white sand.

It stretched before me, a shimmering white blanket that unfurled into the clear turquoise waters.

"So, here is the place I told you about," Icarus said, arms outstretched, smiling. "What do you think?"

Looking around, I couldn't help but be awed by the beauty. The beach was beyond gorgeous, a lovely ribbon of land dotted with towering palm trees. Practically deserted, it seemed unspoiled, as though it hadn't been tread upon since the Carib Indians had inhabited the island centuries ago.

"It is beautiful," I said, taking a few steps toward a palm tree, enjoying the breeze wafting from the ocean waves.

"And most people don't know about it," he said. "So it's nice for taking photos. When you show the picture to someone else who has been to St. Mateo, they will ask you, where did you take that photo? And you will have an interesting story to tell them."

Turning to him, I said, "I don't want to take any pictures. Not of me, I mean."

"You sure?" he asked. "This is a beautiful setting."

"Yes, it is," I said. "And I would like some pictures of the area, but I don't want to be in the pictures."

"You would look lovely in front of that palm tree."

I stared up, slightly irritated, at Icarus. I was sure he said that to all the women he led through the rainforest to see the secret beach. Still, I felt my cheeks warm, and felt foolish because I was sure I was blushing. The hint of amusement in his luminous, bedroom eyes told me that he knew how his compliment had affected me.

"I'm sure," I said, as politely as I could, considering I was still annoyed by the idea that I was just his latest co-star in a play he'd starred in countless times with countless other women. "Anyway, I'm so crazy. I think I left my camera in the limo."

Icarus gave me a sympathetic smile and offered to snap a few pictures of the scenery on his smartphone, but I told him not to bother.

We headed back through the elephant leaves, and I followed him along the path, but something about it seemed different. "Are you sure we're going the right way?"

"Actually," he said, "I just need to make a quick stop."

"A quick stop?" I asked, my pulse racing. "Where?" What I really wanted to ask was why he needed to make a quick stop? What did he need to do? Locate a machete to hack me to death?

"It's just this way," he said, grabbing my hand, forcing me to follow him. "Won't take too long to get there."

"What do you have to do?" I asked, unable to pull my hand away or even dig in my heels to stop our progress, and as we hurried along, I looked over my shoulder and saw nothing but trees. Where was the beach? Which way was the path back to the limo? How the hell was I going to get away from him and—

"Here we are ..."

"Huh? What?" I stammered, glancing up at him and then forward. Before us, several yards away, was a charming thatched-roof bungalow made of bamboo. "What is this place?"

"It's the hotel's spa," Icarus explained, leading me to the door, flanked by hibiscus and oleander. "The spa is known for special body treatments which require ocean water and seaweed from the beach. My supervisor wanted me to make sure that the bungalow was secure. The spa specialist wasn't sure if she'd locked the door."

"Oh," I said, my heart rate returning to normal.

At the door, Icarus released my hand, and I walked toward one of the hibiscus bushes, feeling a bit silly and overwrought for thinking he was trying to kill me.

"Damn ..." Icarus muttered.

Turning to him, I asked, "What is it?"

"The door was still open," he said. "I need to go in and make sure nothing has been stolen. You can stay out here or you can come in, whichever you prefer."

Shrugging, I said, "I'll come inside."

Icarus went inside and I followed, stepping into a cool, dark room with bamboo walls and bamboo floors. A reception area, I guessed. From there, I headed down a short hallway and into a room which featured long panels of gauzy material hanging from the thatched ceiling, forming partitions, billowing like sails in the wind.

"Icarus ..." I said, hesitant as I walked through the gauze, vaguely wondering where he'd gone. The bungalow intrigued me. I couldn't imagine a spa treatment which required someone to travel through a gauzy gauntlet. Considering the nature of the Heliconia Hotel, though, I imagined that the trip through the whispery fabric was meant to be made with no clothes on with the gauze caressing intimate places.

Soon, I was lost among the gauzy panels. Pushing through the fabric, I headed right, trying to find my way.

A shadowy figure, obscured by the filmy fabric, stood on the opposite side of the gauze panel in front of me. Gasping softly, I squinted, trying to make out the face, trying to see through the fabric.

"Icarus?" I asked. "Is that—"

Strong arms encircled me from behind, startling me, but instead of flinching or struggling to twist away, I stood still, my heart slamming.

"Looks like everything is okay in here," he whispered, his lips close to my ear, his deep baritone resonating through me, and I felt a dull throbbing between my legs. "But I need to check the back room. Make sure no bums are using the place to sleep off a bender."

"Okay ..." I said, wondering how he'd managed to slip behind me so quickly when, seconds before, I could have sworn he'd been standing on the other side of the panel.

"Will you come with me?"

"Sure," I said, cringing at the strange, high-pitched squeak in my voice. I thought I heard him chuckle softly as his arms slipped away, and then he stood next to me, taking my hand. The throbbing increased when I saw he'd removed his coat, revealing muscles barely contained by the white dress shirt he wore.

Icarus guided me through a passageway and into another room. After passing through another hallway, we stepped over the threshold and into a large room dominated by a king-sized canopy bed, draped in mosquito netting.

"Well, there doesn't seem to be anyone in here," I said, heart thundering, terrified by what might happen next, and yet curious and even excited.

"No one except us," he said, moving to stand in front of me.

I swallowed again but not for fear this time. A burgeoning lust erupted within me, so intense I was afraid I might not be able to control it, afraid the feeling might compel me to do things I wasn't sure I should do, irrational things. And yet, hadn't I come to St. Mateo to be wild and decadent, not chaste and modest? I'd agreed to come to the Heliconia Hotel so I could live out my most erotic fantasies with good-looking, sexy men.

Like Icarus, who was staring at me as though I was the most beautiful woman he'd ever seen and all he wanted to do in the world was make love to me.

Which obviously wasn't true, I thought, forcing myself to be cynical.

Icarus was probably a master at enticing and entrancing women like me. Women who had allowed anxiety to damn near ruin their careers. Women who needed to get their mojo back in order to get their lives on track.

"It's a little warm in here, don't you think?" he asked, unbuttoning his dress shirt and then unfastening the cuff links. He took his shirt off, and I ogled him without realizing it, enjoying the show, marveling at his muscles and how broad his shoulders were and how he towered over me. When he unbuttoned his pants, I turned from him and stared at the bed, my heart racing. I wasn't sure if I was ready to see him naked. A moment later, I felt him standing close behind me, and figuring that he had no clothes on, I trembled and my heart beat wildly. Part of me wanted to run for my life. Another part wanted to allow the fantasy to play out as the hotel had obviously intended it to. The story line was fairly simple, I surmised. *Woman comes to island and gets spectacularly banged by her hot chauffeur.* It made me excited just thinking about it. But I wasn't sure if I wanted to live out the fantasy. I didn't know if I could ...

Icarus took off my sundress, pushing the thin straps from my shoulders. The flowing, A-line dress dropped to the floor, and I stepped out of it, shivering despite the balmy atmosphere in the bungalow. As he reached around and unhooked my bra, I stiffened as his fingers brushed my breasts, and my nipples immediately hardened. The pink lace bra sailed across the room and landed in the seat of a chair next to a small round table. My panties would be next, I knew, and I didn't know whether to prepare myself or protest, but during my mental debate, Icarus placed his hands on my hips and then inserted his fingers beneath the waistband of the matching bikini-cut underwear. Paralyzed by a jolt of lust, I shivered, feeling his hands trail down my legs as he slid my panties down until they ended in a little pink pool around my ankles. Gently, he lifted my right foot, so I could step out of the underwear, and then my left foot.

He picked up the panties and tossed them onto the chair, and then just like that, I was completely naked.

I felt both embarrassed and liberated. Physically, I had nothing to be ashamed of; in high school and college, I had run cross country, and though I wasn't the most dedicated athlete, I hadn't dropped the fitness routine. I still ran six miles five days of the week. Naturally, my frame was slender, but I had nice curves and cleavage that men paid attention to. Still, I wasn't feeling entirely confident.

Skittish, and wary about what Icarus thought of my body, I decided to crawl onto the bed. I felt something huge and heavy settling next to me. Icarus had joined me in the bed. Still worried about facing him, I flattened my body, lying on my stomach, with my face pressed against the soft, downy pillow.

Gently, he turned me over onto my back. Moving onto his side, propping himself up on an elbow, he stared at me. His whiskey-colored eyes roamed my body, his gaze so intense I swore I could feel it, and when his eyes dropped below my navel, the throbbing made me gasp softly, and I felt an urgent need to arch my hips, an urgent need to be filled completely.

His hand landed on my cheek, his fingers caressing and then trailing along my jawline and chin before moving to my mouth. Parting my lips with his thumb, he lowered his head toward mine.

"Wait ... " I said, panicked.

He stopped, arching a brow seductively.

"I don't want to ..." I stammered. "I mean, I want to but ..."

"Not with me?"

"Not yet ..." I clarified. "I don't want to right now, I mean."

I wasn't sure what I meant or what I wanted. Everything seemed to be happening too fast. And even though I had been told, or warned, it now seemed to me that my fantasies would start immediately, per the letter from the hotel, I wasn't ready to start the fantasy, not just yet. It felt too soon. I needed a moment to prepare. More than a moment, really. *Forever*, I thought. I needed forever to get myself together. Or maybe never, I amended. Maybe never was how long it would take.

"Are you sure?"

"No," I blurted out, feeling foolish and confused. "I mean, yes. I think. I don't know, I mean ..."

"It's okay," he said. "Let's just take our time and see what happens. Everything is all about what you want, remember?"

I nodded, remembering that it was *my* fantasy. Supposedly. Although, honestly, I had never actually fantasized about having sex with a limo driver, so I wasn't quite sure why the hotel had thought I would enjoy this story line. I wasn't really complaining. I didn't know if I was enjoying myself either.

I tried to remember I'd come to St. Mateo to revive, or maybe resurrect, the woman I had been before losing three high-profile cases, but maybe I'd been fooling myself. Maybe I shouldn't have allowed Lisa to talk me into coming to this place. Maybe I didn't know what to do. Maybe I did know, deep down, that sex wasn't going to solve anything. This trip to paradise was a misguided reaction to the deplorable state of my once meteoric career. What I really needed was another chance to successfully litigate a high-profile case.

Closing my eyes, I let out a small sigh.

Icarus's lips brushed against mine, and when I gasped, his tongue slid into my mouth, slow and sensuous and strangely as though it belonged there, as though he had been waiting to kiss me. Eagerly, I opened my mouth to give him more access. I slipped my tongue between his lips as I wound one arm around his neck and the other around his back, kissing him greedily, like a parched woman, swirling my tongue around his in a desperate frenzy.

Without warning, he broke the kiss, and I moaned in protest, but his eyes communicated he had more in mind for me.

A moment later, he pressed his mouth against my forehead. His lips trailed along my hairline, and then he brushed his mouth across my closed eyelids. After a quick peck on the nose, which was playful enough to make both of us smile, he trailed a line of blistering kisses along my cheek and jaw and then behind my ear and down to my neck.

The throbbing between my legs had escalated to an urgent clenching, and it was all I could do not to slip my fingers inside myself and rock against my own hand, and I might have, but I knew it would be so much better if I was patient and allowed the fantasy to run its course.

Icarus dragged his lips across my throat and then moved down to my collarbone and continued on to my shoulder and down my arm to my elbow, wrist, and palm. Taking my hand, he pressed his mouth against my lifeline and then kissed each fingertip.

Taking my other hand, he reversed his order, starting with the fingertip kisses and then brushing his lips against my palm before kissing the inside of my wrist and then trailing his kisses up my arm, past my elbow, and to my shoulder. From my shoulder, he moved to my breasts, taking one nipple in his mouth, licking and flicking his tongue across it while caressing my other breast with his fingers and hand.

The sucking and tugging on my nipples was driving me insane, making it almost impossible for me to keep my hips still. His mouth left my breasts and moved down to my abdomen, and then his lips trailed even lower until he was inches from my navel. But, then he changed course and he trailed his tongue diagonally, down to my left hip. After a few kisses there, he dragged his mouth across to my right hip, and then he inched his mouth down below my naval again and began a dangerously delicious descent toward my—

"Stop," I said, assailed once again by panic. Sitting up, I scooted away from him, avoiding his gaze.

"What's the matter?"

"I'm not sure I want to ..." I took a deep breath, feeling like a ridiculous liar. I suspected we both knew that wasn't true. I was practically soaking wet, and the scent of my desire for him floated around us, like a hypnotic aphrodisiac.

"Then you don't have to," he said.

Glancing at him, I was shocked to see he wasn't naked. He rose to his knees, giving me a full frontal view of the massive bulge in his boxer briefs. My mouth went dry at the sight of it. So big and thick, I didn't think it could possibly be real. Involuntarily, my body continued to prepare for him as a deluge of natural lubrication slipped from between me.

As if sensing my disbelief, he took my hand and helped me to my knees, pulling me closer to him. Dipping his head to mine, he kissed me and then slipped my hand into his boxer briefs. My fingers brushed the wide, slick head. Growing bolder, I inched my fingertips along the shaft and then moved my hand around it, realizing I wouldn't be able to encircle it entirely by touching my thumb to my index finger.

I slid my hand down and then back up, feeling the veins against my palm. I glanced up at him and gasped under my breath, startled by the raw lust in his intense gaze. I could tell he wanted me, and I wanted him, too, and yet, I knew if I gave in and had sex with him, there would be no turning back.

Still conflicted, I moved my hand down again, and his penis twitched against my hand, setting off another round of throbbing between my legs as I imagined what it might feel like if it twitched inside me.

Again, as though he could read my mind, Icarus moved me back down onto the bed and then moved off it to remove the boxer briefs. Completely nude, he was magnificent, but I was worried. I wasn't sure if I would be able to take all of him. Even though I wanted all of him. I needed every inch of him inside me.

Icarus moved next to me, lying on his side. He lowered his head to mine and kissed me, slipping his tongue into my mouth, and at the same time, he trailed a finger along my opening while his thumb brushed my clit. Gasping loudly, I started to rock my hips against the strong fingers twirling in and around my vagina. Opening my legs wider, I arched my back, feeling a delicious ache between my legs. Closing my eyes, I moved my hips in a circular motion against Icarus's nimble fingers, digging my heels into the mattress. A powerful jolt of what I could only describe as electric pleasure sent a charge throughout my entire body, leaving me gasping and shaking as though I'd been struck by lightning.

While I was still trembling, I felt the head of Icarus's penis against the opening of my vagina, sliding along the slick, wet slit, sending more shocking sparks of pleasure through me. Those sparks were nothing compared to what I felt when the broad head pushed inside of me. Clenching around him, I lifted my hips, desperate to have him deeper within me. Searing sparks of pleasure made my body thrash and twitch as Icarus continued, separating the walls of my vagina as he maintained his sweet excavation into me, making his way to my core.

I'd wanted every inch of him, and he was obliging me, sending my body into delightful spasms as he filled me completely. Astonished by the size of him, I wrapped my legs around his waist and spurred him into action, goading him to begin, eager to be screwed like there was no tomorrow.

He began slowly, drawing back and then slipping inside with long, sweeping thrusts. Over and over, he gave me all of his length and thick-ness, retreating and returning until I was gasping and crying out, exploding again. My body trembled and shivered in an orgasmic bliss, leaving me dazed.

Pulling back until only the thick, broad head was inside me, Icarus gave me quick, shallow thrusts, again and again. My body seemed to be breaking apart and then coming back together and then breaking apart again.

Holding me close, Icarus kissed me, thrusting his tongue into my mouth in the same way he thrust in and out of me. Grasping him, I moved my mouth from his as I felt the pressure building between my legs again. As I closed my eyes again, anticipating my next explosion, I felt Icarus's mouth near my ear and heard him asking me how I wanted him to make love to me. Faster? Harder? He trailed a tongue along the edge of my ear before grazing the lobe with his teeth.

He hadn't asked if I wanted him deeper. He was already deeper than I thought was possible. Honestly, I didn't know what to tell him. Fast or slow, it didn't matter. Either way, I knew he could make me come like I never had before in my life, over and over, with an intensity so powerful I thought it might drive me insane.

In response to his question, I could only manage an unintelligible moan. Icarus took it upon himself to thrust faster and then harder. He changed his rhythm more than once as he pushed into me and then drew back, sometimes slow, sometimes faster. He slid into me with unrestrained passion and then with tenderness until I was panting at the searing pleasure rocketing through me.

Soon, his thrusts became more determined and tumultuous. He stared at me with those whiskey-colored eyes as he drove harder, his thickness moving within me in a desperate furor that seemed different somehow as he reached a place I wasn't aware existed, a sensitive spot he stimulated over and again until my body seized, and then it felt as though some sort of sensual detonation went off between my legs, stealing away my breath and all my thoughts and everything I needed to survive.

Seconds later, Icarus had his own explosion, and the vehemence of his orgasm was powerful enough to cause more implosions deep inside me, jerking me violently until I went limp.

Chapter Three

The limousine pulled under the portico and stopped at the front entrance of the Heliconia Hotel.

The grand façade was impressive and reminded me of a tropical version of the palace at Versailles with its arches and rows of columns amid mid-sized palm trees nestled in oversized planters.

The journey to the hotel had taken a little over an hour, due to our bungalow detour. The experience had been indescribable. Never in a million years had I expected to be made love to moments after arriving on the island. The hotel had said the fantasy would start immediately, but I'd thought they'd meant the fantasy was merely being miles away from my disappointing career.

I still couldn't believe it had happened.

Couldn't believe I had done it.

Couldn't believe I hadn't stopped it from happening.

Still slightly dazed, I tried my best to pull myself together and somehow ignore the insistent throbbing between my legs and prepare to get out of the car and check into the hotel.

Icarus opened the door and helped me out of the limo with a polite deference I found slightly strange and distant, considering we had just made love with the sort of wild, reckless abandon reserved for the romance novels I used to read in high school.

Now, he was professional and a little too polished.

I tried not to feel disappointed, but I sensed a broken connection between us, which was ridiculous because I hadn't come to St. Mateo to make a connection. The inconsequential sex was about releasing tension and getting rid of anxiety so I could stop having crazy nightmares. A few mind-blowing orgasms would just be icing on the cake. And yet, I worried I'd become attached to Icarus, for some reason. I hoped not. I didn't want to be one of those women who latched onto the first man who gave them some good sex.

Maybe Icarus was being distant because his role in the fantasy was over. He was "off the clock." The lusty limo driver had played his part. He'd exited stage left, so to speak, and was now back in the real world, where he was a hotel employee who drove a limo.

Icarus escorted me up the grand stairway, where four uniformed bellmen stood at attention. In the expansive, opulent foyer, a young, slim, attractive St. Matean woman was waiting to welcome me to the island and to the hotel. She introduced herself as Liberada and announced she would be my personal assistant for the duration of my stay. "In addition to myself," she went on, "you will have, at your disposal, a personal staff, which will consist of a concierge, a butler, two housekeepers, a secretary, and a driver, Icarus, who you've met."

Nodding, I glanced back at the limo, where Icarus was removing my luggage.

Icarus handed my bags to one of the bellmen, and then without as much as a nod, smile, tip of the hat, or any other acknowledgment to me, he got back into the limo. As he drove off, I couldn't help but wonder if he was heading off to play the sexy chauffeur in some other woman's fantasy, and I felt a weird spark of jealousy. Quickly, I squashed the envy and reminded myself that this experience was supposed to be a fantasy.

As such, I was supposed to enjoy the fantasy, not wrestle with bizarre feelings about a man I'd just met and didn't even know.

Leaving the foyer, I was shepherded down a wide hallway, featuring lots of marble and soaring ceilings, and into a large office, furnished in French Rococo style.

Liberada sat behind the large desk and indicated I should take the chair opposite her.

After explaining a bit about the town, and confirming the length of my stay in paradise, she explained that the history of the hotel's origins was cloaked in secrecy and mystery, obviously.

"The hotel's founder is not widely known, outside of the current owners; however, there are rumors that the hotel was once the private estate of a wealthy French baroness who fell on hard times after the death of her wealthy husband, who left her in debt. To satisfy her creditors, she began offering them certain favors, if you will."

Smiling naughtily, Liberada went on. "Upon her death, it is believed her daughter decided to turn the estate into a hotel. She apparently belonged to a secret society of young noble women, including some members of royalty, who were dedicated to exploring their sexuality in the most decadent ways possible. They were supposedly devoted to debauchery, but due to their positions in society, they had to perform these bacchanal activities in secret. So the baroness's daughter made the hotel available as a place where they could indulge in their wanton desires."

"I see," I said, the throbbing between my legs increasing as I recalled my own wanton debauchery.

"But that's all conjecture and rumor," Liberada said with a saucy wink. "Most likely, this place is owned by rich Arabs."

"Probably so," I said, not sure I really agreed.

"Nevertheless, this is a place of impeccable discretion," she said, the sassiness replaced by stone-cold seriousness. "We take privacy very seriously, and if you feel your privacy has been violated, in any way, you are to please contact me immediately to handle the situation. Sounds good?"

I nodded, thinking that it sounded like she would cut the violator's tongue out to keep him from spilling secrets, but I supposed I was reassured.

"After you decided to stay with us," Liberada said, "you should have received a letter thanking you for choosing to vacation at the Heliconia."

I nodded, remembering the letter I'd received from the hotel after Lisa had booked the trip to St. Mateo.

"Obviously, there were some details about the hotel that had to be omitted, for discretion."

After clearing my throat, I agreed. "Obviously."

"Considering the nature and objectives of the hotel," she began, the naughty gleam in her gaze again, "I must explain that the experiences we offer are categorized according to three different levels. Sensual, sexual, and salacious."

"I see," I said, not sure I really did.

"This is a hotel where you can experience your fantasies," she said. "And we try not to be blunt, but to explain the categories, I find it best not to employ euphemisms."

Worried, I nodded. "Okay."

"Sensual is no penetration, but you will have orgasms, mainly manual and oral stimulation," she said, as though listing the ingredients of some processed snack food. "Sexual, there will be penetration, and if you want to be tied up or whipped or play sex games, you may request that. Finally, salacious is really any perversion you can think of. For example, if you want to screw a goat, we can get you a goat. Sounds good?"

Flabbergasted, and appalled, I gaped at her. "Are you serious?"

"We don't judge," she explained, then shrugged, and said, "So, were you satisfied with Icarus?"

"What?" Thrown by her abrupt question, I felt heat spreading across my face and was terrified that somehow, someway, she knew what Icarus and I had done in the bungalow. And, if so, was it because she had orchestrated it? As my personal assistant, was she responsible for creating my fantasies and making sure they all came true?

"In the past, some of our guests have complained that he's standoffish and not very friendly," Liberada said. "He has been making an effort to be more congenial, and I just wanted to make sure that he was accommodating and that his behavior was to your satisfaction."

Worried by her seemingly coded speech, I stared at her, searching her delicate features for signs that she was well aware of just how accommodating Icarus had been. She gave me a polite, blank "customer service" gaze.

"He was nice," I decided to say, wondering if the hotel had some kind of unofficial rule that fantasies should be experienced but never really acknowledged, and as such, everyone had to be vague and evasive.

"That's good to know," Liberada said. "So, we'll meet the rest of your staff, and they will help you get settled in your room. Sounds good?"

Chapter Four

Standing in the living room of the luxury suite, I looked around, admiring the Baroque and Rococo furnishings, high tray ceilings, triple crown molding, and rows of French doors which opened to a private terrace surrounded by a tropical jungle.

Feeling giddy and decadent, I walked to one of the four couches, grouped in a square with a low coffee table in the center.

I wasn't quite sure what to do next.

I'd met the staff, a deferential group who assured me of their desire to fulfill my every wish during my time in St. Mateo. I was thankful and appreciative, but, since the Heliconia was a fantasy hotel, I couldn't help but wonder if all their talk about vowing to go out of their way to make my stay as enjoyable as possible was just pretense.

However, to their credit, they sought to prove their promises by unpacking my luggage and hanging my clothes in the closet, placing my undergarments in the dresser and arranging my toiletries in neat rows on several built-in shelves in the bathroom.

Walking into the sleeping salon, I figured I probably needed a shower. I could smell Icarus's heady scent on my skin. Maybe some tropical-scented bath gel would help wash away the memories of his kisses, and I might be able to forget the feeling of his lips on my flesh.

As I reached for a bath towel, I thought about the levels of fantasy you could indulge in at the Heliconia.

I'd forgotten to ask Liberada how my fantasy experiences would be categorized, though after my encounter with Icarus, I was sure they would be more than *sensual*. Anyway, I'd come for *sexual* experiences, pun intended. Anything *salacious* would not be tolerated, however.

The hotel's definition of salacious had really thrown me. Did they really offer experiences in bestiality? Was there really some woman out there who actually fantasized about doing it with a barnyard animal? Again, I questioned my rationale for coming to this place.

After my shower, I stepped back into the bedroom. As I was putting on a robe, there was a knock at the door. It was one of the housekeepers. She reached into the pocket on the front of the apron tied around her black dress and pulled out another aqua envelope. "For you."

"Thank you." I took the envelope from her, closed the door, and headed to the couch.

After a moment's hesitation, I opened the letter, pulled out the piece of lambskin, and unfolded it, reading:

Evening experience: Terrace Dinner

Focusing on the word experience, I felt a jolt pass through me, knowing what it meant. Dinner on the terrace would be much more than five courses and a bottle of expensive wine. Another sexy guy would be joining me, I figured.

I wasn't sure if I wanted another fantasy experience.

Correction: I wasn't sure if I wanted another fantasy experience with anyone except Icarus. The thought shamed and sobered me. The point of coming to the Heliconia was to live out lots of fantasies with lots of different guys. I wasn't supposed to get hung up on the first guy who made love to me like both our lives depended on it.

Maybe I was overthinking things. Maybe the sex hadn't been that great. After all, what the hell did I know about great sex? As soon as I'd walked through the doors of Ellison, Zupancic, and Cox, LLC, my sole focus had been my career. I was too busy to indulge in scorching hot sex. Sure, I'd had a few dalliances, but nothing truly mind-blowing, nothing to distract me from my goal of making partner. Maybe what

I'd thought was great sex in the middle of the rainforest with the hottest guy I've ever seen in my life was really just sex that was a bit better than what I had experienced.

Nevertheless, in the interest of not wasting the money I'd shelled out to stay at the Heliconia, I decided to soldier on and see what the hotel had in store for me.

"My name is Joshua," said what the hotel had in store for me.

Standing just outside the doorway of my suite, the star of my current fantasy wore a custom-tailored suit that appeared to have been molded to his lean, athletic frame. He reminded me of an international soccer star. He was good-looking, in a pretty, male model way, with a sculptured face, full lips a bit on the pouty side, and piercing blue eyes incongruous with his golden tan complexion.

Joshua gave me a smoldering gaze as he announced his intentions, which were to be my dinner companion and late-night entertainment, but I wasn't convinced by his fake desire. Maybe I was still drunk from Icarus's sizzling, whiskey-colored stares.

I decided to go with the flow and see how the fantasy would end.

After the polite introductions, Joshua and I walked out onto the terrace. A nice, balmy breeze carried the scent of the tropical flowers surrounding us. The sun had set, but the sky had a coppery glaze, and it spilled onto our setting, casting a golden tint over the outdoor furnishings and the travertine tile and the white hibiscus bushes.

A mixologist showed up a few minutes later to make cocktails for us, and then she made herself scarce, leaving Joshua and me alone to engage in awkward chitchat. Mostly, the conversation consisted of him telling me how good I looked in my dress—one of those bandage numbers that accentuated curves and cleavage—and me being demure.

"So, how do you like St. Mateo so far?"

"It's gorgeous," I said, taking another sip of my mojito. "Breathtakingly beautiful."

"Have you been to St. Mateo before?"

"No, this is my first time."

"You've never been to any other Palmchat Island?"

"No," I said. "Actually, I hate to say this, but before I came here, I hadn't even heard of the Palmchat Islands."

"A lot of people haven't," he said, taking a modest sip of his drink. "We get overshadowed by the U.S. Virgin Islands, but once people discover our islands, they always come back."

"Well, I can see why," I said. "It is a beautiful place."

"So, how did you eventually find out about St. Mateo?"

"A friend told me," I said and took a more generous sip of the mojito.

I had the sinking suspicion this particular fantasy was not going as the hotel had designed it and the ending would be vastly different from what had been intended. The basic story line made sense. *Beautiful hotel guest has dinner with handsome, dashing man who charms her right out of her panties and finds his way into her bed where they make love, passionately and vigorously, all night long.*

The problem was, Joshua was all wrong for the part. Well, not completely wrong, I supposed. He was certainly handsome, so he fit the bill for that part of the description. But he wasn't dashing. His conversational skills were sorely lacking. Not to be blunt, but I found him boring. Talking to him was a chore, and as he continued to pepper me with banal questions about my travel experiences, I racked my brain, searching for some sort of exit out of the stilted banter between us.

I was just about to feign a headache and tell him I wanted to cut the evening short when dinner arrived. Three servers rolled two carts out onto the terrace and began the task of preparing our table. A sommelier followed and educated us on the evening's wine selection. Ecstatic about the intrusion, I struck up a conversation with the sommelier about the wine. I wasn't really a connoisseur, but I was able to ask the sommelier about the composition of the wine he'd selected, how it had been made, and why he thought it would pair well with our menu.

Joshua didn't seem to mind my interest in the sommelier. Maybe because he knew he was the most handsome guy in the room. The servers were decent-looking, but they were average guys with average builds, and I couldn't imagine the hotel casting them in any fantasies.

The servers finished setting the table and then stepped back. Joshua held out a chair for me, and I sat, thanking him. Joshua took his seat, and then the sommelier went through the pretense of presenting the wine selection to Joshua.

After opening the wine, he offered Joshua the cork, which Joshua took from him and then sniffed a few times, furrowing his brow and looking contemplative, as though he actually had a nose to discern whether or not the wine was acceptable.

Then the wine steward offered Joshua a small tasting sample, and Joshua looked at the wine and took a quick sniff before he tasted it. Joshua gave the sommelier a dismissive nod, which I assumed meant the wine was fine to pour, because the sommelier returned the nod and filled our glasses.

The entire scene was so ridiculous to me I almost laughed out loud.

But then I cautioned myself not to throw stones. The fancy dinner fantasy might have been enjoyable to some other woman, and maybe I would have been more enthusiastic if not for my encounter with Icarus in the bungalow.

I couldn't get the torrid lovemaking out of my head. Couldn't get Icarus out of my head either, and I wondered if the hotel would be able to cast another fantasy guy capable of making me forget about the dreamboat with the whiskey-colored eyes.

The servers remained with us during the entire dinner service and were attentive and yet unobtrusive, doing their best to blend into the shadows. As Joshua bored me with more tedious conversation, I felt slightly paranoid, assuming the servers knew what this dinner on the terrace was all about.

The servers and the sommelier were well aware that dessert would not be some fancy confection but instead would be Joshua giving me something better than the famous "Better than Sex" cake. I wondered what they thought, if anything. I wondered if they saw me as some depraved bitch who, for whatever reason, couldn't get a decent lay so she had to sneak off to some island to pay for it. I wondered if they cared at all and decided they probably didn't. Maybe I was hoping they didn't. The idea of them judging me made me angry.

They didn't know a damn thing about me or how I'd sabotaged my own career with bad decisions and faulty strategy, which had been the motivating factor behind my decision to come to the Heliconia Hotel. They had no right to declare me depraved and desperate or think of me as some horny, sex-starved, neglected woman.

Of course, I didn't know what they were thinking, so there was no need to give them the evil eye. Most likely, I was projecting my own feelings onto a group of guys who were probably thinking about getting off work and going home to their own families.

After dinner, the servers and the sommelier got lost in a hurry, leaving me alone with Joshua.

Instead of more small talk, he asked me if I wanted to dance. Confused, I said, "But, there's no music."

Smiling, he said, "Well, I can fix that."

Puzzled, but curious, I watched him walk through the French doors into my suite. A moment later, he returned and soon the melodious strains of a string quartet filled the air.

"Well, that's a neat trick," I said, resolved to be more involved in the fantasy, as he pulled me into his arms.

"I have a lot of neat tricks," he said, voice low, gaze intent on me.

I was sure he did, but I still wasn't interested, and so as not to encourage any more double entendre, I put my head on his shoulder, hoping he would get on with twirling me around the terrace.

We swayed slowly for a few moments to what sounded like Bach. Our movements awkward, we struggled to find a rhythm, but eventually, I relaxed enough to let him lead, though I felt as though I was at a high school prom. We weren't exactly cheek to cheek, but we had our arms wrapped around each other, and there was a bit of space between us, which I was thankful for. I didn't want him pressed close, grinding his erection against me. Especially since he didn't exactly have an erection.

He stared at me with those blue eyes that I should have been more entranced by than I was, and then his head dipped toward mine. His kiss was reluctant and then bold and daring. When he slipped his tongue into my mouth, it didn't feel right. The tip darted in and out, and when I tried to pull away, he became more aggressive, wrapping his muscular arms around me, and plunged his tongue deep into my mouth, nearly gagging me.

Twisting my mouth from his, I pushed away. "Wait a minute, please."

"What's the matter?"

"Nothing," I lied, extricating myself from his embrace, which had slackened. "Just need some water."

"Did I do something wrong?"

I went back to the table and grabbed a glass of lukewarm water. "My throat is a bit dry."

"Look, I'm sorry, okay," he said, "I'm new ..."

"You're new?"

"This is only my second week working fantasies," he said, sheepish and apologetic. "I guess I, um ..."

"Forgot your lines?" I suggested, stepping away from him and walking back to the table to take my seat again.

"I'm sorry," he said, joining me at the table.

"It's okay," I said, relieved he hadn't tried to waltz me into the bedroom to do the horizontal tango.

"I could start over," he said. "I was just a little nervous. I've never done a premium deluxe fantasy before, and I've been anxious about getting it right, and, naturally, I fuck it up."

"Really, Joshua, it's okay. I understand about you being nervous," I said. "To be honest with you, I'm nervous, too. I've never had a premium deluxe fantasy come true for me. I've never had any of my fantasies come true."

"This would have been your first fantasy experience?" Joshua asked, a shocked, stricken look on his face.

"Um ..." I faltered, not wanting to lie but not ready to talk about the encounter with Icarus. "What I meant was, I'm not used to the things I want to happen happening for me, you know."

"Why not?"

"Well ..."

"I mean, you got money, right? Because you're at this hotel and it ain't cheap," he said. "Most people that have money can make stuff happen."

"Well, yes, but ..."

"But?" Joshua prompted, as though he was genuinely interested.

"But, sometimes, the things you want to happen are things that you can't pay for," I said, wondering if maybe he'd remembered his lines and was playing the attentive potential lover. "Things you can't buy, you know."

Nodding, Joshua claimed to understand me, but I didn't believe him. I didn't fault him for not understanding because I wasn't entirely sure I'd done a good job of explaining my feelings. Not that my explanations mattered. I wasn't at the Heliconia for sympathy and understanding. How could I make Joshua understand that I was here to figure out why I was having recurring nightmares about shooting myself?

"So, what didn't happen for you that you wanted to happen?" Joshua asked.

"What?" I asked, surprised by his question, shocked he hadn't lost interest in that particular thread of our conversation. "Oh, um ... too many things to get into right at this moment."

"Yeah, I get it," he said. "You didn't come to this hotel to talk, right?"

"I don't mind conversation," I said, maybe a bit too quickly.

"Okay, well ..." He sighed and then smiled a little and said, "Anything in particular you want to talk about?"

"Tell me about yourself," I said, grabbing my half-empty wine glass, hoping to steer the conversation away from anything about me. "You said you were new, right? Where did you work before you came here?"

"I didn't quit my job to work here," he said. "This is like a part-time gig. I'm really a bartender but not at this hotel. At the sister property, the Hibiscus."

"How did you end up at the Heliconia?" I asked.

"My friend recruited me," Joshua said. "He's been working here for a few years. He was always telling me I could make way more money at the Heliconia doing fantasies. Plus, I'd have all the pussy I want."

Clearing my throat, I said, "Is that right?"

Sheepish, he laughed. "Anyway, my friend was always telling me that the women who come here, they're horny and lonely. Most of them are married to rich old farts that can't get it up, no matter how much Viagra they pop. The women haven't been screwed right in years. They're eager for some good dick."

Affronted, I glared at him.

"Sorry." He gave me an apologetic smile. "But I'm sure that's not the case with you."

Taking a sip of wine, I looked away from Joshua's gaze, which held traces of sympathy and pity he couldn't hide, and said nothing. The woman he'd described, the typical woman who came to the hotel, sounded *nothing* like me. I was at the hotel to distract myself from anxiety-fueled nightmares, but I didn't really belong at this place.

So, why the hell was I booked in a premium deluxe suite at the Heliconia? I wasn't the type of woman who visited a sex hotel to deal with anxiety caused by acute onset career failure. I was the type of woman who would develop a pragmatic strategy to combat anxiety. Or, I used to be. Obviously, that woman wasn't me anymore. Maybe I would never be that woman again. Maybe I was a failure, especially in my ability to make sound choices critical to my success and well-being.

Not one to throw pity parties, I sighed and pushed the defeatist thoughts away.

"Listen, I don't mean to be pushy, but ..." He cleared his throat and glanced to the left, toward the French doors that opened to the bedroom, and then back at me. "Do you want to—"

"No," I blurted out, knowing what he'd been about to ask me. "I mean, I don't but ... not because of you or anything that you did wrong."

"Are you sure?"

"I'm positive," I told him and tried to give him a reassuring smile. "It's me, I'm just ... still sort of nervous and trying to wrap my mind around all of this, you know?"

"Yeah, I get it," he said. "This place is kind of intense."

"Can I ask you," I started, curious about something. "Earlier, you said your friend who recruited you said you'd have the opportunity to be with a lot of women."

"But, he only said that because he was trying to convince me to apply for the job," Joshua said with a quickness that suggested he was worried he'd offended me or said something that would get him terminated.

"I was just going to ask about the men who come here," I said. "Would you have to—"

"Oh, this hotel is for females only," he said. "It's unique that way. Women are not usually catered to, you know. Men have always had the opportunity to live out their fantasies in real life and they are encouraged to, with high-class escorts. But, women are expected to just go buy a romance novel and take care of themselves."

I nodded, thinking his little speech sounded like something he'd heard from the HR manager.

"This hotel will give you whatever fantasy you want," he said. "Well, not whatever you want. Nothing that would hurt anybody."

"Oh, yeah, I get that."

"Some women want just guys to be in their fantasies," he said. "Some just want girls. Some want a combination of both."

"Hmmm ..." I said, distracted, thinking that I just wanted Icarus.

"Well, Ms. Miller." Joshua stood, holding a hand out to me, and I knew the curtain was about to close.

I placed my palm over his and rose. He told me he enjoyed meeting me, said dinner with me was wonderful, and again reiterated how beautiful I was. After he walked me into the bedroom, he gave me a kiss on the cheek and wished me sweet dreams.

Once the door closed behind me, I sank down on the bed, flooded with remorse and relief. Kicking off my heels, I lay back against the pillows and looked up at the ceiling.

I wasn't sure what to think or feel.

I was starting to wonder if coming to the hotel had been a mistake.

DAY TWO

Chapter Five

The next morning, I woke with a massive case of overwhelming regret and panic.

Staring at the ceiling, I tried to remember how the hell I'd allowed Lisa to convince me to come to this place. Why the hell had I thought it would be a good idea? With a shaky sigh, I tried to take a deep breath and calm down. *Maybe I should just leave the island,* I thought. Or, if not the island, then I could leave the Heliconia Hotel. Maybe I could check into another seven-star resort, one that had a nice relaxing spa, and spend the remainder of my time on the island having my skin scrubbed, polished, and wrapped in seaweed or volcanic ash or whatever.

Maybe I needed to forget all this fantasy nonsense and get back to reality. I needed to get on a plane, fly home, and deal with my damn anxiety. Jetting off to some island to screw anonymous men wasn't the answer. Sex wasn't going to restore my career.

Pushing the linens away, I swung my legs over the side of the bed, staring around the bedroom. Early morning light streamed through the French doors like golden gossamer, beautiful and ethereal, filling me with a strange sense of peace and wonder despite the panic fluttering in my stomach. It really was a glorious hotel, and I felt special, cocooned in the majestic, luxurious surroundings.

After freshening up in the bathroom, I went back into the bedroom. Sitting on the edge of the king-sized bed, I picked up the phone on the bed table and pressed the number five, which would connect me with my personal assistant.

"Good morning," chirped Liberada, cheerful. "How did you sleep?"

"Fine," I said. "Can I get a bath and then breakfast?"

"Of course," Liberada sang out. "I'll send Esmerelda immediately. And after breakfast, the concierge will come to see you."

"Why?" I asked, wary.

"He's going to help you plan your day," she explained.

"And by helping me plan my day," I started, probing. "Does that mean he's going to plan another fantasy for me?"

"No, he's really going to help you find something interesting to do today," Liberada said, laughing a bit. "And he doesn't plan your fantasies. Actually, fantasies aren't planned, they are *imagined*. And your fantasies have already been imagined for you. All you have to do is live them out."

Ten minutes later, Esmerelda was in the bathroom, getting the bath ready as I stood in the closet trying to find something to wear. After deciding on an outfit, I walked to the claw foot tub, entranced by the spicy scent swirling through the steamy atmosphere. Esmerelda had created a bathing experience for me. In addition to candles and incense, rose petals floated on the water, and the window was slightly open, allowing a bit of the bathroom's humidity to escape while inviting the song of birds to float in and serenade me as I sank into the water.

Leaning against the neck pillow, I thought about what Liberada had said about the fantasies. All you have to do is live them out. Did I want to live out the fantasies that had been imagined for me? If the fantasies were imagined for me, how could the hotel be sure that I would even want to live them out? The hotel didn't really know anything about me. How could they know what I fantasized about? Shouldn't the hotel make it possible for me to live out fantasies that were actually *imagined* by me?

Was I just overthinking things again?

An hour later, over an opulently presented breakfast of poached eggs, toast, and fresh fruit, I was once more wondering if I should leave the hotel or stick around to see what else they might have in store for me. The concierge, Mr. Queensly, showed up to create an itinerary of events for the day. Sitting across from me, he opened a crocodile planner, uncapped a Mont Blanc pen, and asked, "What would you like to do today?

"What would you suggest?" I asked and then took a sip of my third mimosa.

"You could go on a hike or do some watersports. You could go on a historical tour or do some shopping."

"The historical tour sounds interesting," I said, finishing the mimosa. "What's it about?"

The concierge explained that on the tour, I would visit a series of sugar plantations, colonial mansions of European settlers, strategic outposts used during various wars, a coffee farm, and, finally, a cocoa farm. A private guide would accompany me, providing a running commentary about the history of the island with insight into the culture and economy of St. Mateo.

"You think you might be interested?" Mr. Queensly asked.

"Maybe ..." I hedged, wanting more information about the private guide, wondering if this historical tour was the setting for another fantasy. For some reason, I hoped it wasn't. After the encounter with Icarus, and the epic fail fantasy with Joshua, I wasn't sure I wanted to make love with anyone else.

I was certain I wouldn't do anything ridiculous like get addicted to Icarus—or any other guy the hotel hooked me up with—but once I left the hotel, I'd have to go back to my nonexistent sex life, and I didn't want to be miles away with a craving for something I couldn't have.

"All right, well ..." Mr. Queensly scribbled some notes on a pad in his crocodile planner, closed it, and stood. "I will go and arrange everything, and someone will come for you in an hour or so."

When the concierge left, I changed into linen shorts and a silk tank and then slipped on a pair of gold gladiator sandals with leather straps that ascended to just below my knees. I touched-up my hair, achieving that raven-haired Tinker Bell look I liked and then dusted on a little blush, mascara, and tinted lip gloss. All of that took about thirty minutes, less time than I realized. I wasn't in the mood to spend a half hour pacing around the living room couches, so I called Lisa, something I was supposed to have done as soon as I'd checked into the hotel. But after the fantasy detour on the way to the hotel, I hadn't been able to think straight.

When Lisa answered, she chewed me out for ten minutes for not calling her, venting about how worried she'd been, going on and on, which I let her do. Her bitching was a welcome distraction from the historical tour, which I was becoming more and more worried about. Did I want another living, breathing, live, and in-color sexual fantasy? Physically speaking, I didn't know if I could take another large shaft rammed inside me. I was still a bit sore, although when I remembered why I was sore, it set off a mild throbbing.

Once Lisa got over my "thoughtless ungratefulness," she wanted to know everything about the hotel, and she meant everything. I was forbidden to hold anything back. Naturally, as soon as I began giving her details, she interrupted to question me, which I was used to her doing. Our conversation went on this way until her need for information about the hotel was satisfied.

"Okay, now let's get to the important stuff," she said, mischief in her tone. "Don't keep me in suspense."

"About what?" I asked.

"About the hot-as-hell human sex toys the hotel offers!" Lisa said. "Have you had your first fantasy yet? The hotel said the fantasies start as soon as you get off the plane? Did you have your first fantasy with some scorching hot bellboy? Or was it with the concierge? Or maybe with the chauffeur?"

"The chauffeur?" I squeaked, feeling as though I had to sit down before I fell down. But then I realized I was sitting down. So maybe I needed to put my head between my legs? Or blow into a paper bag? Honestly, I felt like I was going to faint. "Why would I have a fantasy with the chauffeur?"

"I don't really think you would," Lisa said. "I'm sure the hotel can come up with a better fantasy than 'woman gets banged by the hot chauffeur'? That's kind of unimaginative, don't you think?"

"Yeah ..." I stalled, realizing I wasn't ready, for some reason, to tell Lisa about the fantasy experience with Icarus.

"So, have you had your first fantasy yet, or not?"

"You really think the hotel was serious when they said the fantasies would start immediately?" I asked, still wrestling with whether or not to admit the truth. "I'm sure that was just hyperbole."

"I booked the premium deluxe package for you, and when I spoke to the manager, I was told that package includes fantasies that start *immediately*."

"Well, it's okay if they don't start *immediately*."

"No, it's not okay," Lisa said, her voice rising an octave. "You should have already had a fantasy experience by now. That's what you paid for!"

My best friend's words hit me like a series of punches in the gut. The sex with Icarus had been paid for. By me. He was, to be blunt, just a ... prostitute. I was just one of the many clients he'd serviced. That bungalow deluxe premium experience had just been some seedy, immoral transaction, sex for cash. An experience he'd probably provided before to countless other female guests.

The realization upset me, which was crazy. There was no reason to get upset. After all, it had been a fantasy experience. I couldn't take any of it personally.

"Who's your personal assistant?" Lisa demanded. "You need to call her and—"

Three sharp knocks on the door startled me, stealing my attention from Lisa's outrage. "Hey, Lisa, listen, let me call you back, okay? Somebody is at the door."

"Okay, but call your assistant and let her know you didn't get—"

"I will, I will," I said. "I have to go."

"Just a minute," I called out, tossing my cell phone on the coffee table and standing. Walking to the door, I took a deep breath and debated cancelling the historical tour. Whoever was at the door—probably one of the housekeepers—could relay the message to the concierge for me.

I opened the door and my heart damn near exploded, beating wild and frantic. Icarus stood just outside the door, tall and broad-shouldered, more handsome than I remembered.

Again, I thought my knees might buckle, but I somehow managed to stay on my feet.

"Ms. Miller," he said. "How are you this morning?"

"Fine," I said, disappointed by how whispery my voice sounded. "How are you?"

"I'm well," he said. "Thank you for asking. Are you ready to go?"

"Go ... where?" I asked, confused, reeling from his presence and the memories of what we'd done.

"The historical tour?" He gave me a slightly curious look.

"Oh, right ..." Embarrassed, I mumbled something about getting my purse and then hurried away, into the bedroom, where I hyperventilated and then chastened myself for behaving like a silly fangirl and then took more deep breaths and admonished myself to snap out of it because he wasn't the best-looking guy on earth.

Except, to me, he was ...

Okay, so what? The point was I needed to act like a grown damn woman and not a silly virgin. Resisting the urge to scream, I grabbed my bag and headed back into the living room. I wished for the courage to saunter out, hips swaying provocatively, as if I was on the runway.

But my legs were still shaking, and it was all I could do to successfully put one foot in front of the other.

"So, you're my tour guide?" I asked as we left my suite.

"Your tour guide will be Jessie," he said, with brisk, detached efficiency. "I'll be driving."

"Oh," I murmured, disappointed.

Icarus led me to the main building, through the opulent foyer, and down the steps of the front entrance where several limousines were parked.

Walking toward the car, we passed two women who seemed to be leaving. Standing on the sidewalk, they waited, watching as their luggage was placed in the trunk. The women couldn't have appeared more different. One was tall and corpulent, dressed in what looked like a flowing, flowery tent, with blonde curls trailing down her back. The other woman was small and thin, in an expensive business suit, with her hair yanked back from her forehead and coiled in a slick knot at the nape of her neck. And yet, they both wore the same expression— slightly dazed, sullen, and a bit forlorn. I couldn't help wondering if they were sad to be leaving or upset and regretful they'd come to the Heliconia. Had their experiences been worth every penny? Or had the fantasies cost them more than they'd realized?

Up ahead, a woman got out of the limo parked in front of my limo, stumbling and laughing. She seemed a bit tipsy, and from the half-lidded stare she gave her driver as she allowed him to guide her up the stairs, I had a feeling she'd had the "hidden beach spa bungalow" delight, as well, and had also enjoyed it immensely. She was unabashedly advertising her enjoyment while I had tried my best to make sure no one would be able to guess what had happened on the way to the hotel.

They didn't need to guess, I realized now. I was sure the entire hotel staff knew what happened during the limousine rides to and from the airport.

At the limo, Icarus opened the door and helped me inside. He climbed in with me and closed the door. Immediately, my heart started pounding again. Although, honestly, it had never really stopped. His presence was overwhelming, and intoxicating, permeating my senses. I feared I might do something ridiculous, like crawl into his lap, throw my arms around him, and—

"Do you need anything while we wait for Jessie?" Icarus asked.

I stared at him, dumbstruck by his question. Or, *lust-struck*, rather, because I wanted to say *you*. I need you. But that was ridiculous, because I didn't *need* him. I wanted him, maybe. I didn't need him.

"No, thank you," I said, as polite as possible.

"You sure?" he asked, his gaze intense and a little unfathomable, making me wonder if maybe I'd given him the wrong answer. Maybe he'd wanted me to tell him that I needed ... what? Him? No, that couldn't be right. I had to be misinterpreting his looks, misreading him. Most likely, he was just giving me good customer service. Liberada had said he was trying to be more congenial and accom-modating.

There was a knock on the window.

Icarus said, "That's probably Jessie." He opened the door, got out, and exchanged morning pleasantries with the tour guide, who turned out to be a cute, young St. Matean girl with a warm, engaging smile. She got into the back of the limo, introduced herself, and then launched into her spiel, telling me about the historical sites we were scheduled to visit.

Barely listening, I was too busy peering through the darkened windows as Icarus strode to the front of the limo. His confident stride caused an intense fluttering below my navel, and I desperately wanted another fantasy experience with him.

Something Lisa had said sobered me, though, like ice water in my face. *You paid for that fantasy.*

The experience with Icarus hadn't really been a fantasy. It had been business. The business of fooling women into believing their sexual wishes were coming true. The hotel was selling wet dreams at top dollar. The worst part was, I'd bought into the illusion, and I had a feeling it would cost me more than the money I'd paid.

Chapter Six

"So, how was the tour?" Liberada asked later that afternoon, around two p.m.

Looking pretty and professional in her aqua silk blouse and slim white pencil skirt, she'd sailed into the living room of my suite, announcing she had stopped by to make sure I'd been satisfied with the historical tour.

Sitting next to her on the couch, I assured her that I'd found the tour to be a very interesting introduction to St. Matean culture and history. "And I enjoyed the chocolate and coffee samples, as well."

"And was Jessie to your liking?" Liberada asked, in a sly way, as though her mind was in the gutter.

"Jessie was a great guide," I said. "Very informative with a good personality."

Nodding and smiling, Liberada scribbled on a piece of unlined paper in an aqua-colored portfolio made of ostrich. Notes about Jessie's performance, I assumed.

Thinking about Jessie's *performance*, during the tour, I kept wondering if the tour guide would take me off and try to have her way with me, but she made no advances, neither overt nor subtle. Her smiles were always sincere, not seductive or suggestive, and I figured she really was a tour guide and not part of the fantasies.

For some reason, I was glad. I had never been with a woman before, and I had never desired or fantasized about a sexual experience with another female, so I wasn't sure what I would have done if she would have made a move.

Even if Jessie had been a guy, I would have rebuffed him. I wouldn't have felt comfortable with Icarus driving while another guy and I were getting it on in the back seat, separated only by the partition, which may or may not have drowned out my moaning. I wouldn't have liked wondering what Icarus would think about me, spreading my legs so easily for anyone the hotel offered. And yet, wasn't that why I was there? To have as much mind-blowing sex with as many men as possible? Wasn't earth-shattering sex supposed to cure my anxiety?

But, wasn't I fooling myself? Really, how the hell could multiple orgasms revive my dying career?

"And did Icarus mind his manners?" Liberada asked, a little of that mischief in her gaze.

For his part, Icarus was just my driver, and I realized his role had been significant but limited.

He was polite and professional, and though he smiled at me from time to time, there was no indication he remembered our encounter. I tried to resign myself to his polite aloofness, but it was disheartening, knowing he wasn't willing to share a secret glance with me. Our encounter had meant nothing to him. But why should it? My stay at the Heliconia was nothing more than an enhanced fantasy where I was supposed to have encounters with lots of different men. Icarus was one of many. He obviously knew, and had accepted, I was at the hotel to be with lots of different guys like the other guests.

"Icarus was very, uh ..." I stopped for a moment, struggling for the right word, and finally managed to say "he was very mannerly."

Liberada's gaze was both cunning and clever, as though she knew some naughty secret about me I wasn't aware of—yet. I cautioned myself not to overanalyze, especially since my ability to analyze was iffy these days.

"So, I do have another reason for visiting you," she said, smiling brightly, like she was about to tell me I was the winner of some billion-dollar lottery. "I am not sure if you are aware of this or not, but the Palmchat Islands—and St. Mateo, in particular—are known for their breathtaking, magnificent waterfalls, and we happen to have our very own waterfall here on the grounds of the Heliconia Hotel."

"Really?" I said. "I didn't know that."

"The falls are spectacular," Liberada gushed. "And this is the best time of the day to visit them. The midafternoon sun sparkles on the water like diamonds as it rushes over the cliffs."

"That does sound lovely," I said.

"So, I was thinking you could go and see them now," she said. "And then you can come back and have a nice bath and a nap, sounds good?"

"Yes, but how do I get to the falls?" I asked.

Liberada smiled and opened her ostrich portfolio. "I have a map for you."

I took the piece of paper she handed me and stared at it, frowning. The map was crudely drawn, as though by some kindergarten child. "Do you have a better map than this one?"

Liberada shook her head and gave me an apologetic smile. "I'm sorry we don't. But don't worry, if you get lost, I'm sure you'll come across someone to help you find your way."

"Well, if you think so," I said, wary of the sassiness in her gaze.

"Have a great time," she said and then left my suite.

Thirty minutes later, dressed in khaki shorts, a pink tank top, and hiking sandals, I headed down a wide path through the rainforest behind the hotel. Staring at the map, I tried to make sense of the vague markings and evasive instructions. Turn left by the bird of paradise. Turn right by the bamboo tree. Well, which damn bamboo tree? The forest was littered with bamboo. And banana trees. And bird of paradise and heliconia and dozens of other shrubs, low-lying branches, and hanging vines.

Even though I probably wasn't going to find my way to the falls, I found the tropical scenery peaceful. Birds chirped and called and sang. The sun winked through the canopy of broad leaves high above me.

Another twenty minutes passed and I stopped to get a bottle of water from my bag. After a few generous sips, I was contemplating giving up the search for the falls when I heard a branch snap, some-where behind me. Heart slamming, I spun around, praying it wasn't one of those wild pigs I'd read about during my research of the islands.

Nothing was behind me, however. Worried, I tried to peer between the jumble of leaves, imagining I could see the crazed black eyes of a rabid boar, ready to come charging out of the bushes and—

"Excuse me."

Gasping loudly, I turned to the left, in the direction of the voice, stumbling slightly.

"Whoa, you okay?" The guy caught my arm, helping me stay on my feet.

"I'm fine," I said and looked up at him. He was very handsome, tall, with lean muscles, like those of a champion swimmer. Not the thick solid heavyweight prizefighter build like Icarus but—

Why the hell was I comparing Icarus to this random stranger? Why was I even thinking about Icarus?

"Didn't mean to scare you," the good-looking stranger said and gave me a smile, which was nice in a sort of male model posing for an ad campaign way.

"That's okay."

"I'm kind of lost," he said.

"Where are you trying to go?"

"I was supposed to meet my friends at some waterfall near the Heliconia," he said. "My friends heard about the waterfall on the hotel's property. Apparently, it's only for the enjoyment of the hotel's guests, but my friends said people sneak onto the property all the time. Problem is, it's hard to find the falls without a map, which the hotel has, but for guests only."

I laughed and then said, "I don't think you could find it with the map the hotel gives you. At least, I haven't been able to find it."

"You're staying at the hotel?"

I stared at him, slightly suspicious, suddenly aware that I was out in the middle of the rainforest, maybe miles away from the hotel.

There was no telling what could happen to me. There was no telling if the guy was telling the truth. Maybe he wasn't really going to the waterfalls. Maybe he was some local guy, aware of the hotel's secret purpose, who stalked the rainforest, looking for female guests to attack.

Sure, I had my cell phone, but the good-looking stranger could probably grab it and knock me over the head with it before I got a chance to call the hotel.

And yet as I stared at those amber eyes, I got a flash of discernment. I remembered Liberada saying I would find someone to help me if I got lost. Recalling her sly gaze, I realized I was in the middle of another fantasy.

The stranger was too gorgeous and sexy to just be some random guy who was trespassing.

I decided to play along. "Yes, I'm staying at the hotel, and actually, I was on my way to see the waterfalls. They gave me a map, but I can't figure it out. You want to see it?"

"Sure," he said. I pulled the map from my bag and gave it to him. He made a show of studying it, and he furrowed his brow as he turned the paper this way and that way, as if he really needed a map to get to the falls. I would have bet he had taken lots of women to the waterfalls before, playing the role of the lost hiker in this premium deluxe fantasy.

After a moment, he declared that I was right, the map sucked, but he thought it might give us some assistance.

"Okay," I said, still playing along, trying not to snicker. "I'll follow you."

I figured he'd lead me right to the falls, but to his credit, he made a few wrong turns. Eventually, we were able to hear the falls, and after a few more turns, we pushed through a wall of tall hibiscus and came to a large clearing.

The scene before me wasn't quite as majestic as the hidden beach I'd seen when Icarus had pushed past the elephant leaves. The falls were beautiful, just as Liberada had promised. Framed by the blue sky above and the surrounding rainforest, it was like a private, secret oasis. The water rushed over a cliff and plunged into a clear turquoise pool that shimmered in the midafternoon sunlight. From the edge of the tropical forest, we stepped onto a bank of white sand, which angled down to the water.

Laughter rang out beneath the rushing roar of the water, and then the handsome stranger called out, "Hercules! Hermes!"

Hercules and Hermes, I thought, rolling my eyes at the kitsch of the names—which I didn't believe for one minute were real names—when two good-looking, well-built guys emerged from behind the waterfalls, walking toward us, shirtless, the clear water lapping around toned, tight abs, I understood why they'd been given the names of Greek gods.

They stopped in the middle of the pool, calling back to the stranger, telling him that the water was nice and he should come on in.

"Who's your friend?" the taller one asked. He was buff and dark with dark curly hair, closely cropped. The guy standing next to him was just slightly shorter but a bit more muscular and with a more olive complexion.

"I'm not sure. We just met." He turned to me, smiled, and then asked, "What's your name?"

"Quinn," I said, no longer wary, convinced that all three guys were part of this waterfalls fantasy.

Less convincing, however, was my resolve to live it out, my willingness to go through with it. I knew the fantasy would involve sex, but I wasn't sure which one, if any of them, I wanted to be with. My body still craved Icarus, but maybe sex with another man would help to dampen my desire. Last thing I wanted to do was fall for him.

"What's your name?" I asked.

"Apollo," he said.

"Apollo ..." I repeated, trying not to giggle. Of course, his name was Apollo. Another island Greek god.

"So, Quinn," Apollo said and started to take off his shirt. "You wanna go in?"

"I don't have a swimsuit," I said, my heart pounding with worry and excitement.

"Quinn doesn't have a swimsuit," Apollo said and dropped his T-shirt, revealing an abundance of glistening, rock-hard muscles. Around his neck, there was a thin, gold chain, and hanging from it was a medallion. About the size of a silver dollar, it was positioned between the swell of his hard pecs.

"No clothes allowed!" the water gods called out.

Panic sizzled through me, settling in my stomach and then quickly dropping lower, below my navel, and then even lower, where it turned to desire and propelled me toward a decision I knew I would regret.

And yet, I felt trapped in the grip of some kind of obsessive compulsion, or compulsive obsession, I wasn't sure. I only knew that the feeling was overwhelming, and I couldn't stop myself from stepping out of my hiking sandals and then taking off my pink tank top and my khaki shorts.

Standing in my underwear, though, that "ice water in my face" sobering feeling returned. The feverish desire waned and the panic intensified. What the hell was I doing? Was I really about to strip naked in front of three guys I didn't even know? Was I actually going to skinny dip?

Apollo moved to stand in front of me. Heart thudding, I stared up at him. His lusty, half-lidded gaze turned the panic back to desire. Reaching out, Apollo unfastened the clip holding the two demi-cups of my bra together and then pushed the cups back, exposing my breasts. My nipples hardened as he slipped the straps off my shoulders. The other two watched as Apollo undressed me. Aware of their gazes, I felt something primal within me roaring louder than the falls, something intoxicating. When Apollo tugged my panties down, I didn't protest ...

I wanted them off. I wanted to be naked and wild and wicked. A breeze danced across my nipples. Gasping in delight, I rushed into the water, laughing and splashing.

In the water, they surrounded me like a trio of hunky water gods, kissing every inch of my body, quick pecks, teasing me. Dipping beneath the water, they taunted me with fingers that brushed lightly but never lingered, enough to send me into a frenzy of intense longing and need. The balmy water was like liquid silk, but it didn't feel nearly as good as the hands exploring my body, the fingers everywhere at the same time.

It was all so decadent, for me, at least. Maybe old hat, or boring and blasé, for some girls, but the combination of water and hands all over my body was delicious and wicked. They stroked slightly, fingertips near my opening but never going inside. Tongues darted quickly against my nipples. Moaning, I slid my own hands beneath the water, determined to take care of myself if they weren't in the mood to please me.

But one of them grabbed my hands and brought them out of the water and behind my back.

Apollo wrapped his arms around my waist, pressing me against his hard erection. "Are you ready, Quinn?"

Unable to speak, I was desperate to grind against him, anxious for release, and yet I wasn't really sure. Was I ready? Could I really have a foursome with three guys? Did I want to do that? Was that really my fantasy?

"Quinn?" Apollo prodded, his gaze uncertain.

"No, I don't want to ..." I shook my head, pushing away from Apollo, my heart slamming, fear and shame battling within me. "I'm sorry. I thought I did, but ..."

"Bitch, are you serious?" Hercules scowled at me. "Do you know what kind of hotel you came to?"

"Hey, if she ain't interested, she ain't interested," the other guy, Hermes said, turning and heading out of the water. "This is actually very convenient for me. I got other shit I need to take care of."

Scoffing, Hercules sneered at me as he followed Hermes out of the water. "Can't stand when silly, scary bitches waste your time. Whatever. That bitch wishes she could take all twelve of these inches."

"Twelve?" Hermes laughed as he pulled on a pair of cargo shorts. "Fool, you wish."

After slipping back into their clothes, the two water gods went off down the path, disappearing into the trees, laughing and joking, largely at my expense. I didn't care what they thought of me. What mattered was what I thought of me. I had a feeling I wouldn't have thought very much of myself had I gone through with the orgy. I'd made a lot of bad decisions during the past six months, but I was happy a foursome wouldn't be another irrational choice I'd have to lament and regret.

"Okay, those assholes are gone, so ..." Apollo slipped an arm around me again. "Now, it's just me and you, and that's all it should be. Just us ..."

"I don't think so," I said, sidestepping, avoiding his kiss as he bent his head toward mine. "Sorry ..."

"You don't think so?" He moved toward me, eyes narrowed, filled with an emotion I couldn't identify or understand. "Why don't you think so? Why don't you want to have a fantasy with me?"

"I just ..." I tried to swallow, but my mouth felt like cotton, and my heart was beating so wildly it was roaring in my ears. His aggression scared and confused me. I fought the urge to cry, desperately wishing I could be the woman I'd once been, the cunning mediator who would disarm a hostile witness and de-escalate a threatening situation.

"You think I'm not good enough for you?" he challenged, eyes hard, cold. "You think I won't get hard enough? You think I won't go deep enough? Fast enough? You think I won't have you screaming my name? You think I won't make you forget about every other man you ever been with?"

"No, I never said ..." I took a deep breath, praying his strange anger toward me would subside and I wouldn't be assaulted or raped. "Listen, I didn't mean to upset you, I just—"

"Go fuck yourself," he spat and then turned, sloshing water as he headed away from me.

DAY THREE

Chapter Seven

"The hotel actually planned an *orgy* for one of your fantasies?" Lisa groaned. "Maybe you were right. Maybe you shouldn't have gone to the Heliconia."

"*Maybe* I was right?" I laughed, staring at the burger and plate of fries I'd ordered. Moments before Lisa's call, I'd been taking part in one of the hotel's excursions, a trip to a picturesque fishing village. Scenic and quaint, the village's main attraction was the waterfront. Colorful boats bobbed in the briny water beneath the weather-beaten wooden plank boardwalk, which was lined with a variety of souvenir shops and restaurants, one of which, the Lovely Lobster, I was sitting at right now, enjoying a lunch break from the tour.

The guide had been leading our group—seventeen women, some of them raucous, others reticent— along narrow streets, pointing out Caribbean architecture, explaining the history, for the better part of the morning, and I'd found his narration informative and interesting.

"Okay, you were absolutely right," Lisa admitted.

"Don't think the Heliconia is for me," I said. "Maybe I can go over to their sister property, the Hibiscus."

"Well, before you leave, I think you should tell Liberada how rude and nasty that Apollo guy was," Lisa said. "Who the hell does he think he is? He needs to do something about that misplaced anger."

"I never have to see him again, so I'm not going to worry about it," I said, not in the mood to relive the unpleasant experience by the waterfalls.

I still couldn't believe I'd stripped naked in front of three men I didn't know, but I was glad I hadn't gone through with the orgy. I suppose it might have been sinful fun. Having three men pleasure me at the same time might have been heaven. Beyond hedonistic. A salacious experience, even if there were no goats involved. Maybe I shouldn't knock it since I hadn't tried it.

Nevertheless, I was sure regret and self-recrimination would have replaced lasciviousness and lust. The experience would have left me feeling guilty and anguished. I wasn't the woman I once was, but I knew I couldn't be the kind of woman who paid for sex. I would have to find some other way to get over the anxiety derailing my career. Sex wasn't going to help me start winning cases again.

Reaching for a lukewarm fry, I said, "Let's talk about something else, okay? You still online dating?"

Later that afternoon, back in my suite, I called housekeeping to request a bath. The heady incense, rose petals, and slight breeze sneaking through the window was just what I needed to ease my anxious mind.

After soaking for almost two hours, I grabbed a plush oversized towel to dry off and then dropped it on the floor. Naked, I headed into the bedroom and stopped abruptly, frowning.

There was an aqua envelope on my bed.

Panic nearly knocked me out. I knew what the aqua envelope meant. Another fantasy. My heart kicked against my rib cage. I wouldn't have another fantasy. Because I *couldn't*. I didn't want to experience any more fantasies; I didn't care how good-looking or sexy the guy was. I was ready to leave. I wanted to get the hell off the island, go back to the United States, and maybe pop a few pills to deal with my anxiety, the way Lisa had originally suggested.

Hesitant, I sat on the edge of the bed and picked up the envelope. I didn't want to open it. I wanted to rip it to shreds. But, despite my reluctance, I lifted the flap, extracted the note, and read ...

Check your phone for an important message

Frowning, slightly annoyed, I debated whether or not to comply. After all, I wasn't going to participate in another fantasy at this damn hotel. I was getting the hell off this island as soon as possible. So, I didn't need to check my phone to find out about the next guy the hotel had hired to bang me into oblivion. If the hotel had sent me a text, I could reply with a message of my own, telling them to send my final bill because I was checking out early.

After grabbing my cell phone from my purse, I sat on a chaise in the corner and checked my text messages. Not surprisingly, I had one, which I opened.

Video images filled the screen of the smartphone, and for a moment, I was confused as I stared at the woman in the video. She was on her back, writhing and moaning as the man on top of her thrust into her. Moving in a frantic rhythm, she clutched the man's shoulders, and when her head turned, the camera zoomed closer and I saw her face clearly ...

I knew the woman, even though I hardly recognized her as she frowned from the pleasure, her eyes crazed with lust. I knew the man making love to her, too, recognized the sensuous, animalistic power of his huge, magnificent body.

It was Icarus.

And it was me.

It was Icarus making love to me in the spa bungalow.

Staring at the video, I felt something imploding within me, as though my foundation was collapsing from the inside out, and the very essence of me was deconstructing, and decomposing, quickly being destroyed. Paralyzed, I stared at the screen. A scream churned in my gut, desperate to escape, but I couldn't remember how to open my mouth and let it out. I wanted to throw the cell phone across the room. I wanted to smash it into a million pieces. But I couldn't move.

All I could do was stare at the screen of the cell phone, terrorized, horrified.

The video ended abruptly with a still shot of my face, frozen in an almost painful ecstasy.

And then, a deep, distorted voice, like some evil malevolent being, spoke ...

"Ms. Miller, you certainly put on quite a show. But I'm sure it's a performance you don't want anyone to ever see. However, lots of viewers will enjoy it, unless you make sure they don't see it. But how can you make sure that your 'Sex and the Chauffeur' porn doesn't end up all over the Internet?"

Horror intensified, multiplying inside of me.

"Well, Ms. Miller, it's simple. I'm willing to sell you this video. I only have one copy, and the sale will be final. It will cost you one hundred thousand dollars. I want this money in cash, unmarked bills with different serial numbers. I'll give you five days to get the money to me. Don't go to the police. If you call the cops, I'll know about it, and then the deal will be off, and your porn video, 'Sex and the Chauffeur,' will be immediately released to your law firm and then to the public. Don't try anything stupid unless you want all your colleagues to know you went to a sex hotel and paid to be screwed by men you don't even know. On day five, I will contact you and tell you where to bring the money. Once again, you will be watched. If you contact the authorities, I will ruin your life."

The evil, terrifying voice stopped, leaving behind an odd silence, as though sound no longer existed.

At once, a strange mania came over me, and for a moment, I thought I might laugh. Maybe it was some strange joke? Maybe I was dreaming? Maybe this was some kind of hallucinogenic manifestation of my anxiety, which still plagued me? As I continued to stare at the freeze frame of my orgasmic bliss, the panic returned, pulling me under, drowning me, and I realized I was sobbing uncontrollably, gasping for air as the phone slid from my hand, and I slid to the floor.

Time passed, though I wasn't sure how much, and eventually, the tears subsided and the fear retreated. As I pulled myself back onto the chaise, one question screamed through my mind, demanding to be answered. Who had sent the text message? Who the hell was black-mailing me? How could I find out?

It took me a while to marshal my thoughts, but I remembered the damn aqua envelope. How had it gotten in my room? Who had put it on my bed? Liberada? The butler? One of the maids?

Hands trembling, I called the housekeeper and told her I needed to see her immediately and it was urgent. She showed up about five seconds later, attentive, and yet there was a nervous wariness in her gaze. Wasting no time with polite formalities, I held the aqua envelope up and asked, "Did you deliver this?"

"Yes, ma'am," she said, her voice a quivering whisper. "I was told to deliver it to you."

My heart shot into my throat. "Who told you to deliver this to me?"

The housekeeper said, "Your driver."

"My driver?" My heart dropped into my stomach. "What are you talking about?"

"Your driver told me to deliver the note," she said, her face clouded with worry. "I know I shouldn't have done it. We're not supposed to have unauthorized contact with any of the guests, but—"

"Wait a minute," I stopped her, confused, my heart slamming. "You said ... my *driver?*"

"Yes, your chauffeur." Nodding, the housekeeper said, "Icarus."

Chapter Eight

Your driver told me to deliver the note ... Icarus.

I wasn't sure how many hours had passed since I'd questioned the maid about the aqua envelope, but the shock, confusion, and rage still roiled within me. Something wicked and sinister stirred my emotions, whipping me into a frenzy of hate and fury. I was livid, outraged, seeing blood red. I didn't understand anything. *Your driver told me to deliver the note ... Icarus.* Why? There were too many questions and no answers. I didn't know what to think, didn't know what to do. It was still so damn hard to fathom what the maid had told me. I didn't know how to believe the truth.

Icarus had secretly taped our encounter in the spa bungalow, and now he was blackmailing me.

It didn't make sense. Why would Icarus blackmail me? How could he? I had thought that maybe he and I ...

I didn't want to admit what I'd thought, what I had wanted, wished, and hoped. Those longings were an indictment of my irrational anxiousness, and I burst into bitter tears.

All I could do was sob, uncontrollably, and as I collapsed to my knees on the floor, I didn't think the tears would ever stop.

But they did.

It took about an hour, but I stopped crying. Anger replaced my sadness. But, truly, to call what I was feeling anger didn't do it justice. I was seething with rage, all of it directed at one person—me.

I wouldn't be filled with anger and hate if not for one person—Icarus. Did he really think he could blackmail me and get away with it? Did he think I wouldn't confront him? I wanted to know why he was trying to extort money from me. He was going to tell me why the hell he wanted to ruin my life.

Determined to get answers from Icarus, I picked up the phone and pushed the number five, my direct line to Liberada. "Good afternoon, Ms. Miller, how may I help you?"

Her effervescent accent pissed me off, but I knew I was directing my rage at the wrong person, and so I took a breath before I said, as pleasantly as I could manage, "Hi, Liberada. If it's not too much trouble, I would like to go for a drive."

"Any place in particular you want to go?"

"Well, I ..." Trailing off, I stammered something incoherent and then said, "I haven't been to any of the beaches yet, so maybe ..."

"Okay, no problem," she said. "St. Mateo has some of the loveliest beaches in the Caribbean. Copper Beach is only five minutes from the hotel, so you really don't need to have someone drive you—"

"Oh, but afterwards, I'd like to do some souvenir shopping," I said quickly, my heart thundering in panic. "I mean, if that's okay?"

"That will certainly be perfectly okay," she said, her tone even brighter, if that was possible. "Remember, Ms. Miller, your wish is our command."

"That's good to hear," I said, my hands shaking, a slight tremor in my voice. "So ... can you tell Icarus that I'll be ready in ten minutes?"

The limo door opened and Icarus reached in to help me out.

I stared at his hand, hesitating. I didn't want him to touch me. Or look at me. Or even know who the hell I was because I wished to God that I didn't know him, that I'd never met him. I wished I had never let him make love to me.

As I allowed Icarus to help me out, the feel of his hand closing over mine gave me a jolt of excitement and ecstasy that enraged me. I felt my body betraying me, and I knew that, deep down, I didn't regret our lovemaking in the bungalow. Just the opposite, I relished it.

I wanted more of it, wanted more of him. Which made no sense. How could I still want a devious son of a bitch who was trying to blackmail me?

Outside of the limo, the ocean breeze whispered across my face as I looked around. My heart started to pound louder than the waves crashing against the sugary white sand. The fragrance of salt and fruit swirled around me, and tears pricked my eyes.

I recognized the familiar surroundings, the palm trees and the turquoise waters.

After I'd ended the call to Liberada, I had grabbed my purse and my cell phone with the offensive video and headed out of my suite. Icarus had been waiting in the open-air marbled lobby for me, and he'd mentioned that Liberada had told him I wanted to go to the beach.

As we pulled away from the hotel, Icarus turned onto the main road, and I wasn't really paying attention to where he was going. I was aware of the car gliding along the winding roads, but I was too busy thinking of what I would say to him once we were alone.

I was sure he knew I'd received his little blackmail note. Most likely, he thought this impromptu trip to the beach wasn't really as spontaneous as it seemed. It would be a chance for the two of us to discuss his extortion demands.

When the limo stopped and Icarus opened the door for me, I had no idea where we were, and it really didn't matter. I didn't want to sunbathe or shop for souvenirs. All I wanted to do was tell Icarus I would never give him one hundred thousand dollars.

"You know where we are?" Icarus asked.

Irritated, I gazed at the palm trees and the white sand and the way the sun danced on the water. Why the hell would he bring me here? Why would he think I would want to come back to the hidden beach? To the place where we first made love? And why was this damn beach making me feel so forlorn and nostalgic, making me reminisce about things I was so desperate to forget?

Glancing left, my gaze followed the sand as it rushed toward the tropical forest. Despite myself, I focused on the wall of elephant trees, knowing that the bungalow was behind those large, waxy green leaves.

"What the hell are we doing here?" I demanded, trying not to remember our lovemaking in the bungalow. It had been an earth-shattering, exciting experience, one of the best in my life. Now, it was tainted and spoiled, since I knew he'd been secretly videoing the entire encounter.

"You wanted to go to the beach."

"Look, I ..." I cleared my throat. "I need to talk to you about—"

"My note," Icarus said. "You got it?"

"Yeah, I got it," I said, my voice trembling as I tried to focus on my rage and not the crushing disappointment threatening to overwhelm me.

"Well?"

His blatant eagerness was appalling. Was he so aggressively mercenary that he wouldn't even try to be sly and subtle with me? Why had he bothered with blackmail, I wondered, scowling at him. Wouldn't it have been easier for him to just point a gun in my face and demand that I give him my purse?

"Quinn?"

Pushing the sadness away, I let the anger take over. It traveled from the pit of my gut and over to my shoulder, down my arm, and to my hand. I slapped him. The blow was pretty hard, surprisingly, considering that he was much taller than me. The brunt of my slap landed against his lower jaw, but my nails got a piece of him, slashing his chin.

Shocked, he stared at me. Livid, I matched his gaze, even though I ran the risk of becoming mesmerized by those soulful, whiskey-colored eyes.

"What the hell is your problem?" he demanded.

"What is my problem? What is my ... how the hell can you ask me that when ... my problem is ... " I took a deep breath, hardly able to get the words out. "You are not going to get away with this!"

"Wait a minute, what the hell are you talking about?" Icarus grabbed me.

"I'm talking about your text message with—"

Confusion crossed his features. "What text message?" He shook his head. "I didn't send you a text."

"Liar!"

"Quinn, will you please calm down and listen to me!"

"No, I will not calm down, and get your hands off me!" I said, trying to twist away from him. "You are not going to get away with blackmailing me! I am going to the police, and I am going to have you arrested!"

"Blackmailing you?" He frowned, looking genuinely confused. I couldn't tell if he was really shocked or if he was a damn good actor. At that moment, I didn't give a damn. I just wanted to get the hell away from him.

Pushing away, I turned and started walking, trudging through the soft, powdery sand, not caring where the hell I was going, as long as it was the hell away from Icarus.

"Quinn, wait! Listen, I don't know what the hell is going on," he said. "I don't know why you think I'm trying to blackmail you, but—"

I faced him. "Stay away from me, okay."

"Quinn, listen to me," Icarus said. "I don't know anything about blackmailing you. I don't know—"

"You asked me if I got your note and I did," I told him. "I read your damn note."

"I don't know what note you read," Icarus said. "But, it wasn't the note that I sent you."

"The maid told me that you told her to deliver that note to me," I said, yanking away from him, stepping back even though I wanted to step closer, into his arms. What the hell was wrong with me? How could I still want him, knowing he was plotting to extort money from me? Was I nothing more than one of those sex-starved women Joshua had described? *Eager for some good sex.*

I was beginning to understand why I'd lost three cases, back to back to back. Obviously, I'd lost my mind, in addition to my sense of logic, pragmatism, and discernment. There was no other explanation for my attraction to Icarus except stark raving lunacy. The woman I thought I was would never be controlled by lust, allowing desire to impede her judgment. Problem was, the old Quinn was missing in action, but I needed to find her, quickly, before the new Quinn made any more ridiculous decisions.

"I did tell the maid to deliver the note," Icarus said. "But, my note said—"

"I know what the note said," I told him, taking a few more steps back, irritated by how the sight of him made me swing wildly from lust to rage and back to lust. "And you need to know that I'm not going to let you blackmail me!"

"Quinn, I—"

"Go to hell!" I told him. "And don't worry about taking me back to the hotel. I'll get a damn cab."

Chapter Nine

Back at the hotel, I paced back and forth in the living room, trying to control my scattered thoughts, trying to make sense of what was happening to me.

Feeling crazy and desperate, I walked from one couch to the next, sitting down and then jumping up. One moment, I was nervous and jittery and convinced that my life as I knew it was over. The next second, I was calm and introspective, certain I would find a way out of the mess I'd made of my life.

Nevertheless, I wasn't sure what was going on with Icarus and didn't know what to believe. Was Icarus telling the truth? Or had he lied to me? Was he the blackmailer? If so, why would he go through the grand pretense of trying to make me believe he hadn't sent that text message? Was he playing some kind of psychological game? Trying to mess with my head? Trying to make me think ... what? I didn't know. Everything was too confusing.

Once again, I couldn't think. I needed a fresh perspective. I needed someone else's opinions and ideas and thoughts and deductions to help me come up with some conclusions and a plan to deal with my situation.

Grabbing my cell phone, I called my best friend Lisa.

"My life is ruined," I blurted out, close to tears, when Lisa answered.

"What? Wait a minute, what are you talking about?" Lisa demanded. "Quinn, calm down and tell me what the hell is going on, okay?"

It took a few deep breaths, and several times I had to stop and get myself together so I wouldn't burst into tears, but eventually, I was able to confide in Lisa. After I'd finished, there was an odd pause, during which I'd wondered if the line had been accidentally disconnected, but then Lisa said, "Pay him."

I jumped up from the couch, my heart pounding. "What?"

"Pay the chauffeur and then leave that damn island."

"I'm not going to pay him," I said, confused and offended by her suggestion. "I'm not letting him get away with this!"

"You don't have a choice, okay," Lisa said, a fierce demand in her voice. "Pay him, and then tell him you want to see him erase the video, and then get on a plane, and—"

"If I pay him once, what's to stop him from blackmailing me again?" I asked, pacing the length of the couch. "He's probably got a dozen copies of that damn video!"

Lisa sighed. "I know but—"

"No, I can't," I said, circling the couch counterclockwise.

"Quinn, think rationally, okay?"

Sinking to the couch again, I said, "I haven't been able to think rationally for the past six months, and I doubt if I'll start right now."

"Listen. That devious limo driver is going to have you all over the Internet," Lisa said. "He said the whole world will know. The story will be anxiety-ridden prominent attorney makes porn video."

"I know that," I said, panic exploding within me again.

"Then you know there's too much at stake for you to play around with this guy," she said. "You'll give your grandfather a stroke and your dad a heart attack! And what about the partners at Ellison, Zupancic, and Cox?"

"Oh God ..." I whispered, remembering the moral turpitude clause in the employment contract I'd signed. If the video was released, the firm could fire me, and no other prominent self-respecting establishment would want their reputation tainted by my seedy antics.

"Do you really want everybody at your firm to know that you went to a sex hotel?"

"Yeah, because you told me to," I said, flushed and yet chilled, my body going hot and then ice cold, intermittently. "I never would have come to this place if you hadn't insisted that I needed sexual healing to get over my anxiety!"

"Wait a minute, are you blaming me?"

"It's your damn fault that I'm in this mess!" I yelled, unable to temper my irrational thoughts. "You wanted me to come here! It was your damn idea! If I hadn't listened to you then none of this would have happened!"

"Yes, it was my idea," Lisa admitted, her tone curt and clipped. "But I didn't put a damn gun to your head!

Incensed, and yet with no argument to dispute her, I said nothing, just drew my feet beneath me and stared at nothing, no longer trying to get hold of the emotions warring within me.

"Look, I don't mean to make you feel worse about all this," Lisa said. "And, honestly, I think I got so upset because ..."

"Because?"

"Because I do feel responsible," Lisa said. "You're right, I pushed you to go to St. Mateo. I convinced you that you would feel better about yourself if you had a bunch of crazy sex."

"Like you said," I told her, "you didn't put a gun to my head. I could have said, no, I don't want to go, I don't want to have sex with anyone."

"But, if I hadn't told you about the hotel—"

"Lisa, it's not your fault," I said. "Really, it's not."

"Okay, maybe it's not completely my fault," she said. "But, I am somewhat to blame for this hell you're going through, and I want to help you."

"There's really nothing you can do."

"Except be there for you," Lisa said. "I could fly down there. I have some vacation—"

"No, no, don't do that," I told her. "You don't have to disrupt your life because of my stupid choices."

"You wouldn't have made those choices if I hadn't—"

"Lisa, don't, okay? Assigning blame is not going to solve the problem."

"A hundred thousand dollars will solve the problem," Lisa said. "You've got to pay that asshole and then leave that damn island."

"I know that."

"Do you, really?" Lisa asked. "Quinn, you only have five days to get the money. I think you should call your banker and start getting things in motion. It's not going to be easy to get a hundred thousand dollars cash."

"Yeah," I said, distracted by the worry and panic threatening to overtake me. "I know."

After the call with Lisa, I stood, walked across the living room to the French doors, and stepped out onto the terrace. The warm breeze with its floral fragrance entranced me. Lying on one of the chaise lounges, I closed my eyes and tried to relax, tried to forget about my problems for a moment or two. Despite the turmoil in my life, I dozed off.

It wasn't a peaceful, refreshing nap. My subconscious conjured up a virulent nightmare, one in which I was running through the forest. Someone was chasing me, and they had a gun. Every now and then, I heard a gunshot and the petals of a hibiscus flower would explode as the bullet tore through it. Eventually, I tripped, and when I scrambled to my knees, my pursuer stood before me, pointing a gun in my face.

Trembling and cowering, I stared up into the face I knew well. My own face. As all my anxiety dreams had before, this one ended with me shooting myself.

With a crying gasp, I awoke, shaken and slightly disoriented, my heart slamming. Pulling my knees to my chest, I scanned my surroundings, wary, half-expecting to hear gunshots. Another anxiety nightmare. The first one since I'd arrived in paradise, which was supposed to have stopped the crazy dreams. Disappointed and discouraged, I realized I still wasn't close to being over the anxiety. And maybe, I wouldn't get over the anxiety until I discovered what was fueling it.

Why had I started making foolish decisions six months ago? What was driving the illogical self-sabotaging tendencies threatening my career?

I wasn't sure, but somehow, someway, I needed to figure it out.

DAY FOUR

Chapter Ten

"Oh, Ms. Miller," said the housekeeper as she was about to leave my suite after delivering my lunch—niçoise salad, fruit, and a dirty martini.

After a third sip of the olive-brined vodka, I glanced up at her. "Yes?"

"I almost forgot," she said, walking back into the dining alcove, slipping a hand into the wide pocket on her aqua-colored apron. "This is for you."

Paralyzed, I glared at her. "What is that?"

She held an aqua-colored envelope toward me. "I think it got lost. The butler said he found it in the trash."

"In the trash?" I eyed the envelope, suspicious, reluctant to take it.

The housekeeper shrugged. "That's what the butler said. Then he saw your name on the back of it, and he told me to give it to you."

I nodded and then said, "Just leave it. I'll open it later."

The maid gave me a polite nod, then placed the envelope on the table, and left, wishing me a wonderful day on her way out.

Taking a few more sips of the dirty martini, I studied the envelope as though it was a rattlesnake, coiled and ready to strike. Wary, with trembling fingers, I pulled the note from the envelope and stared at it.

Quinn, call me. Icarus. Beneath the bold, decisive strokes, there was a phone number. Hope rose in me, filling me with elation, but I fought to ignore it.

Confused, I read the note again, over and over. The more I read the words, the less they made sense and the more puzzled I became. Had Icarus been telling me the truth? *I don't know what note you read, but it wasn't the note that I sent you.* Or, had he bribed the maid to deliver the envelope and give me some lie about the butler finding it in the trash? He had to know I was suspicious of him. Maybe he'd decided he needed to fool me into thinking that he was innocent, and on my side.

Was it possible that Icarus was blackmailing me in plain sight, right in front of my face?

Despite my doubts about him, I wanted Icarus to be innocent. I needed him to be innocent. Because if he wasn't, then how could I continue to allow the attraction and feelings I'd developed for him to run rampant. Common sense dictated I should hate him and want him behind bars for his attempt to extort money from me.

Couldn't rely on my common sense these days, though.

I jumped up, abandoning the lunch I had no appetite for, and hurried into the bedroom to get my cell phone. I sat on the chaise and, with the note from Icarus on my lap, I called the number he'd scrawled across the pale aqua paper.

The phone rang several times, and then the answering machine came on. I ended the call, not wanting to leave a message. Anxious to talk to Icarus, I decided to go to the front atrium and ask one of the staff members to find him.

While waiting to talk to a desk assistant, I wandered out of the foyer and to the front entrance.

The circular drive in front of the hotel was teeming with activity, limousines arriving and departing. Chauffeurs opened doors, helping women out. Drivers closed doors after helping women into the back-seats of their respective cars. Bellmen hurried to load and unload expensive luggage while young, slim, attractive St. Matean personal assistants strode out to welcome whichever sex-starved woman had been assigned to them.

In the midst of the frenzied activity, I sidestepped over to a marble column, hoping to spot Liberada. As my eyes drifted to and fro, I spotted Icarus. I froze, and something plummeted within me as I watched him escorting another woman out of a limo. Envy rocked me, and I nearly collapsed. Realistically, I'd suspected that Icarus had been assigned to more than one guest, but having the proof of my suspicions right in front of me was too much to bear.

As he and the woman ascended the stairs, Icarus glanced in my direction. Our eyes met as he walked past me, but there was no recognition in his gaze, and a moment later, he looked away.

I went back to my suite, feeling stupid and naive. Crawling into bed, I buried myself beneath the covers and sobbed myself to sleep.

Hours later, I woke and found the room flooded with a copper golden glow. The sun was setting. The clock on the bed table told me it was a few minutes after six. Shocked that I had slept so long, I stumbled out of bed and into the bathroom where I took a long, scalding shower, trying to wash away the shame and guilt, trying to refresh and awaken a sense of determination and decisiveness.

Wallowing in bed and crying wasn't going to make my problems go away. I needed to analyze and evaluate my predicament, come up with options, make some decisions, formulate a plan, and carry it out. Easier said than done, I thought, stepping out of the shower. But I couldn't just curl into a ball and die. I had to try to use all of the perceptive and resourceful skills I employed as a litigator to figure a way out of this predicament.

After drying off, I slipped into a robe and went into the bedroom. Moments later, there was a knock at the door. Housekeeping, I figured. Probably here to inquire about my dinner plans. Not in a rush, I went into the living area and opened the door.

Icarus stood before me. Lust flooded me, like a shot of adrenaline, leaving me dizzy and weak. My attraction to Icarus was too powerful and hypnotic, like a drug.

We stared at each other for a moment too long before I asked, "What the hell do you want?"

"I want you to know that I didn't send that blackmail note," he said. "I would never do something like that, I would never blackmail anyone. But especially not you."

The earnest sincerity in his gaze made me feel horrible for thinking he could be so conniving and mercenary. And yet, I was worried by my lack of wariness, wondering if my desire for him was causing me to ignore the signs of his treachery.

"I know you didn't send it," I said, even though I didn't really know, I was just hoping. "I got the letter you wanted me to have."

"I don't understand," he said. "If you got my letter, why did you say—"

"I got two letters," I told him, stepping back, allowing him entrance.

"Two letters?" he asked, confusion in his gaze.

"I don't really know what's going on," I said and closed the door. "But, one of the maids told me that she was told to deliver a letter to me, and she said it was from you. And it was that blackmail letter."

"What was the maid's name?"

"I don't know. I don't think I asked her." I turned to him. "And I don't think she was one of the original four housekeepers I was introduced to when I met the staff assigned to me."

"What did she look like?"

"She had a very light complexion," I said, remembering. "Dark curly hair pulled back into a ponytail. Does she sound familiar to you?"

Frowning, Icarus looked contemplative. "Sort of, but not really. Matean women come in various complexions from light to dark and every shade in between."

"I need to find out who that maid was," I said, my mind churning. The time for tears and self-recrimination had passed. It was time to figure this mess out. "And once I do, I can find out who told her to deliver that blackmail letter to me."

"Maybe I could help with that," Icarus said.

"How?" I asked, encouraged by the determination in his gaze. He seemed to be just as upset as I was about the blackmail demand and was, perhaps, committed to helping me find out who the hell was trying to make my life hell. I was hopeful but cautioning myself. I still didn't know if I could trust Icarus. He might be trying to trick me into thinking he was for me when, really, he was against me. I didn't like feeling so paranoid, but I didn't think I could afford to let my guard down completely.

"I could talk with your housekeeping staff," Icarus said, walking to one of the couches. "One of them might know the housekeeper with curly ponytail."

"I hope so," I said, sitting next to him. "I need to know who sent me that damn blackmail letter. I might not be able to do anything about it, because I was told not to go to the police."

Icarus frowned. "Where is the letter? I want to read it."

"Actually, it wasn't a letter," I said. "It was a text message. The note in the aqua envelope said something like you have an important message on your phone."

"Well, let me see the text message."

Panic made my gut twist, and I stared at him, hesitating.

"Quinn ..." Icarus prompted.

Biting my bottom lip, I looked away, conflicted. If Icarus was really the blackmailer, then he would have already seen the video because he would have sent the video. And he would know what the text message said because, again, he would have been the man behind that awful, evil distorted voice.

After a weary sigh, I stood and went into the bedroom to grab my phone from the night table. Back in the living room, I accessed the offensive text message and showed it to Icarus.

"It's me and you," he said after the evil, distorted voice ended.

Nodding, I said, "When we were together in the spa bungalow."

"The first time we made love," he said, staring at the final image, the frozen shot of my ecstasy, the results of his passionate lovemaking. "Somebody must have been in the spa with us."

"The doors were unlocked." I reminded him. "I assumed that was part of the fantasy, but maybe not."

"Maybe whoever filmed us broke into the spa before we got there," Icarus said.

"Maybe they were waiting for us," I said. "Maybe the person knew you were going to bring me there. Maybe they knew that would be my first fantasy."

Icarus looked away and then cleared his throat. "Um, maybe I shouldn't ask this but do you have a hundred thousand dollars ...?"

Staring at him, I tried to discern if he was asking because he was curious, or because he was trying to make sure I had enough money to pay him.

"No, I don't," I said, watching his expression. I was looking for some sign of horrified disappointment, but what I saw looked like concern and worry. "Well, I mean, I have access to money, so ..."

"So coming up with a hundred thousand dollars won't be a problem for you?" he asked, a strange look on his face, one I couldn't really understand.

"Getting the money won't be a problem," I said, unable to fathom the emotions behind those whiskey eyes.

"Listen, um ..." Icarus cleared his throat again and stood. "I should probably go and find the maid who delivered the blackmail note. I'll let you know what I find out."

Chapter Eleven

Icarus returned later, around nine p.m.

"Hey," he said, giving me a quick squeeze as he walked into my suite. Exhaling a nervous breath, I closed the door behind him and then turned, anxious to learn what he'd found out.

"You okay?" he asked, genuinely concerned.

"Yeah," I said, and shrugged. "I'm fine. Did you find out which one of the housekeepers delivered the note?"

Nodding, he took my hand and led me to one of the couches. After we sat, Icarus explained that he had asked a maid named Sandy to deliver his note to me, and she had. But Sandy told him that as she was leaving, she'd seen another maid walking into my suite—a maid Sandy didn't recognize. The maid Sandy didn't recognize told Sandy that she was new and was filling in for another maid who had called in sick. Sandy didn't question the new maid. The new maid told Sandy that she had an envelope to deliver to me, and Sandy told the new maid to put it in the bedroom with the other note. Then Sandy and the new maid left my suite.

"So, who was the new maid?" I asked.

"Sandy couldn't remember what her name was, so I asked Libera-da," Icarus said. "She didn't know anything about a new maid. So, I talked to a friend of mine in security. There are surveillance cameras in the hallways, so we took a look and I saw who the new maid was."

"Do you know her?" I asked, picking up on a hint of familiarity in his tone.

"Her name is Stazia Zacheo. And she's not a new maid," Icarus said. "She used to work here, but she was fired a year ago. She got caught stealing from the guest suites. She's not even supposed to be on this property."

"So, how the hell did she get on the property and into my room?"

"Somehow, she snuck into the hotel to deliver that blackmail letter to you."

"So, she's working with the blackmailer, you think?" I asked.

"I'm going to find out," Icarus said. "I'm going to talk to her."

"I want to come with you," I said.

Icarus shook his head. "I don't think that's a good idea."

"Why not?" I asked, trying to ignore the suspicions of him that had returned. "I want to know who told this Stazia girl to give me that letter."

"So do I," he said. "But she's not going to be honest if you're there. I can talk to her, Matean to Matean."

"And she'll tell you the truth?" I asked, wary of his claim.

"She'll be straight with me," he said and then added, "or else."

Apprehensive, I wanted to ask or else what, but I pushed the doubts away.

"After I find out what Stazia has to say, I'll be back."

Nodding, I sighed.

"It's going to be okay," Icarus said.

"If you say so ..."

"I do say so," he said, lifting my chin, making me look at him. "Trust me, okay?"

I nodded, but I couldn't stop the tears trailing down my cheek. After Icarus kissed the tears away, he left, leaving me alone in my room with nothing but scattered, confusing thoughts to keep me company as I paced around the living room. I couldn't stop thinking about Stazia Zacheo, the fake maid who'd managed to slip into my hotel suite. Who was she working with? Would she really tell Icarus who the blackmailer was? And if she did, then what? I couldn't go to the cops and tell them. I would still have to pay the blackmailer. I couldn't let the world see that sex tape. What was the point of talking to Stazia?

Still, not long after Icarus left, I began obsessing about his conversation with the fake maid, Stazia. What were they talking about? Was she telling him who the blackmailer was? Afraid I might go out of my mind, I called Lisa and updated her on everything.

Not surprisingly, she thought Icarus's reason for talking to Stazia alone was bullshit.

"I don't trust that guy, Quinn," Lisa announced. "I mean, the maid told you that Icarus asked her to deliver the blackmail note to you."

"That's what I thought, too," I said. "But then I got the note that Icarus actually wanted delivered to me, remember? The note with his number on it that the butler found in the trash. The maid told me that."

"Icarus could have told the maid to lie and tell you that," Lisa said. "I think that asshole is trying to gaslight you."

Lisa and I continued to discuss, speculate, and analyze the depressing, disturbing events occurring in my life, but eventually, she had to go. Again, I was left to pace around the suite, waiting for Icarus to return, but he never did.

Neither did he answer his cell phone when I called the number on the letter. As time passed without word from him, I grew increasingly worried. Soon the worry turned to suspicion. My doubts about Icarus returned, leaving me weak, feeling like a desperate fool.

As ten p.m. became eleven p.m., I was in full panic mode, enraged, believing Icarus had made a complete fool of me. I was pissed at myself for allowing the deception. Why hadn't I voiced my suspicions when he insisted on going to talk to Stazia alone? Why had I believed him when he'd claimed the fake maid wouldn't open up if I was around when he questioned her?

Eleven p.m. rolled into midnight, and I was stalking back and forth throughout the suite, wanting to scream and throw things but somehow managing to keep it together.

Sometime before one in the morning, I stomped into the bedroom, dived into the bed, and pulled the covers over my head.

DAY FIVE

Chapter Twelve

The next morning, knocking woke me up.

Groggy, half-awake, I staggered to the door and yanked it open.

"Good morning," the maid said in that annoying, cheery St. Matean accent. "How are you today, Ms. Miller?"

Irritated, I asked, "Can you come back later?"

"Yes, ma'am," she said. "But will you want your bath and breakfast?"

I wanted to slap her. "What part of come back later do you not understand?"

Her eyes widened with shock and she dropped her gaze. "Yes, ma'am. I'm sorry. I didn't mean to—"

"No, I'm sorry," I said, pissed at myself for hurting her feelings. "Please. Forgive me. I didn't sleep well. I wasn't feeling very good."

"Do you need to see the hotel doctor?" she asked, sincerely concerned, making me feel even worse for snapping at her so viciously.

"No, no ... " I stopped, then sighed, and said, "I just ... it doesn't matter. I just need a bit more sleep."

"Sorry I disturbed you."

"No, no, listen, I will have breakfast," I said. "But no bath, I'll just take a shower. Maybe in about two hours. Can you come back then?"

When she returned, around eleven a.m., my mood had not improved, but I kept the attitude and anger to myself because *myself* was who I was mad at.

As she poured my coffee, she asked, "Did you get your note?"

"My note?"

"I left an aqua envelope on the coffee table for you."

Suspicious, I glared at her. "Who told you to do that?"

"No one."

"No one?" I asked, doubtful.

"I mean no one *told* me," she said. "It was on my task sheet."

"Task sheet?"

"A daily list of tasks I'm required to perform for each guest," she explained. "But that task—delivering the note to you—wasn't on the official task sheet, which is printed from the computer. It was written on a sticky note. It said, 'Deliver aqua envelope in your task box to Ms. Miller'."

"What is a task box?"

"When a guest wants something like a special brand of shampoo or something not normally stocked in the suite," she said, "that item will be placed in our task boxes to be delivered to the guest."

"And who would have put the envelope in your task box?"

"Sometimes the concierge or the personal assistant," she said. "Usually, we don't know who specifically assigns the tasks, but it will be one of our supervisors. Maybe the butler. Maybe the head housekeeper."

After the maid left, I grabbed the aqua envelope from the coffee table and ripped it open. Trembling, I read the note inside of it, staring at the words written in small, neat, block print:

Below you will find an outline of the instructions you are to follow for the delivery of the payment for the video. Follow these instructions completely. Any deviation from these instructions will result in immediate release of the video all over the Internet.

1. Wrap the money in newspaper. Make five separate bundles of $20,000 each
2. Put the money in a large beach bag

3. Take the beach bag to Golden Lizard Beach, which is located behind the hotel
4. At Golden Lizard Beach, there is a unisex/family locker room. Go to the locker room and put the beach bag in locker/safe number 17
5. Use the code 2868 to lock the safe
6. Leave Golden Lizard Beach and go back to your hotel suite

You are to act alone. Under no circumstances are you to contact or alert the police in any way. Your every move is being watched and the video will be released immediately if you try anything stupid.

Dizzy and enraged, I sat on the couch, reading the blackmail demand letter over and over, scarcely able to believe that it was real, hardly able to fathom how my life had taken this disastrous turn. Part of me struggled to figure out who the hell could be blackmailing me. Thinking about what the maid had told me, I realized that whoever had wanted the letter delivered to me had to have known about the housekeeping "task list" and "task box" system. The person knew the maid on duty would carry out the task without question, assuming a superior had assigned it.

I had to consider that maybe one of the supervisors at the hotel might be the blackmailer. Maybe Liberada. The lovely personal assistant knew about all of my fantasies. She may have even *imagined* some of them. She might have told Icarus to take me to the spa bungalow because she'd planned to set me up. Suddenly, I wanted to confront Liberada, to demand the truth from her. But as soon as I jumped up from the couch, my indignation was tempered by worry. If Liberada wasn't blackmailing me, then the real blackmailer—who claimed to be watching my every move—might think I was trying to get Liberada to help me contact the authorities. Or, maybe—

A knock on the door interrupted my scattered, disorganized thoughts. I opened the door. Icarus stood in front of me, dressed in his custom-tailored chauffeur's uniform, reminding me of the first time I saw him.

"Where have you been?" I asked, not caring if I sounded like some kind of nagging fishwife. "Why didn't you come back yesterday?"

"That's why I'm here," he said. "I wanted to tell you what happened."

Crossing my arms, I said, "I'm listening."

"I looked for Stazia all night," Icarus said. "She wasn't home. I wasn't able to find her."

Nodding, I shrugged. "Well, I guess you tried."

"I won't stop looking."

Saying nothing, I stared at him, desperately wanting to believe him.

"Why are you looking at me like that?"

"Like what?" I asked, trying to ignore how damn good he looked. And smelled.

"Like you don't believe me."

"Maybe I don't," I said. "You say you were looking for her, but I don't know that for sure."

Icarus said, "You have to trust me, Quinn."

"What if I don't know how to trust you?" I asked.

"How many times do I have to tell you," Icarus said, his eyes solemn and grave. "Blackmail is not my hustle, okay?"

"What is your hustle?"

"Nothing criminal," he said, a touch defensive. "Nothing that would hurt anyone. Strictly legit. My plan is to make an honest living."

"Doing what?"

"One of my aunts passed away a few years ago, and she left me a house," he said. "A huge, run-down place on the east side of the island, close to Pirate's Beach."

"I read about Pirate's Beach," I said. "Fodor's said it was the best beach on the island."

"May be the best beach," he said, his grin wry. "But, it's on the east side of the island, near a few neighborhoods that tourists are told to avoid."

"I read that, too."

"There are some poor areas and some crime, but the majority of the people who live there are good, honest, hard-working people," he said, with the same pride he'd displayed the first time I met him, when he'd given me commentary about his island home. "Most of them work in the tourism industry, in the hotels and restaurants and excursion companies.

"Anyway, the house was left to my aunt by her husband. He was from Ireland and had a bit of money. After he died, my aunt went a little batty," he said, giving me a quick rueful smile that faded quickly. "She didn't really keep the place up. She didn't keep herself up, either, that's why I made sure to check on her two or three times a week."

Looking away, I warned myself to take what he'd told me with a grain of salt. I didn't want to be touched by Icarus's kindness toward his aunt, an old woman who had obviously been unable to manage the difficulty of being a widow. I didn't want to be fooled by his compassion. The sweet nephew act might have been just an act, designed to make him appear caring. For all I knew, he might have tricked his aunt into leaving him the house. He might have employed coercion or even resorted to forgery. I couldn't assume he was being honest with me, even though I hoped he was telling me the truth.

"Anyway, I want to fix the house up," he said. "Turn it into a small hotel."

"You need money for renovations," I said, assigning a motive for blackmail to him, though I was starting to have trouble with my own suspicions of him.

"Which is why I'm going to get a home improvement loan," he said, bestowing me with a smile that was beguiling and reassuring in a way which made me think he had decided not to be offended by my doubts of him.

"Well, while you were looking for Stazia," I said. "I received another aqua envelope."

"What did it say?"

"Don't act like you don't know what it says," I told him.

"What is it going to take to make you believe me? I want to help you," he said. "I'm *not* trying to blackmail you. If I was, trust me, leaving you notes on hotel stationery is not how I'd do it. If I was blackmailing you, I wouldn't be playing these bullshit games, okay? I would have just come to you, showed you the video, and then told you how much it would cost you to make it go away."

Conflicted, confused, I stared at him, struck by the honest

sincerity in his gaze, desperate to believe him and yet still not sure I should.

"Maybe you'll believe me when I help you find out who the blackmailer really is," he said. "And I think the best way to do that is to pay him."

"Of course, you do."

Exhaling angrily, he shook his head.

"Look, I want to believe you," I said. "But can't you see how hard it is when you're telling me to pay the blackmailer? Shouldn't you tell me not to pay him? Or her?"

"If you don't pay," he said, "the blackmailer is probably going to upload the video to a whole bunch of Internet porn sites, and I know that's not what you want."

"So why do you think paying the blackmailer will help us find out who he is?" I asked, purposely using inclusive language in an attempt to set my suspicions aside. For the moment.

"Well, you haven't shown me the second demand letter," he said. "But, I'm guessing it mentions something about where you need to leave the money."

Nodding, I got the letter and handed it to him.

"I have an idea of how we can find out who the blackmailer is," Icarus said, after reading the letter. "After you drop the money off, I can go to the drop-off location and video the blackmailer. I'll go ahead of you and find a good spot, a place where I won't be noticed but where I can get good footage. And then you'll come and drop the money off and leave. Then someone will come to pick up the money. I'll film everything and then follow that person wherever they go or find out if he meets with anyone, or whatever. Then you'll have every-thing you need to—"

"Go to the police?" I shook my head. "I can't do that."

"Keep the blackmailer in line," he said. "You'll have video of him accepting an extortion payment. That's a crime."

"But what if the person who comes to pick up the money isn't the blackmailer?"

"It probably won't be the blackmailer," Icarus said. "It'll be the person who leads us to the blackmailer."

I nodded, silently conceding it made sense, but I was still antsy. Something could, and most likely would, go wrong with our plan.

Icarus sighed as he removed his phone from his jacket and stared at it.

"What is it?" I asked.

"Work," he said. "I'm late. I need to get going. The guest I'm supposed to pick up is early."

"So, you're picking up another hotel guest," I said, my voice hollow.

Insane jealously seized me, leaving me panicked and distraught. But why? Icarus was not my husband, boyfriend, friend with benefits, or secret lover. We had no commitment to each other. There was no allegiance or devotion between us that he had to respect. He was nothing to me. So, why couldn't I stand the thought of him with another woman, even though I had no claim to his fidelity?

"Well, I guess you should get going," I said, unable to get control of the envy roaring through me. "You've got to pick up some woman you're going to screw in the bungalow ..."

"Why do you think I'm going to have sex with the lady I'm picking up from the airport?"

It was my turn to be utterly confused. "So, you're not going to have sex with this woman?"

"No, I'm not."

"You expect me to believe that?" I asked. "I know what's going to happen after you pick her up."

"Actually, no, you really don't," said Icarus.

"What?"

Exhaling, Icarus said, "I should have told you this sooner but ..."

"Told me what sooner?"

"We weren't supposed to have sex."

"What were we supposed to do?"

"Did Liberada explain the fantasy levels to you?"

"Yes." I nodded, wishing he would get on with it. "Sensual, sexual, and salacious."

"Well, employees of the hotel are categorized the same way," Icarus explained. "Employees are considered either sensual arts, sexual arts, or salacious arts."

"And your category is?"

"None of the above."

"I don't understand."

"I'm just a chauffeur," he said, his slight grin sheepish. "I'm just supposed to stop at Plantain Pass so you can take a nice photo before I drive you to the hotel."

"Which means you aren't supposed to have sex with the guests," I said, my heart beating wildly with relief.

"I'm sorry," he said, sincere and contrite. "I shouldn't have made love to you. I knew it was wrong. I knew I could lose my job if management ever found out."

"Then why did you?"

"Couldn't help myself," Icarus said. "When I first saw you, I wanted you, so much that I was willing to risk my job at the hotel, which isn't something that I can afford to do."

Stunned, I stared at him. I wasn't sure what to think. As he gazed at me, I had a feeling he wanted a response, but I wasn't sure what to say.

"Listen, I gotta go," he said and turned from me. "I'll talk to you later."

Chapter Thirteen

After Icarus left, I went to the couch and sat down, still dumbfounded by what he'd revealed about our experience at the hidden beach. I couldn't stop thinking about his confession, his reason for making love to me even though he could have been fired. *Couldn't help myself.*

I didn't really know what to think. I didn't know if I should allow myself to feel beautiful and desirable enough to cause a man to risk his livelihood to be with me, to make love to me.

I couldn't lie to myself; his confession had done wonders for my self-esteem, my self-worth, and my ego. I cautioned myself not to read too much into his reasons for making love to me.

Besides, I needed to call my banker.

Four hours later, after a grueling, gut-wrenching marathon conversation, I finally ended the international call and threw my phone across the room, terrified and frustrated. Pacing the living room, I went over the conversation with my banker, growing increasingly panicked and horrified until I was damn near paralyzed with fear.

Sometime later, after the sun had set, a brisk, staccato knock on the door of my suite made me jump. Heart thundering, I went to the door and opened it. Icarus walked in and I collapsed into his arms. As I sobbed, he closed the door and guided me over to the couch.

"What's wrong, Quinn," he asked, wiping tears from my cheeks. "What happened? Did the blackmailer contact you again, or—"

"My life is over," I cried, dropping my face in my hands. "It's ruined and it's my own damn fault!"

"Sweetheart, your life is not over," Icarus said, taking my hands from my face, forcing me to look at him. "Now, calm down and tell me what happened? Why are you so upset?"

Exhaling a shaky breath, I told him about the phone call to my banker. "There's a problem."

"What's the problem?"

"I'm not going to be able to get the money."

Worry in his eyes, Icarus asked, "Why not?"

After another deep breath, I explained, telling Icarus what my banker had told me. The Palmchat Islands only had two banks, and neither was a Chase Manhattan, which was where the bulk of my funds earned interest. The island's fiduciary needs were serviced by Palmchat Island Bank and Global Caribbean Bank, both of which had branches in town, but that wouldn't do me any good since I wouldn't be able to stroll into the bank, fill out a withdrawal slip, and ask the teller to pony up one hundred grand.

Like the blackmailer had said, it might take up to five business days to wire the funds from my account to Global Caribbean—hence the five days the blackmailer had given me to secure the funds. But the problem wasn't actually with the wire transfer of funds. That could be done in twenty-four hours, my banker explained. The problem was with the reality of withdrawing so much cash at one time. Simply put, the island's banks didn't have a hundred thousand dollars in cash available to give to me. As a result, they would have to make provisions to secure the cash I needed from their parent institution in Miami.

"And how long would that take?" Icarus asked.

"Five to seven days," I said, trying to breathe, blinking back fresh tears. "Which I don't have!"

"Quinn, look at me," Icarus said, taking my face in his hands. "I think I can help you."

"What?" Confused, I stared at him. "I don't understand. How can you—"

"Let me explain," he said and then went on to tell me his idea. After he'd given me the details and patiently answered all my questions, I wasn't sure I could get on board with it.

"So, I hate to keep making you go over everything, but—"

"It's okay," he assured me. "We can go over it as many times as you need to until you feel comfortable."

Nodding, I said, "So, Chase can transfer the funds from my account in the U.S. to your account at Global Caribbean in the Cayman Islands," I said, looking at my trembling hands, trying to find a way to reconcile Icarus's idea.

"Once the money is in my account in the Caymans," he said, "I can authorize my cousin—"

"Your cousin?" I asked, my head spinning with confusion as I tried to make sense of his idea, which still made me uneasy.

"He's an assistant vice president at the Grand Cayman branch of Global Caribbean," Icarus explained.

Convenient, I couldn't stop myself from thinking. There was a problem with me getting the money to the blackmailer by the deadline, and all of a sudden, Icarus had a solution. With the help of one of his family members, I could get my hands on the cash I needed to pay the extortionist, but I would have to trust Icarus at a level that unnerved me, and that I wasn't sure I'd be able to do.

"And the bank in the Caymans will have the cash available for me?"

Icarus nodded. "People deposit millions into the Caymans. Sometimes bags of cash, according to my cousin. So, they'll have the money."

"And then how will we get the money from the Caymans to St. Mateo?"

"My cousin will bring it to St. Mateo personally," Icarus said, staring at me. "You can charter a plane for him."

"And how long will it take to get here from the Cayman Islands?"

"My cousin can be here in a few hours with the cash," Icarus promised.

Sighing, I stood and walked away from the couch, toward the wall of French doors, looking out to the terrace. In the waning sunlight, the lush scenery had a dark golden glow. Palm trees, hibiscus, plumeria, bird of paradise ... and, of course, heliconia.

I scowled at the fuchsia-and-orange tropical flower.

The name of the flower was a direct association to the hotel, a place I was slowly coming to loathe despite its luxury and opulence and focus on catering to its guests' every whim. But, really, it wasn't the hotel I hated. I despised my decision to come to the hotel. I hated how I'd allowed my anxiety to dictate my actions.

"What are you thinking?"

Rolling my neck, I turned to Icarus and said, "I'm just wondering if this is the best way to do it."

"Or, maybe ..." Icarus stood and began walking toward me. "You're wondering if you can trust me?"

Speechless, I stared up at him. "What?"

"You don't want to transfer the money to my account because you think I won't withdraw it for you, don't you?" Icarus asked, frowning. "You think I'd keep it in my account? You think I would steal your money?"

I wanted to tell him he was wrong. Wanted to tell him I trusted him and I knew he wasn't going to stab me in the back, but that would be a lie. Because that was exactly what I was thinking. Icarus's grand scheme to get the money to the blackmailer involved putting *my* cash in *his* bank account. If that happened, then technically, the money would be his at that point, and he wouldn't have to give it to me.

I didn't want to think that, and deep down, I guess I didn't think he could be that cold-blooded, but ...

"It's a lot to deal with." I sighed, shaking my head. "I'm just trying to wrap my mind around it."

His frown eased into a look of uncertainty. "Quinn, I'm not a thief or a blackmailer."

"I know you're not," I said, not really convinced of that statement. "I'm just really stressed out."

"It's going to be okay," Icarus said. "You'll pay this asshole off, and I'll get video of it, and then you'll be able to put all of this behind you. It'll be over and you can forget about it."

Nodding, I looked at my feet. I supposed Icarus was right. I had come here to conquer the angst that threatened to ruin my professional career, but now I couldn't focus on what had brought me to St. Mateo because I was living a real-life nightmare.

After I paid the extortion demand, the nightmare would be over. But, would it really? Why did I have a horrible feeling that giving the blackmailer the money would be the beginning of my bad dream?

DAY SIX

Chapter Fourteen

"You have to work?" I stared at him, my heart plummeting as I started to tremble. "But, I don't understand? I thought you had the day off?"

"I thought so, too, but I got my weeks mixed up," he said, placing an oversized aqua-colored beach bag on the coffee table. "I'm off next Friday, not this Friday."

"Well, is there anything you can do?" I asked, as he sat down across from me instead of joining me on the couch where I was seated. "Can you ask to take a vacation day or—"

"I tried to switch shifts, but nobody would do it," he said, sullen, disappointed. "I can't believe this. The one damn day I need off."

"What are we going to do?" I asked, feeling jittery and desperate.

"What do you mean?" he asked, his whiskey-colored eyes dropping from me to the beach bag. "You have to deliver the money."

Apprehensive, I stared at the aqua-colored beach bag, knowing its contents—one hundred thousand dollars, unmarked bills, non-sequential serial numbers, per the blackmailer's instructions.

Moments ago, while I was half-heartedly picking at the eggs benedict I'd ordered for breakfast, Icarus had arrived at my suite to deliver the funds I would need to pay off the blackmailer. As he explained yesterday, the funds had been wire transferred to the bank in the

Caymans. His cousin had facilitated the receipt, deposit, and immediate withdrawal of the money, and then had flown to St. Mateo. Icarus had taken possession of the box, counted the money, and certified the amount—one hundred thousand dollars.

In the bedroom, Icarus removed the money from the box and spread it out across the king-sized bed. Shell-shocked, I'd stared at the money, still not quite believing everything had gone so smoothly. I had been certain something would go wrong. Maybe the wire transfer wouldn't go through for some weird reason, but the wire transfer had occurred with no issues.

Then I became paranoid that Icarus would tell me there was some problem with his account in the Caymans and he wouldn't be able to withdraw that much money. Or, maybe the bank didn't have that much cash on hand. But the one hundred-thousand-dollar cash withdrawal hadn't been a problem.

Finally, I thought that maybe Icarus's cousin would steal the money. Or maybe something would happen to the plane.

Nothing went wrong.

And, for some reason, that just didn't seem right.

After I counted the cash, verifying the amount, Icarus and I wrapped the money in newspaper, per the blackmailer's demands, making five bundles of twenty thousand dollars each, and then shoved the bundles into an oversized beach bag I'd bought yesterday in the hotel's gift shop.

"Well," I said, staring at the money-stuffed aqua-colored beach bag. "I guess that's that. All I have to do now is deliver this money to the son of a bitch."

"Quinn, you know I wanted to be there when everything goes down," Icarus said. "This is killing me that I won't be there. I hate disappointing you."

"It's okay—"

"No, it's not okay," he said. "It's just that I'm in a dicey position right now. I'm on Liberada's shit list."

"Why?"

"She found out about the letter I had delivered to you," he said. "The maid told her. Anyway, if I didn't need this job—"

"But, you do need it," I said. "And I know why. You explained that to me, and I want you to be able to renovate your house and realize your dreams of opening your own hotel."

"I'm still letting you down, though," he said. "I told you I would help you and—"

"You didn't let me down," I said.

"But you're in this position because of me," he said. "I shouldn't have made love to you. Now, you're paying for my mistake. If I hadn't gone too far, then—"

"Listen to me," I said. "It's not your fault that—"

"Just a second," he said, reaching into his jacket. "My cell phone."

I nodded, glad for the interruption.

"I'm sorry," he said, staring at the display screen. "I really need to get going."

"Okay ..." I said, reluctant to see him leave or let him go, desperate to cling to him. "So ... do you want to meet later, or ..."

"Actually," he said. "This lady I'm driving today is going on an island tour. She wants to see all of St. Mateo, which will take about eight hours, so ..."

"Okay, well," I said, trying to keep the disappointment from my voice. "Tomorrow then?"

Smiling, he lifted my chin and kissed me. Then he left. After he closed the door behind him, I stared at it for a long time, unable to move. His kiss had seemed reluctant, almost polite, with a fatalistic note of finality that worried me. Slowly, I was able to turn from the door and take a few steps. Making my way into the bedroom, I couldn't help but think that he hadn't agreed to meet me tomorrow.

I couldn't dwell on that or what it might or might not mean.

I had a blackmailer to pay off. And I had to get evidence of the money drop, which could be invaluable. Might be just what I needed to keep the extortionist from demanding more money. I was disappointed Icarus wouldn't be able to film the pickup of the extortion payment, but he wasn't the only person capable of operating cell phone video.

I had to find someone else to get surveillance for me, I realized, feeling somewhat like my former self, and I knew just who to ask.

Chapter Fifteen

"Can you do me a favor?" I asked, grabbing the maid's wrist, pulling her into my suite, and then closing the door.

"A favor?" she asked, eyes wide, as though she didn't understand the meaning of the word. I realized that doing a favor for a guest might be strange to the staff. They had been trained to provide luxury and comfort and excellent customer service. At a hotel where every whim was catered to, guests didn't need to ask for favors, and therefore, the request was met with hesitation.

"I need you to get a message to Joshua," I said, wishing I knew the last name of the blue-eyed lothario who didn't quite seal the deal during our terrace dinner my first night at the hotel. "Do you know him?"

"Yes, but ..."

"But?"

"I'm not sure I should," she said. "We're not supposed to have unauthorized contact with guests, and if I give him your message—"

"I know, but, please," I implored her. "This is very important."

Looking at her shoes, she said, "I could get in trouble."

"I could pay you," I said, desperate. "A hundred dollars. Two hundred."

She glanced up, the trepidation replaced by a hint of larceny. "Five?"

After forking over five one-hundred-dollar bills to the maid, which she pocketed with a judicious smile void of any shame, I sent her off with a note for Joshua. He arrived twenty minutes later with the same initial hesitation the maid had displayed. No longer fooled by the staff's contrite reluctance, I said, "I'll give you a thousand dollars to do me a favor ..."

Joshua agreed without going through the pretense of being worried about the no unauthorized contact with guests rule. I explained what I needed him to do, and we went over the plan several times.

After Joshua left, I took a deep breath and prepared myself to deliver the money.

I put on a bikini and then slipped on a sheer cover-up. With sunglasses covering my eyes and Chanel flip-flops on my feet, I grabbed the beach bag and left the suite, my heart pounding with each step I took. As I walked through the airy, opulent, marbled breeze-ways, I passed several members of the staff, each clad in the hotel's signature aqua colors. Jumpy and paranoid, I did my best to avoid any gazes. There were lots of cheerful, smiling hellos, but I could barely mumble a reply. I could barely breathe, or put one foot in front of the other, my legs were shaking so bad.

All I could think was that I was being watched. The blackmailer's note had warned I would be under constant surveillance as I went to deliver the money. Any attempt to contact the police, or any other person in a position of authority, and all bets would be off. The video would be immediately released to the Internet.

I hailed a cab and when the driver asked me where to in a cheerful, carefree St. Matean accent, I managed to tell him "Golden Lizard Beach" despite the roaring in my head and my racing heart. He engaged me in polite conversation, asking me the typical questions. Was this my first time to the island? How long was I staying? How was I enjoying myself so far?

It took every ounce of what little strength I had left not to tell him I wasn't enjoying myself. I was being blackmailed by some asshole who planned to release a sex tape of me if I didn't give him a hundred thousand dollars. I took a few deep breaths and tried to disassociate myself from my predicament. Pretending to be just an average tourist, I was able to converse without screaming or opening the door and jumping out of the moving car, which I was tempted to do.

At Golden Lizard Beach, I paid the driver and got out. Crossing the parking lot, I found the path leading to the little shack where they sold burgers, fries, and frozen drinks. I circled the burger shack, smiling at a couple sitting at the half-moon bar. Also at the bar was Joshua, and seeing him, I was flooded with a piercing relief that almost made my knees buckle. Our plan involved him sitting at the bar, having a drink, and looking at his cell phone, which he was doing, but he wasn't really scrolling through his Facebook feed. Surreptitiously, Joshua was filming me, getting video of me as I walked around the bar and then went on to the family locker room, which was behind the restrooms. His instructions were to follow me into the locker room and continue filming me. After I left, Joshua would remain in the locker room to film whoever came to pick up the blackmail money.

After passing the restrooms, I went to the locker room and walked inside. It was cool but humid, and though it was clean, the cement floor was damp and the smell of sun and wet hair permeated the air. The thatched roof allowed a bit of a breeze as I walked past three changing stalls and two showers to the back of the room, where there was a wall of self-serve lockers.

I found the locker with the number seventeen stenciled on it and shoved the beach bag inside. Then I closed it and pressed the code the blackmailer had given me into the keypad.

Walking out of the locker room, I saw Joshua standing just outside the entryway, still looking at his phone. To his credit, he didn't even look up as I walked straight toward him, making sure he had good footage of me before I left the shed.

Hesitating, I slowed my stride as I stepped on the path that snaked toward the bathrooms, pretending as though I was looking in my purse for something. Truthfully, I didn't want to leave. I wanted to stick around and make sure Joshua got video of the person who would come to pick up the money, but I'd been warned that the blackmailer had people watching me. I couldn't take any chances. I had to trust that

Joshua would earn that thousand dollars I'd given him and get the footage I needed.

Trembling, I paid the driver and got out of the cab, a hundred thousand dollars lighter.

The money in my bag had weighed me down, physically, mentally, emotionally, and spiritually. I was glad it was no longer in my possession. It was now shoved into one of the self-serve lockers at Golden Lizard Beach, waiting to be removed by some bastard who thought nothing of terrorizing me. As much as I hated the extortionist, I knew he wasn't solely to blame for making my life hell. I was complicit in his scheme. My actions had made it possible for him to blackmail me.

With a weary sigh, I walked through the luxurious open-air reception foyer, oblivious to the efficient, expedient staff and the smattering of eager, smiling, female guests. What I wanted most of all was a glass of wine and then a nap, one I wouldn't wake up from for several hours.

"Ms. Miller! Ms. Miller ..."

I turned. Liberada was hurrying toward me, slim and confident in her customary aqua dress shirt, white pencil skirt, and kitten heels.

"I was going to call you," Liberada began with her usual cheerfulness. "But since I saw you, I figured I'd just stop you and let you know that James will be your chauffeur for today. So, if you want to leave the hotel—"

"James?" I cut her off, confused.

"Icarus called in sick," said Liberada, rolling her eyes in derision. "So James—"

"Wait a minute, what?" I stopped her, my heart slamming. "Icarus called in sick?"

"He's not working today." Liberada shook her head. "Some kind of stomach bug, he claims."

"Are you sure?" I asked, panicked. "Because I thought I saw him earlier."

"He called about five this morning," Liberada said. "I don't think it was Icarus that you saw. Anyway, James will be available if you need him, sounds good?"

It sounded like my worst nightmare. But I didn't want to jump to conclusions, didn't want to think the worse. Still, my mind was reeling with paranoia and suspicion. Why had Icarus lied to me? Where was he? He'd told me he couldn't film the money drop-off because he had to work. So, why would he call in sick with some lie about a stomach bug? I didn't want to think about what I suspected, so I didn't. I pushed the doubts away.

Back in my suite, I checked my cell phone. Joshua had sent me a text message. I was expecting the video of the money drop. Instead, the message read: *Got the video but phone is dead. Texting from friends phone. Will send video as soon as phone charges.*

Irritated and frustrated, I resisted the urge to hurl the phone across the room. Resigned, I called one of the housekeepers and told her to bring me a bottle of wine. "Would you like cheese and crackers with that?" she suggested. "Sure, fine," I said and then replaced the phone on the receiver base.

With a shaky sigh, I trudged to the couch and plopped down on it, praying the wine would come soon and that the text would too ...

DAY SEVEN

Chapter Sixteen

Around five p.m. the next day, I got the text from Joshua I'd been waiting for since yesterday.

The video of the money drop.

Dropping down onto the couch, I watched the video. My pulse jumping, I stared at the images, narrating them in my head.

I arrive at Golden Lizard Beach, carrying a large beach bag, with a haunted, nervous look on my face.

I walk past the bar and then head to the locker room.

I walk to the wall of lockers, open one, stuff the beach bag inside, close the locker, and then set the combination.

I leave Golden Lizard Beach.

For the next ten minutes, I watched a static shot on the screen, an image of the wall of lockers at the back of the changing shed. The image jumped several times, and I figured it was because Joshua was moving his phone ever so slightly, making sure that he appeared to be looking at the screen, should anyone see him.

Then, almost abruptly, a man walked into the shot but at an angle where I could only see the back of him. Carrying a medium-sized gym duffle bag, he was tall and very muscular, wearing jeans and a dark gray T-shirt, which seemed to cling to his well-built physique. The tall hunk walked to the wall of lockers at the back of the shed. Joshua used the camera's zoom function to get a closer shot, and the image jerked and jumped, but seconds later, I could see that the man stood in front of locker seventeen. The tall guy punched in a code and opened locker seventeen—the locker where the one-hundred-thousand-dollar payoff was stashed.

My heart nearly exploded. I was looking at the blackmailer, I was sure of it. If not the blackmailer himself, then this was someone the blackmailer was working with, someone sent to pick up the money. Didn't matter who it was, though. I'd given Joshua instructions to follow whoever came to retrieve the beach bag, so if this tall, well-built guy wasn't the blackmailer, then I was sure he would lead me to the true culprit.

The tall guy reached inside the locker and pulled out the large beach bag I'd left behind. Closing the locker, he placed the beach bag into the duffle bag, and then he turned ...

And when he turned, for several seconds, he was facing the camera phone.

His face was clearly shown, and then there was a shaky, jerky zoom into his face.

A scream stuck in my throat.

I knew the man who had removed the money from locker seventeen.

Icarus.

Chapter Seventeen

Glancing across the road, I stared at the house, a small, pale blue, one-story Colonial sitting in the midst of palms and frangipanis. The modest home, with its yellow door and security bars on the windows, was in a neighborhood on the east side of the island officially called Hilaire-Honoré, but which the locals referred to as "Double-H", or "Dub-H."

An hour earlier, when I'd given the cab driver the address, he'd looked shocked. From his dubious looks, I imagined he wondered why I was leaving the plush, luxurious, seven-star Heliconia to go to a disenfranchised neighborhood where tourists never ventured.

As the cab sped along, I stared out the window, oblivious to the tropical scenery rushing past. Towering palm trees and turquoise waters couldn't compete with the images I couldn't get out of my head. The video Joshua had filmed played over and over in my mind, as though on a loop.

Icarus removing the bag from the locker in the dressing shed at Golden Lizard Beach. Icarus getting into his Jeep and driving away from the beach parking lot. Joshua had continued to follow Icarus even after he'd left the beach, as per my instructions, and had captured Icarus navigating the narrow, twisting streets of the dense, raucous neighborhood. Eventually, the Jeep escaped the island squalor and made its way to a relatively quiet enclave of small but well-kept houses, most of them painted in creamy pastels, cocooned by tropical bushes, with oyster-shell driveways.

And there I was now, standing on the side of the road, dressed in shorts, a T-shirt, and deck shoes, clutching the strap of the small cross-body purse hanging from my shoulder. I had come to the "Double-H" to confront Icarus about his vicious blackmail scheme.

At seven in the evening, the sky was deep lavender with slashes of blue and pink and gold, a gorgeous St. Matean sunset. As a balmy breeze drifted past me, I realized I didn't want to confront Icarus about the money. I didn't care about the cash or even want it back. What I wanted was to know *why?* Why did Icarus blackmail me? Why did he dream up this elaborate scam against me?

Icarus's lies hurt the most. He'd pretended to care about me, pretended he was on my side and eager to help me.

Thinking about his betrayal and how stupid I'd been to believe his lies, my blood boiled and my hesitation fled. Once again, I was adamant about confronting him. I wanted an explanation for his cold-blooded treachery and he was going it give it to me—or else.

"Icarus! Open the damn door!" I said, pounding my fist against the yellow painted wood, not caring who could see me or hear me, not caring if any neighbors were peeking out of their windows, trying to locate the source of the commotion.

"Open this damn door!" I demanded, continuing to pound my fists. "Let me in! Open the—"

The door swung back, abruptly, and I stumbled over the threshold, stopping just short of colliding with the island guy standing inches away, scowling at me.

"What the hell is your damn problem?" he demanded. "Beating on the door like some crazy woman! What the hell do you want?"

Confused, I stepped back, staring at him. Astonishment and bewilderment hit me, like a vicious right hook followed by a stinging left jab. I knew this guy who was standing in the doorway scowling at me, though I couldn't remember his name. And even if I could, I knew he hadn't given me his real name anyway. He'd given me a fake name. A fantasy name. He'd given me the name of the guy he played in my "Waterfall Fantasy."

"What's your name?" I asked.

"Apollo," he said.

Dumbfounded, I stared at the guy I'd met on the trail to the waterfalls, the one who pretended to be lost and yet was able to lead me to the waterfalls where he and his two friends—

"What do you want?" he asked, still scowling.

"Where is Icarus?" I asked. "I need to talk to him. It's important. Is he here?"

Shrugging, the guy said, "Nope." He started to close the door, but I put my hand out, stopping him.

"Wait a minute," I said. "I really need to talk to him. Do you know where he is? Do you know when he's coming back?"

"Why the hell you think Icarus is coming back here?"

Confused, I asked, "Doesn't he live here?"

"Icarus don't stay here," he said, scowling at me.

"But, I know he came to this house," I said, remembering the video. "I saw him. Earlier, he came here."

"I don't know what you think you saw, but ..." he trailed off, frowning. "You know what? You look familiar."

"What?"

"Don't I know you?"

"Um, no, I don't think so," I stammered, wary.

My indignation had fled the scene, leaving behind a paralyzing fear that told me it was time to get the hell out of the Double-H. Coming to this house to confront Icarus had been a mistake. A stupid, horrible mistake. What the hell had I been thinking? Who did I think I was? Some take no prisoners tough girl, kicking ass and taking names? True, I was not one to let people walk all over me or push me around, but make no mistake, I was not a badass.

"Yeah, I think I do know you," he said, grabbing my wrist, pulling me toward him. "Can't remember your name, but I never forget a face, especially a face as pretty as yours."

"Look, since Icarus isn't here, or doesn't live here rather," I said, my tone casual despite the terror racing through me as I tried to extricate my wrist from his grip without calling too much attention to my actions. "Then I should just go. Sorry I bothered—"

"Actually, it's no bother at all," he said. Tightening his grip on my wrist, he pulled me into the house and shoved me toward a ratty threadbare love seat in a small living area, a space no bigger than a twelve-by-twelve square.

Stumbling, I took a few ungraceful side steps to avoid banging my leg on a mirrored coffee table and turned just as he slammed the door and faced me.

My heart kicked. I was trapped. Apollo was blocking my exit, standing in front of the door, arms crossed over his bare chest, smiling a predatory grin that turned my blood to ice.

"I should go," I said, scarcely able to breathe, speak, or think. The panic flooding me was so intense I felt like I would drown in it. "I'll just talk to Icarus later."

"I thought you wanted to wait for Icarus to come back."

"Well, I changed my mind," I said. "I'll try to call him later."

"You're the woman from the waterfalls, aren't you? You're the one who didn't want to make love," he said, leering at me as he caught his lower lip between his teeth and then slowly released it, looking as though he might be in the mood for hot, dirty sex. "We could've had a good time that day. We could have a good time now, just you and me. I didn't want to share you with Hermes and Hercules. As soon as I saw you, I wanted to have you all to myself."

"You know what, maybe I should just go," I said, blood rushing to my head as I tried to walk around him, but he blocked me.

"Relax, okay," he said, placing his hands on my shoulders as he looked down at me. "Don't be nervous. We're going to have a good time while we wait for Icarus to come back. And maybe when he comes, he can join us. We can screw you at the same time."

Heart in my throat, I struggled to tell him, "I don't think—"

"You ever tried double penetration?" he asked, his erection evident in his black boxer's pants. "You'll like it. I'll be in your ass and he can be in your—"

"Listen," I said, trying to stay calm. "I shouldn't have come here."

"I'm glad you came," he said, his hand landing on my face, caressing my cheek. "And I can't wait to make you come. Over and over."

"I think I should go back to my hotel," I said, voice trembling.

"It's a long way back to your hotel," Apollo said, his hand sliding down my neck. "And it's getting dark. Cabs don't like to come to the Double-H after dark. I'll probably have to drive you back to the Heliconia."

Icy sweat slid down my back. "I can call the hotel, and I know they'll send someone to come and—"

"Why don't you just stay here," Apollo said, but it wasn't a suggestion, it was an order. "Icarus should be back soon."

"I don't think that's a good idea," I said, moving away from his grasp, heading around him.

His hand clamped around the back of my neck, stopping me. My legs trembled, turning to jelly. Apollo jerked me against him, his penis, huge and hard, pressing against my back. "I think it's a very good idea, baby," he whispered, sticking his tongue in my ear.

Alarmed, I moved my head away. "Stop it!"

"Don't you wanna have some fun, baby?" Apollo asked, his voice husky as he reached around, delved his hand into the side of my tank top, through the armhole, and grabbed my left breast, yanking the nipple.

My panic mutating into anger, I used the heel of my right foot to kick him in the shin. Yelping, Apollo stumbled back, releasing my breast. Encouraged by his pain, I turned, intent on kicking him in the balls, but he must have guessed what I had planned for him, because he slapped me—hard.

Crying out in pain and shock, I stumbled back as he stalked toward me, growling curses. Turning, I lurched away from him, toward the galley kitchen, desperate to find the back door, knowing I wouldn't get past him if I tried to escape through the front door. But the kitchen didn't even have a window, let alone a back door I could escape out of.

Frantic, I looked over my shoulder. Apollo was walking toward me, casual and yet predatory, like some kind of jungle cat, a teasing glint in his gaze as he stalked me. Whipping my head back to the kitchen, I scanned the area, looking for some sort of weapon, anything I could use to wound him, maybe a pot or pan I could whack him with, stunning him long enough so that I could get away.

My eyes swept the kitchen from the refrigerator to the stove and then back again, stopping at the sink, positioned between those two appliances. There, in a plastic dish rack, I saw what I needed. A large butcher's knife. Without thinking, I rushed toward the sink, grabbed the knife, and turned.

An open hand cracked across my face so hard I saw lights popping and feared my jaw had been dislocated. Crying out, I stumbled back, the knife dropping from my grasp and clattering across the stained, sticky linoleum tile. Feeling nauseated from the sloshing in my head, I dropped to one knee, struggling to get my bearings.

"Get up, bitch!" Apollo grabbed my arm and pulled me to my feet.

"Let go of me!" I screamed, trying to yank away from him.

"Shut up!" he said, and his hand came toward my face again, quick as a cobra's strike, and yet I was able to see that this time his hand was closed just as I felt the stinging blow of his fist near my left temple. My knees buckled and I felt my legs giving way as my eyes fluttered. Desperate not to lose consciousness, I struggled to keep my eyes open as darkness converged, but it was no use.

The blackness pulled me into its boundless depths.

Chapter Eighteen

Words whispered around me, floating through my head, which ached slightly.

The pain at the base of my skull wasn't nearly as bad as the throbbing just above my left ear. Groggy and nauseated, I struggled to open my eyes, desperate to understand why my head hurt so badly. I couldn't figure out how to move and couldn't remember how to lift my eyelids so I could see where the hell I was and what was going on.

"Quinn ..." a voice said. "Sweetie. Wake up, Quinn. Honey, you have to wake up."

Alarmed, I tried to force my eyes to open. Who was calling me sweetie and honey? The voice sounded familiar, but—

"Quinn!" The voice was insistent, hoarse with tension and fear. "Wake up!"

I felt as though I was floating up toward something, some type of surface, but I was rising too fast, and before I could prepare myself, I had burst through the barriers in my mind. My eyes opened and I stared at the face hovering over me—a handsome face. The face of the man who thrilled, entranced, and hypnotized me. The face of the man who had betrayed me in the worst possible way. Icarus.

"Quinn, what happened?" Icarus asked, gently trailing fingers along my cheek. "Quinn ..."

"Get away from me," I said, my voice weak and whispery as I struggled to orient myself as I rolled over onto my hip and pushed to a sitting position. I couldn't remember where I was, though my surroundings were becoming vaguely familiar. I was absolutely certain that Icarus was the enemy. He'd stabbed me in the back. He'd pretended to be on my side when all along he was setting me up for the ultimate kill.

That's why I was here, I realized. I was at this house because Icarus had come here. After he'd picked up the money I'd left in the locker at Golden Lizard Beach—per his instructions—he had driven to this house. Joshua had filmed him parking his Jeep in the oyster-shell driveway, getting out and walking to the door.

The same door I'd banged on, I remembered.

"Quinn ..."

"Leave me alone," I said, swatting a hand at him as the clouds in my head began to dissipate and I started to remember how I'd gotten to the house and why I was there. "Get away from me!"

"Quinn, listen to me," he said, his gaze intense, filled with apprehension. "You need to tell me what happened."

"Tell you what happened?" I looked at him, wary of his tense stare. "What are you talking about?"

"What happened?" Icarus repeated, his voice insistent. "Tell me—"

"Get away from me!" I practically howled at him, stumbling back. "Stay away from me! You liar! You evil bastard! I know what you did!"

"What I did?" he asked. "What—"

"I saw you!" I said as the kaleidoscopic haze of confusion drifted away and my mind started to clear.

"You saw me? What? Where?"

"At Golden Lizard Beach!" I said. "I saw you go there, to the locker room where the lockers are! I saw you go to the place where the blackmailer told me to deliver the money, and I know why you went there!"

"No, Quinn, I can explain why I was there."

"I don't need your explanation!" I said. "I know why you were there! Because you are the blackmailer! You went there to get the money—"

"That's not true, I swear to you," he said. "You have to believe me. I can explain why I was there."

"Can you explain to me why you lied and said you couldn't video the blackmailer because you had to work? Can you explain why you told Liberada you had some stomach virus and couldn't come to work?" I demanded. "Can you explain why—"

"Yes, Quinn, I can explain everything!" Icarus said, grabbing my arms and staring at me. "And I will explain everything, but not right now! Because we have a much bigger problem to deal with!"

"What bigger problem?" I asked, my anger waning as the panic in his gaze worried me. "What the hell are you talking about?"

"Henri," he said.

"Henri?" I shook my head, confused. "Who is Henri?"

"Henri Monteils," Icarus said.

"Who is Henri Monteils?"

"What do you mean, who is he?" Icarus asked. "You don't know him?"

"No, I have no idea who he is," I said, wary.

"Then why did you come here, to his house?" Icarus asked.

"I didn't come here to talk to Henri Monteils," I said. "I came here to ask you why the hell you blackmailed me! I came here because I saw you come here after you took the beach bag out of the locker in the changing room at Golden Lizard Beach!"

"How did you see me?" Icarus asked. "You followed me?"

"I had you followed," I said. "When you said you couldn't video the blackmail money drop, I found someone else to do it. I told them to follow whoever came to get the money. And when I saw the video, the person who came to pick up the money was you!"

"I said I can explain," he said, as though he was struggling for patience. "But, right now, you have to tell me what happened to Henri? When you got here, was he—"

"When I got here, I was looking for you," I repeated. "But you weren't here. Some other guy came to the door. I recognized him from the hotel. I don't know his real name."

"His real name is Henri," Icarus said. "At the hotel, he goes by Apollo."

Apollo. The guy from the waterfall fantasy I'd rejected. *You're the one who didn't want to make love. We could have had a good time that day.*

"I didn't know his real name was Henri," I muttered. "I asked him where you were, and he said he didn't know. He said you didn't live here. So, I said I would leave and call you later, but he said I should stay ..."

We could have a good time now, just you and me.

Trembling slightly, I said, "He wouldn't let me leave."

"He wouldn't let you leave?" Icarus asked. "Why not?"

"He made some vulgar comments about me, you, and him having a threesome," I said, struggling to focus, feeling as though I needed to remember exactly what had happened. "But, I kept telling him I wanted to leave. He grabbed me and then ..."

"And then?" Icarus prompted. "What happened?"

Get up, bitch!

"I thought he was going to rape me," I said, the memory so acute it was as if I was experiencing the panic and terror all over again. "He had blocked the door so I couldn't leave. I was so terrified. I had to get away from him, and so I ran into the kitchen to find something to defend myself with, and I found a knife and I grabbed it and ... "

"And then what happened?" Icarus asked. "When you grabbed the knife, what did you do?"

Fearful and wary, I glanced away from his piercing gaze, terrorized and confused by the unfathomable look I'd seen in his whiskey-colored eyes. Had it been doubt? Suspicion? But that made no sense. Why the hell would Icarus be suspicious of me? I wasn't the criminal. I hadn't done anything wrong. I certainly hadn't lied to him and conned him out of a hundred thousand dollars.

"Quinn, I need to ask you something very important, okay?" he said, placing a hand beneath my chin and lifting my head, forcing me to look at him. "And I need you to be honest with me."

Saying nothing, my heart beating chaotically, I glared at him.

"When you grabbed the knife," Icarus said. "Did you stab Henri? Quinn, did you kill him?"

Staring at Icarus, stunned by his question, I opened my mouth to scream, but no words came out.

Because I had no words. I didn't understand what Icarus was asking me. *Did you kill him?* Why would he ask me something like that? How could he possibly think that I would—

"Quinn ..." Icarus grabbed my hands and pulled me to my feet. "Did you—"

"I didn't kill anybody!" I tried to twist away from Icarus, but it was impossible. He was bigger and stronger and had no problems guiding me out of the living area and into a short hallway that led into a small bedroom.

It was dominated by a large bed, and on top of the pale yellow quilt, Henri was sprawled on the bed with a butcher's knife in his heart, half of the blade and the hilt jutting out of his blood-covered chest. Horrified, my stomach twisted from the gruesome sight.

Trembling, I turned to Icarus.

"We need to call the police," I said. "We need to tell them ... we need to ... tell them ..."

"Tell them what, Quinn?"

"The truth!"

"And what's the truth?" Icarus asked me. "Do you even know? Do you know what happened? Do you know who killed Henri?"

"I know that I didn't kill him!" I said. "I know that and I want the police to know that I did not stab him! And I don't know who did, but I didn't kill him!"

"What if they don't believe you?" Icarus asked.

Bewildered, I asked, "What?"

"What if the police don't believe you?"

I stared at him, confused. "Why wouldn't the police believe me?"

"Because it doesn't look like you *didn't* kill him!"

"I don't understand."

"Quinn, you have blood all over you," Icarus said. "Henri's blood!"

"What?" I shook my head, panic and mania taking over as I glanced down at my shirt and saw the dried, rust-colored smears. "Oh my God!"

"Quinn—"

"How did his blood get on me?" Hysterical, I grabbed the hem and lifted the shirt. "I don't know how his blood got on me!"

"Calm down!" Icarus ordered.

"I want it off!" Crying, I pulled the shirt up and stretched it out away from me at the same time, desperate to get it off, and trying not to get the bloody fabric on my face or anywhere near me. "Get it off me!"

"Quinn, don't—"

"I have to get out of here!" Flinging the bloody shirt away from me, I bolted out of the bedroom, through the hallway and into the living area, gasping and gulping, desperate to get out of the house. My eyes on the front door, I sprinted to it, grabbed the knob, twisted it and yanked it open.

"Quinn, wait!" Icarus grabbed me, hands clamped around the back of my arms like shackles.

"No, leave me alone! I have to go!" With a feral strength I wasn't aware I had, I wrenched away from him and fled out of the house and into the night.

Chapter Nineteen

"We should call the cops," I said, lying on the velvet-tufted chaise across from the wardrobe in the bedroom of my hotel suite. "We need to let the police know what happened to Henri."

"I'll call them," Icarus said.

After my mad, panicked dash from Henri's small blue house, Icarus had followed, chasing me before I accidentally ran into the road and got hit by a car. Crying and shell-shocked, I couldn't calm down as my mind swirled with images of blood and knives.

Somehow, Icarus managed to calm me down enough to walk me to his Jeep. Inside, he gave me a jacket to put on. Now, I cringed, remembering my desperate flight out of the house, clad in only shorts and a see-through lace push-up bra.

After arriving back at the Heliconia, Icarus escorted me to my room, guiding me along a deserted maze of hallways at the rear of the hotel, making sure we didn't attract the attention of any staff or guests who might question my frantic, disheveled demeanor.

"What are you going to tell the police?" I asked.

"I'll just say I want to report that a man was stabbed and give them Henri's address."

"You're not going to mention me?" I stared at him, biting my bottom lip, wary of my own reasons for asking the question. Was I asking because I didn't want him to mention me, or because I couldn't believe he wasn't going to be honest with the cops?

"Why would I mention you?" Icarus sat on the corner of the bed, diagonally across from the chaise.

"Because I was there," I reminded him. "I had Henri's blood all over me."

"They don't need to know that."

"So, you're going to lie to the cops?" I asked, my tone a mix of condemnation and relief; wasn't sure if I was glad, or disappointed in his decision.

"I'm going to make sure you don't get arrested for something you didn't do."

What he said made sense, but it felt wrong. "How do we know I didn't?"

"What do you mean?" Icarus said. "You told me you didn't stab him."

"I don't *remember* stabbing him." I jumped up and started to pace, wringing my hands, near hysteria. "But what if I did and I just don't remember? What if—"

"What if we talk about what you do remember," Icarus suggested. "Tell me the whole story."

"I don't even know where to start."

"The beginning."

"The beginning is when I saw that video of you taking the beach bag out of the locker at Golden Lizard Beach!"

"I told you I can explain."

"But you haven't explained," I reminded him. "So when will you?"

"First, let's figure out what you remember."

"I remember seeing that video of you," I persisted. "You took the beach bag out of the locker and then you got in your Jeep and drove to Henri's house. You knocked on the door, and someone opened it. I couldn't see who because of the angle of the video—"

"Who did you get to follow me?" Icarus interrupted.

"Don't try to change the subject," I warned. "Tell me why you took the money!"

"Because I had suspected Henri was the blackmailer, but I couldn't prove it," he said. "So, I took the money and went to his house to confront him. I planned to offer him a deal. If he confessed to the extortion scam—on camera—then I would give him the money. You would have a videotaped confession which would, hopefully, stop him from trying to extort more money from you."

"Why didn't you just tell me that you wanted to change the plan?" I asked, not sure I believed him.

"I know our original plan was that I would follow whoever came to pick up the money," Icarus said. "But I started thinking, what if that person had been told to pass the money to someone else."

"Then you would have followed that person," I said.

"Right, but then I got worried," he said. "What if it became like a shell game, with one person passing the money to another person and then that person passing the money to someone else? What if one of the people removed the money from the bag and put it into a briefcase, or something, without me knowing about it? I would still be following whoever had the beach bag, not realizing that the money was no longer inside of it until the last person dropped the empty beach bag into a trash can somewhere. I just didn't want that to happen."

I stared at him, wondering if that sincerity in his soulful eyes was just a ruse. His reasoning for the last-minute change of our original plan seemed to be based on paranoia, but I understood it. The blackmailer didn't trust me, obviously, and probably hadn't expected me to follow his instructions about not going to the cops. The extortionist would have taken steps to make sure he, or she, would not be discovered. Still, something about Icarus's story seemed fishy, farfetched.

"What happened when you went to Henri's?" I asked. "Did he take your deal? Do you have his confession?"

"Henri wasn't there."

Convenient. The word came to me, but I wasn't sure if I really thought that or if I was allowing Lisa to influence me.

"So, tell me this," I said, folding my arms. "Where is the money now?"

Icarus shook his head. "I don't know."

"You don't know?"

"The money wasn't in the beach bag," he said.

"I don't understand."

"Remember I told you I was afraid the blackmailer would play some kind of shell game with the ransom pickup?" Icarus asked. "Well, I was right. By the time I got to the locker room, that shell game was already in play, only I didn't realize it until later, after I had left Henri's place."

"Wait a minute," I stopped him. "Are you telling me that the beach bag you removed from locker number seventeen at Golden Lizard Beach was empty?"

"It wasn't empty," he said. "Inside, there were five bundles wrapped in newspaper."

"The five bundles of money we wrapped in the newspaper," I said.

"That's what I thought," he said. "But, something didn't seem right, so I opened one of the bundles. It was a small paperback book. There were paperback books in all of the bundles."

"So, someone took the money out of the bag, replaced it with paperback books that had been wrapped in newspaper, and then put the bag back in the locker?" I rubbed my eyes and then stared at him. "That's crazy. Why would the blackmailer do that?"

"I don't know," Icarus said. "But, like I told you, Quinn, we have bigger issues to deal with."

Apprehensive, I sighed and decided to mull over his story later, maybe with Lisa, who would provide her usual suspicion and insight.

"Henri's murder." I nodded, realizing he was right.

"You were going to tell me what you remember?"

"I don't really remember anything else that I haven't already told you," I said, jumping up to pace. "I thought he was going to hurt me so I grabbed a knife, and then I turned and I think ..."

"You think what?"

"I think he hit me," I said. "I think he knocked me out. Because the next thing I remember is you telling me to get up."

Icarus sighed and stood. "Try to see if you can remember anything else."

"I don't think I will," I said. "Are you leaving?"

"Before I call the police," he said. "I want to go back to Henri's and look for your shirt."

My heart kicked. "My shirt?"

"The shirt that had blood all over it," he reminded me. "You took it off at Henri's place, remember?"

"Because I had to get it off," I said, defensive, trying to ignore the escalating panic I felt. "I didn't want that bloody shirt anywhere near me. I remember I threw it ... somewhere."

"I'll find it," he said, assuring me, though I could have sworn I'd seen a flash of doubt in his gaze. "And then I'll get rid of it."

"What if you can't find it?" I jumped up and hurried to him.

"It's got to be at Henri's house," he said, embracing me. "I'll find it."

I wrapped my arms around his waist and clung to him, pressing my face against his T-shirt as the tears fell.

"It's going to be okay," he said, and when I lifted my head to look up at him, he pressed his lips against my forehead. "I'll be back as soon as I find your shirt and then I'll call the police, okay?"

"Okay," I said, nodding, trying not to cry, and resisting the urge to tell him to hurry.

"Listen, while I'm gone, try to relax," he said. "Maybe have the butler bring you a glass of wine. Something to take the edge off."

After Icarus left, I returned to the bed and lay across it, knowing I wouldn't be able to relax enough to get a decent night's sleep. Most likely, I wouldn't close my eyes tonight, and on the off chance I did, I would be haunted by images of Henri, stabbed to death, lying in bed with a knife protruding from his chest—a brand new night terror to replace the crazy courtroom killing nightmares.

Sighing, I thought about the unease and restlessness I had endured from my recurring dreams. Since I'd met Icarus, I'd had only one nightmare, but I couldn't celebrate tension-free sleep just yet. I still needed to identify the cause of my angst, but there was no time for introspection or analyzing, not with the horror show my life had become.

Icarus's suggestion to have a glass of wine was tempting; though I doubted pinot grigio would be able to lure me away from the ledge I wanted to jump off. Nothing would.

Well, maybe there was something. Sex. Specifically, sweaty, scorching sex with Icarus. I wasn't sure if I could trust him or believe his wild rationalizations. I didn't think falling into bed with him was a good idea, no matter how much I wanted to be with him.

DAY EIGHT

Chapter Twenty

"Quinn," Icarus began. "There's something we need to talk about."

"What?" I asked, heart pounding.

At a little after eight in the morning, we sat at the small bistro table on the terrace outside my bedroom, surrounded by lush, tropical flowers bathed in golden sunlight. Icarus had returned after midnight. I had still been up, waiting for him to tell me what happened when he went back to Henri's place to look for my shirt, but Icarus said we would talk in the morning.

I fell asleep in his arms, imagining it was what I did every night, because I wished I could. In the morning, there would be grave conversation, possibly bad news, panic, and worry. Last night, I gave myself permission to pretend that Icarus was my husband. I imagined a scenario where we were on a third honeymoon in paradise. He loved me, and his passion and desire for me would never fade.

That was my fantasy.

But, like most fantasies, it would never be real, never come true.

"I didn't call the cops," he said.

My heart sank. I knew why Icarus hadn't informed the police about Henri's murder. "Because you didn't find my shirt, did you?"

"I didn't get a chance to look for it," he said. "The cops were already at Henri's house. As soon as I turned on his street, I saw all the cop cars, so I just drove by his house."

"You think the police found my shirt?"

"I don't know," he said. "But I don't think you should stick around to find out."

Heart slamming, I asked, "What do you mean?"

"I think you should leave St. Mateo," he said. "You should take the first flight back to the states."

Confused, I just stared at him, not sure what to say.

"I was looking up the flights before you woke up," he said. "First flight out is around one o'clock tomorrow. But it was sold out. And so was the next one, which was taking off around six in the evening. Usually, there are only two flights in and out of St. Mateo each day."

Reeling, still shell-shocked by his suggestion, I found myself asking, "What about Sunday?"

"The second flight on Sunday still has some seats," he said. "It leaves at eight Sunday night, heading to Miami. From there, you can go back home, wherever that is."

"Okay, fine, if that's what you think I should do," I said, trying to manage the disappointment and sadness coursing through me. "I'll leave St. Mateo on Sunday."

"I think that's for the best," he said and then added, "even though I wish it wasn't."

"What?"

"You should leave," he said. "But that doesn't mean I want you to go."

"You don't?"

"I want you to stay here with me," he said. "But, I know that's impossible. Even if this stuff hadn't happened with the blackmailer and with Henri, your fantasy still would have come to an end."

Near tears, I nodded. Reality could be cruel, I realized.

"I know you have a life back in the United States," he went on. "You have to go back there and live it."

"It's not much of a life," I said.

"What does that mean?" Icarus asked. "It's not much of a life?"

"It means ..." I shook my head, not wanting to talk about the sad state of my career in these final moments of my fantasy. "Nothing. It doesn't matter. What matters is that you don't want me to go."

"You thought I did?"

"I didn't know what to think," I admitted. "I was just hoping that maybe ..."

"You were hoping what?"

Looking at him, I didn't know how to say what I felt or if I should admit I'd been hoping Icarus might feel something for me. I didn't really know how to define what I wanted him to feel. Something like what? Something like ... falling in love?

Startled by the wayward direction of my thoughts, I buried them. Asking Icarus to fall in love with me was too much to ask of him, myself, and of our situation. For the two of us, it could be nothing more than an island fling.

"I was just hoping that you wanted me to stay here," I said. "But I guess leaving would be best."

"If you stay in St. Mateo," he said. "I think you might be accused of killing Henri."

"But, I didn't kill him."

"I know that," Icarus said. "But the cops might think differently. They might find evidence that shows you were at his house when he was killed. Or, maybe someone saw you at Henri's."

"Like a neighbor, you mean?" I asked, my heart slamming wildly, as I tried to remember whether or not I'd seen anyone else in the immediate area of Henri's house.

"Did you notice any neighbors outside?" Icarus asked. "Did you see anyone walking down the street?"

"I don't know," I said. "I mean, I don't think so, but ..."

"But?"

"But, I wasn't really paying attention," I said. "I was so angry, I was literally seeing red. I wasn't thinking about my surroundings. All I wanted to do was—"

"Confront me," Icarus said. "You wanted to accuse me of blackmailing you."

"Icarus—"

"It's okay," he said. "I get why you might not believe me. I realize that some of the things I've done may have seemed suspicious to you, but I want you to know that I would never try to blackmail you."

I nodded, though I didn't know what I was acknowledging. Was I letting him know I believed him? Or had it been some automatic nonverbal response because I wasn't sure what to say to him? I didn't know what to believe about him.

The question remained: Did I think Icarus had blackmailed me? Did I believe he'd plotted an elaborate con to take me for a hundred thousand dollars? Did I think he was still conning me? I didn't know. I just wasn't sure about anything. So many horrible things had happened, and I didn't know what to think.

Except maybe Icarus was right. Maybe I should flee the island to avoid being thrown in jail for a crime I hadn't committed.

Even if it meant I would never see Icarus again.

Chapter Twenty-One

"I knew you couldn't trust Icarus," Lisa said, triumphant, as though she was vindicated.

Sighing, I paced around the plush, tufted couches, my cell phone on speaker as I held it in my palm.

Icarus had left several hours ago, and during that time, I'd called Lisa to update her on the latest events in my continuing nightmare—from Icarus telling me he wouldn't be able to video the money drop to seeing Icarus on the video.

I told her about going to the little pale blue house to confront Icarus, but instead I'd encountered Henri, the guy from the waterfall fantasy. He'd knocked me unconscious, and when I woke up, Icarus had been there, asking me if I had killed Henri.

"But, you didn't," Lisa said, adamant. "You wouldn't stab somebody to death."

"Unless I did," I mumbled, biting my lip.

"What the hell are you talking about?"

"Lisa, I don't really remember what happened after Henri hit me," I said. "What if I regained consciousness and grabbed the knife and—"

"That's not what happened," Lisa said. "You know what happened? I'll tell you what happened. Henri knocked you out, and then Icarus came back to the house, and he and Henri fought, probably argued about the money that Icarus got out of that locker at the beach."

"I don't know, Lisa," I said. "I don't think—"

"Well, I do think that," Lisa said. "Somebody has to think that Icarus is a blackmailing murderer because you sure as hell don't want to believe it!"

"It's not that I don't want to believe it," I said. "I just don't think it's true."

"You don't want to believe it because Icarus is giving it to you good," Lisa said. "He's giving it to you like you never got it before, and you don't want to give him up. But if he's a blackmailing murderer, then you can't have anything to do with his ass."

"He's not a blackmailing murderer," I said, once again questioning my decision to come clean to Lisa about my burgeoning relationship with Icarus.

"Quinn, you know that you have questions about why he took the beach bag out of the locker and why he went to Henri's house," Lisa said. "And you know you're skeptical about his bullshit answers, which don't add up."

"Yeah, but—"

A knock on the door, loud and persistent, interrupted me, and I told Lisa I would call her later.

I opened the door. "Quinn Miller?" said a tall, well-built, good-looking man. His smooth complexion reminded me of coffee with a swirl of cream and honey. Wearing dark slacks and a light-green button-down cotton dress shirt, he seemed to be in his early thirties, maybe. The muscles and the handsome face worried me. Was he the star of my next fantasy? God, I hoped not.

"Yes," I said, a sliver of worry slicing through me. "I'm Quinn Miller."

"Ms. Miller, my name is Detective Richland François."

My heart kicked and my attempt to swallow the lump in my throat almost made me choke.

"Do you mind if I ask you a few questions?"

"Questions about what?" I asked.

"Would it be okay if I came inside?" he asked.

"What is this about?" I asked. "I really don't have time for this. I have a spa appointment in fifteen—"

"It's about a man named Henri Monteils," he said.

"Why would you want to ask me about a man named Henri Monteils?" I asked, stalling, trying to think of what to do, worried about what to say. "What makes you think I even know someone named Henri Monteils?"

"Well, you must know him," the detective said. "You went to see him yesterday evening. You want to tell me what that was about?"

"What makes you think I went to see him?"

The detective sighed. "Ms. Miller, I think you better come with me."

"Why?" I asked, stepping back, tempted to slam the door in his face. "I don't understand what any of this is about."

"Henri Monteils was killed yesterday," the detective said. "You need to tell me what you know about that."

Pulse racing, my stomach leaped as I shook my head. "I don't know anything about—"

"I think you do," said the detective. "And I would like you to come down to the police station."

At the police station, in the dank, dimly lit interrogation room, I sat at a cold, metal table that was bolted to the floor, trying not to have a damn heart attack.

When the door opened, I nearly jumped out of my skin. Detective François stepped into the room, his dark eyes kind, and yet I sensed shrewdness in his gaze, as though he was sizing me up. While he examined me, I imagined he was trying to figure out how to coax me into incriminating myself.

Criminal defense was not my area of expertise, but I knew better than to talk to the cops without a lawyer. So, why the hell would I allow this detective to question me without any representation? The rational part of me probably thought I was somewhat still smart enough to answer questions without incriminating myself. All I had to do was tell the truth and trust the detective to have enough sense to know I wasn't a killer. The detective would surely determine that I couldn't have murdered Henri Monteils.

"So, Ms. Miller, before we get started, would you care for something to drink?" the detective asked as he closed the door and walked to the table in the center of the room. "Water? Coffee?"

I shook my head, rebuffing his attempts to play the gracious host, probably trying to disarm me, get my guard down, and fool me into thinking I could trust him with all my dirty little secrets.

"Well, then, why don't we begin with the basics," he suggested, asking me to provide vital statistics.

"Harlequin Annette Miller," I said in a flat tone after he asked for my full name.

"Interesting name," the detective said. "Harlequin. Very pretty."

Sneering at him, I snipped, "No one calls me Harlequin."

"Do people ever call you Harley?" he asked, as though he was actually interested.

"People only call me Quinn," I said, crossing my arms as I glared at him.

Nodding, he asked, "And Miller is your maiden name?"

I nodded.

"And, just for the record, you are a U.S.-born citizen visiting the islands, correct?"

"Correct."

"Where are you from?"

After I told him, he asked, "And you are an attorney?"

Again, I nodded, employing a strategy I would sometimes give my clients, which was to rely on nonverbal responses, when possible, and to not expound upon their answers. Most people wanted to explain themselves, but doing so while under oath was risky. In the courtroom, anything you accidentally said could be intentionally used against you.

"Why did you come to St. Mateo? Business? Vacation?"

Sex, I thought wryly, but I said, "Vacation."

"For how long?" he asked, scribbling across a yellow legal pad. "And also, when did you arrive?"

Sighing, I answered his questions.

"How do you like St. Mateo?"

Exhaling, I asked, "What do you want to ask me about Henri Monteils?"

Following a tight smile, the detective said, "And you're staying at the Heliconia? I'm curious, why did you pick that hotel?"

Despite the open curiosity on his face, I knew the detective had some opinion about my choice of hotel. Probably, he pegged me as some gold digger married to a rich geezer who couldn't get it up, looking for, as Joshua had told me, "some good dick."

Shifting uncomfortably, I asked, "What does that have to do with what you think I know about the man who was stabbed?"

A hint of amusement in his eyes, the detective leaned back and stroked his chin. "Interesting you should say that."

"Say what?" I asked, panic and apprehension sneaking up on me.

"The man who was *stabbed*," he said. "I told you Henri Monteils had been killed. Never said *how* he was killed. So, tell me, Ms. Miller, how do you know Henri Monteils was stabbed to death?"

Shell-shocked, I stared at the detective, desperate to come up with some plausible reason for how I knew Henri had been stabbed.

"Maybe you know because you stabbed Henri Monteils."

"That's not true." Shaking my head, I said, "I didn't stab him. I would never—"

"A neighbor saw you pounding on the door," he said. "This neighbor said you were demanding that Henri Monteils open the door."

"I don't know what the neighbor—"

"You recognize this, Ms. Miller?"

Trying not to scream, I stared at the object the detective had placed on the table between us, like a gruesome centerpiece. Inside a clear plastic evidence bag was my tank top, covered in Henri's blood, dried to a dark, rusty brown.

"Looks like a tank top," I said, remembering how I'd practically ripped it from my body I'd been so desperate to get it off.

"It was found in Henri Monteils' house," the detective said. "A witness identified it as the shirt that the woman who was banging on Henri's door was wearing."

My heart dropped into my churning gut as I struggled to breathe.

How could this be happening to me? Was I dreaming? Trapped in a nightmare? Nothing about this situation seemed real. It was all like some bizarre hallucination. Why the hell was I sitting in the interrogation room of some island police station being questioned about a murder I couldn't have possibly committed?

"Know what else we found when we searched Henri Monteils' house?" The detective asked, his expression smug. "A burner phone with two very interesting text messages that Henri sent."

Holding myself rigid, I stared at the detective, praying I wouldn't betray the fact that I knew about the messages he referred to.

"He was blackmailing you, wasn't he?"

Stricken, flummoxed, I sputtered, "Yes, but—"

"And you killed him, didn't you?"

I shook my head. "No!"

"Ms. Miller, we have a lot of evidence against you," the cop said. "Are you sure you don't want to just tell us the truth? Save us a lot of time and money. Save you a lot of embarrassment."

"Embarrassment?"

"If you cut a deal with our prosecution team," the cop said, "they can keep this whole sordid mess out of the papers. Nobody will have to know that you came here to have a little fun at that sex hotel."

My heart thundered as I glared at him.

"I know all about the Heliconia." He gave me a mirthless, judgmental smile. "The seven-star hotel that caters to lonely, desperate women who are starved for attention, longing to be touched."

Ashamed, I dropped my head.

"You checked into the Heliconia for some good stuff," the detective went on, a hint of ridicule in his derisive rant. "You want it long and thick. You want it to last forever."

I kept my eyes averted.

"You're a high-powered attorney, but you work at one of those good-old-boy conservative firms where the men are given most of the credit and the women really should be home taking care of the kids and the house," he said. "But not you. You're determined to prove yourself. Determined to make partner even though you know those good old boys don't think you're good enough. They're waiting for you to fuck up so they can tell you that you're just not partner material. The last thing you need is a sex tape floating out there on the Internet for those good old boys to see. You know that tape is gonna fuck up your whole career, which hasn't been going very well, has it? Funny thing is, those good old boys might have given you a chance to redeem yourself, but if they see the tape, you can forget it. Goodbye making partner. Goodbye job at that prestigious law firm. It's a paralyzing, sobering thought. So, you decide to pay the guy. But then you realize if you pay him once, you'll be supporting this guy for the rest of his life because there is no way he didn't make a dozen extra copies of that video where you're getting it in the ass—"

"I didn't kill him!" Enraged, I pounded my fists on the table.

The cop scoffed and then chuckled sardonically as he leaned back in his seat. "Ms. Miller, let's not go through this pretense, okay? We both know you killed Henri Monteils. You went to his house to confront him."

"I didn't go there to ..." I shut my mouth, worried I'd already messed up and said too much.

"So, you did go there," the cop said, catching the significance of my slip—inadvertently, stupidly, I'd put myself at the scene of the crime. "But ... maybe you didn't go to kill him? Maybe you went there to get the evidence of your indiscretion? And, maybe he didn't want to give it to you? Maybe he wanted more money? And that pissed you off and you snapped and—"

"This conversation is over," I told him. "I'm not saying another word until I talk to a lawyer."

"You're not saying another word until you enter your plea to the judge," the detective said, scowling as he stood.

"My plea to the judge?" I stared at him, feeling something within me imploding.

"I'm arresting you, Ms. Miller," Detective François said.

"Arresting me?" I whispered, aghast and outraged.

"For the murder of Henri Monteils."

Chapter Twenty-Two

"I'm in jail ..." I whispered, clutching the phone with trembling fingers.

There was a pause, and then Icarus said, "Jail? Why are you in jail? What the hell happened?"

"I've been arrested for Henri's murder," I said, determined not to cry despite the tremor in my voice and the panic twisting my gut.

After I was booked—fingerprints, mug shot, the works—another deputy escorted me to a small, windowless, dingy room, allowing me some privacy to make a phone call. My first thought was to contact Lisa. What could she do from thousands of miles away except worry about me? I didn't want to put her through that.

Next, I contemplated calling my dad. My father could have gotten me out of this horrific situation, but I didn't want my dad to find out about my shameful, deplorable actions. As it was, Dad thought I was off at some retreat meditating, which he'd thought was a good idea. "You need to exorcise Ellison, Zupancic, and Cox from your spirit, mind, and soul." I couldn't bear the thought of Dad knowing the truth, which he would find out if I called him for help. I didn't want him to be disappointed by my visit to a sex hotel.

Exhaling, I stared at the faint traces of ink on my fingertips.

"The police arrested you for Henri's murder?" Icarus echoed, as though he hadn't understood a word I'd said, as if I was speaking a foreign language. "What? How? Why?"

What, how, and *why* were questions I didn't have answers to, but I told Icarus, my tone halting and hoarse from sobbing, about the evidence and the witnesses the police had against me—the bloody tank top, the cab driver, and the neighbors who had seen me banging on Henri's door like a woman scorned, ready to unleash my hellish fury.

"Doesn't seem like enough evidence to charge you with murder," he said.

"There's also the text messages," I said. "The messages from the blackmailer to me were found on a burner phone in Henri's bedroom. Henri was the blackmailer. You were right."

"Sonofabitch," Icarus muttered. "I knew he was behind it."

The question was, as Lisa had pointed out when I'd updated her, how had Icarus found out Henri was the blackmailer? When had he found out? And why hadn't he told me the moment he knew, or even suspected, Henri had tried to extort money from me?

Those questions begged answers, but later, not right now.

"Okay, listen, don't worry," Icarus said. "I'm going to get you out of there."

An hour later, Icarus showed up with his cousin, a criminal defense attorney named Octavia Constant. Short and stocky, and yet brisk and efficient in her red power suit, Octavia had an engaging smile and attentive light brown eyes, slightly magnified by the thick lenses of her black-rimmed glasses.

Octavia—Icarus affectionately called her "Tavie," and she teasingly referred to him as "Ish" after Ishmael, his last name—had a passionate exuberance and natural warmth about her that I found comforting. Despite my predicament, her confident attitude gave me hope.

A few minutes after five o'clock in the afternoon, Octavia had secured my release on my own recognizance, which I was thankful for because I wouldn't have to spend the night in jail.

"That's the good news," Octavia said as she, Icarus, and I sat at a table in the interrogation room.

"And the bad news?" I asked, my heart skittering.

When she told me, my heart dropped. The recognizance bond was contingent upon the surrender of my passport to the authorities.

"What if I refuse?" I asked. "I'd rather pay the bail amount."

"If you refuse, the prosecution will argue that bail should be denied because you are rich, which makes you an automatic flight risk in their mind," she explained. "The only way to keep you on the island is to make it impossible for you to leave. Because of the criminal charges, the U.S. Embassy would refuse to issue you a temporary emergency passport."

"So basically, if she refuses to surrender her passport," said Icarus, "then she has to stay in jail until her trial."

"Exactly," said Octavia. "Despite the fact that St. Mateo is a U.S. territory, it is not easy to extradite a citizen born in the United States back to the island. There's a strict burden of proof, and it could take four to five years with no guarantee that the request will be granted despite the evidence against you."

Icarus volunteered to drive back to the hotel to get my passport and bring it back to the station, and then it was another two hours before I was officially released. Exhausted, enraged, and terrified, I walked out of the police station just in time to experience another glorious St. Matean sunset.

Following Octavia and Icarus down the steps and to the wide sidewalk, I glanced about at the throngs of pedestrians, tourists, and locals, smiling and laughing, caught up in animated conversations, and felt a stab of envy and longing. Everyone seemed so frivolous and jovial, enjoying life, and I was a few steps away from running into the street and in front of one of the jitney buses that sputtered along, backfiring and belching exhaust.

Octavia announced that she would get her car. While Icarus and I waited for her to return, he said, "I'm sorry about that passport issue."

"It's not your fault," I said.

"But if you had your passport," Icarus said, the muscles in his jaw tightening. "Then you could leave the island and then you wouldn't have to worry about this bullshit murder charge."

I stepped back as a group of European tourists, led by a guide speaking what sounded like German, or maybe Polish, ambled past us, and then said, "Maybe the murder charge isn't bullshit."

"What do you mean?" Icarus looked at me, obviously confused and a little skeptical.

"We're not sure that I didn't kill Henri," I reminded him.

"I'm sure that you didn't kill him," Icarus said.

"What if I don't remember killing him?" I looked up at him, searching his gaze. "I remember picking up the knife when Henri came at me. I remember thinking I had to do whatever it took to defend myself, even if whatever meant killing him, so maybe I—"

"You didn't kill him."

Shaking my head, I said, "But, what if—"

"There's my cousin," Icarus said as he grabbed my hand and pulled me toward the little hatchback that Octavia had parked next to the curb.

DAY NINE

Chapter Twenty-Three

"We need to clear Quinn's name, Tavie," Icarus said, the next day. "How do we do that?"

"Well, you could look for clues to prove that you didn't do it," Octavia said. "But, of course, that's easier said than done."

"That's more like damn near impossible," I complained, trying to temper my rising fear and frustration. Nine in the morning was too early for a spike in my blood pressure, but it was impossible to stay calm.

"Then we do the damn near impossible," Icarus said. "We'll find the evidence we need to prove that Quinn didn't kill Henri."

"Actually, you'd be better off looking for another suspect," Octavia said. "Right now, the cops are convinced that Quinn killed Henri because they don't have any other options. They need someone else to consider. Find them someone else who could have killed Henri."

"How am I supposed to do that?" I asked, anger overtaking the fear. "How am I supposed to find out who else might have wanted Henri dead?"

"I actually have an idea of who we should talk to," Icarus said. "Henri's sister, Doris. If Henri had some kind of beef with somebody, she would know."

After grabbing a yellow legal pad from a cabinet in the bamboo wood credenza behind the desk, Octavia took a seat in her big, leather chair, uncapped a pen and said, "Okay, Quinn, tell me everything."

Alarmed, I said, "Everything."

She nodded. "Henri was blackmailing you, right?"

"Yes."

"And you paid him?"

I nodded and then explained about the video of the money drop. Octavia seemed excited about the video until Icarus told her it showed him removing the blackmail money from the locker at Golden Lizard Beach. As an explanation for his actions, Icarus gave his cousin the same story he'd given me—he'd planned to use the money as bait to lure Henri into confessing he'd blackmailed me.

"Why was Henri blackmailing you?" Octavia asked, scribbling furiously on her yellow legal pad. "What did you do?"

"It's my fault," Icarus said.

I shook my head. "Icarus, don't—"

"Your fault?" Octavia frowned at her cousin. "I don't understand."

Icarus said, "Henri had a video of me and Quinn ... together."

"A sex tape of you and Quinn?" Octavia asked. "Hmmm ... we need to make sure it doesn't get leaked. Ish, do me a favor? Go tell my assistant I need a Motion to Suppress, like the one she did in the Valencia case. Please?"

"Motion to Suppress?" I asked, the attorney in me wondering if Octavia was employing the correct strategy. Of course, I couldn't throw stones, especially since my strategic efforts had failed my clients.

"If this case goes to trial," she started, "and we're going to make sure it doesn't, but just in case, I like to file a motion to keep the details of my cases out of the newspapers. Don't want potential jurors making up their minds months in advance, you know?"

Thankful for Octavia's foresight, I nodded. The last damn thing I needed was someone accidentally seeing the story of my arrest online.

Octavia said, "I'll file a motion, today, for a gag order."

"Will that stop the cops and the prosecution from talking to the media?" Icarus asked.

"Maybe, maybe not," she said. "But, it will stop them from talking to the press until the judge can rule on the motion. Let me get my assistant working on that. I'll have it filed before noon."

"How long will it take for the judge to rule on the motion?" I asked, making a mental note to do some research on the Palmchat Island judicial system.

"Depends on how many cases he's got on his docket," she said. "But, a week or two, at least."

"That gives us time to prove that you didn't do this," Icarus said. "And then there'll be no need for them to talk to the papers."

Octavia cleared her throat. "Ish, can you do that favor for me now?"

After Icarus stood and walked out of his cousin's office, Octavia leaned back, eyeing me shrewdly. "So, I'm wondering ..."

Wary, I asked, "What?"

"What made you choose the Heliconia?" Octavia asked. "You don't look like the type of woman who normally goes there."

"I thought that ... well, it doesn't matter what I thought," I said, not wanting to get into my personal issues. "I'll tell you this: I wish I had never gone to that damn hotel."

"A lot of women end up feeling that way," she said. "It's a nice premise. But, you have to be very careful when you go to a place like that. Because it's all fun and games until somebody gets blackmailed."

Sighing, I nodded.

"Or ... falls in love."

Stricken, panicked, I stared at her. "What are you talking about?"

"I'm talking about your feelings for Icarus," she said. "You've fallen for my cousin."

"No, I'm not in love with Icarus," I rushed out, feeling desperate and confused.

"Oh, come on ... I saw the way he was looking at you," she said. "And the way you were looking at him. Maybe you two haven't fallen in love, but you've fallen into something, and I think it's a bit deeper than lust."

Swallowing, I looked away, not sure what to say.

"But you didn't come here for relationship advice," she said. "You need a legal strategy."

"Which will be?" I said, thankful for the opportunity to move the topic away from my feelings for Icarus.

"We've got to find another suspect," she said. "Someone who had a stronger motive and a better opportunity to kill Henri than you did."

"Sounds like you want me to find the real killer."

"That may be the only way for you to stay out of jail," she said. "Right now, the cops think they've got their man—or woman, rather—and they're not looking for any other suspects. So, we have to do our own investigation."

"How?" I asked, though I had a feeling my commercial litigation skills—if I could get them working properly—might be useful.

"Well, Ish can help with that," she said. "Every now and then, he does a little freelance investigative work for me. I've just opened my practice in St. Mateo—I used to practice in the USVI—and I'm from here, but I've been gone awhile. Ish knows everybody and people tell him stuff they wouldn't tell me."

I nodded, hopeful.

"Look, I know it probably seems like your life is collapsing around you," she said, "but we're going to get you out of this mess, okay? So, not that you want any motivational platitudes—"

"Motivational platitudes would be nice, actually."

"Well, then, stay strong," she said and smiled. "And keep the faith."

Chapter Twenty-Four

"I hate to say this," Doris started, shaking her head. "But, I'm not even surprised that Henri is dead."

"You're not?" I gaped at her, not sure how to process what she'd said.

A little after nine o'clock that night, my nerves were on edge as I sat at small table across from Henri's sister, a petite St. Matean woman with a compact body like a gymnast, nothing but sinew and muscle. She had a slightly vague resemblance to her brother, and I noticed she was wearing the same gold medallion necklace that had been hanging from Henri's neck when I'd first encountered him on the path to the waterfalls.

Driving from Octavia's law office back to the Heliconia, Icarus had said, "We can go talk to Henri's sister after I get off tonight. Should be around seven."

"You want me to come with you?"

"You don't want to talk to her?"

"Maybe she won't want to talk to me," I said, worried. "I was arrested for killing her brother. I'm sure she knows that. Octavia's gag order can probably stop the story from showing up in the *New York Times*, but I doubt we can do anything about island gossip."

"St. Mateo is like a small town," Icarus confirmed. "Everybody knows everybody's business."

"Maybe you should talk to her alone," I suggested, but Icarus didn't think that was a good idea. Doris would want to talk to me, he'd promised, especially when I told her that I hadn't killed Henri. Doris would be able to discern that I was telling the truth and would want to help us find out who really killed her brother.

"What do you mean by that?" Icarus asked, obviously shocked by Doris's chilling admission. "Why are you not surprised that he's dead?"

"All them get-rich-quick ideas he always coming up with," the sister said. "I try to tell him it's not going to work. The Bible say when you dig a ditch for somebody, you gone fall in it yourself. And that is what happened to Henri. He done got caught in the trap he try to set for you."

Doris's words seemed harsh, but her solemn eyes told the story of her sorrow over her brother's murder. Her fatalistic, philosophical sentiments were most likely some attempt to assign meaning, or maybe even blame, to a devastating, hopeless situation.

When we'd arrived, Icarus and Doris greeted each other with easy, comfortable familiarity, and then he introduced me and explained to Henri's sister exactly why we were there. As he'd warned me, he was honest with Doris about who I was—the woman who'd been arrested for killing her brother. "But, Ms. Miller didn't do it," Icarus had said. "The police have the wrong person. That's why we want to talk to you. We want to know if you know of anybody else who might have killed Henri."

Doris had given me a shrewd look, and for a moment, I didn't know if she would collapse into sobs or start screaming like a banshee while she attacked me. After a moment, she allowed us to come inside the tiny home. In the small kitchen, Doris offered me a seat at a table that was just a bit bigger than a snack tray, and Icarus stood in the entryway.

"I think when he went to work for the Heliconia, that was the worst thing for him," Doris said and then took a swig from the plastic bottle of Coke she'd taken from the mini-fridge. "Something about being around all them rich people put a bitterness in his heart. And, all of a sudden, he got to get out of the double-H. He can't stand the east side no more. He do whatever he have to so he can leave this place, like it's so horrible. It's not the worst place in the world. It's good people here. Kind people. We care about each other. Friendly people with a good heart. But, Henri want to leave, he want to be rich, so he come up with this plan."

"And what was his plan?" I asked, even though I knew all about Henri's wicked schemes.

"Henri say all the women who come to the Heliconia are rich," Doris said. "He say they got more money than they need. He come up with an idea to force one of these rich ladies to give him money. He say he going to video one of ladies when she naked, doing one of her fantasies. Then, he will tell the lady, you give me money or I put the video all over the Internet."

"But how did Henri decide to target me?" I asked. "Did he find out I was coming to the hotel and do some research on me or something?"

"Wasn't planned like that," Doris said. "I ask Henri, what lady you gone do this to? He say, it don't matter."

"Wait a minute," I said, my heart hammering. "Are you saying I was chosen at random?"

"Didn't matter to Henri who the lady gone be, he say," Doris said, pursing her lips in disgust. "All that matter is she rich and got the money to pay him."

Dumbfounded, I glanced at Icarus, who was frowning, and then back to Doris, whose sympathetic gaze I couldn't bear. I looked away, toward the little picture window above the sink. Focusing on the wilting herbs growing in the mason jar filled with water, I tried not to cry.

I wanted to scream at the injustice and unfairness of this hell I was going through. A nightmare I could have avoided if only I hadn't been making love with Icarus in the spa bungalow when he decided to put his disgusting extortion plan into action. It was like a punch in the gut, knowing Henri hadn't specifically targeted me. The blackmail scheme wasn't even about me. It was about Henri finding a rich woman, any rich woman, to extort money from.

The blackmail attempt had been a random attack, which bothered me and made the whole sick, twisted situation worse. I wouldn't be dealing with blackmail demands and a first-degree murder charge if I had changed my mind about going to the Heliconia Hotel to deal with my anxiety.

"What I think is that he got killed by one of them fools he was working with," Doris said, rolling her eyes.

"Fools Henri was working with," Icarus said. "What fools? Henri was working this scam with other people?"

"They thought they were so smart," Doris spat, tone dripping with scorn. "They thought that they would get away with it. Henri say they gone call themselves the alliance."

"The alliance?" Icarus asked.

"Henri was in some kind of alliance?" I asked, trying to follow her, praying I wouldn't miss a crucial clue.

"Henri didn't come up with this idea by himself," Doris said. "He had help. So-called friends. I told him not to get involved with them, that he couldn't trust them."

"What friends?" Icarus asked.

"Nick and Sam, for sure," Doris said. "And Stazia."

"Stazia," I echoed, thinking of the fake maid who'd left the black-mail letter in my suite.

"Maybe one other person, but I'm not sure because I told him I didn't want to know anything about it," Doris said. "I told Henri I didn't want the cops asking me no questions, you know, if the plan didn't work out. And it didn't. I knew it wouldn't. But, I didn't think ..."

Trailing off, her eyes brimming with tears, Doris looked away, shaking her head.

Disquieted by her display, I thought of reaching across the table to place my hand over hers, but I hesitated, not sure how my gesture would be received.

"Did you tell the police about all this?" Icarus asked, getting the conversation back on track. "You told them that Henri and some other hotel workers decided to blackmail one of the guests?"

"I absolutely did," she said and then sighed. "But I don't know if they take me seriously, you know? Because I don't have no proof of what I say. It was not like Henri write this idea down. He tell me about it, and so the police say, that is hearsay. Then they say they already know who killed my brother."

"I know the police told you I killed him," I said, my heart slamming. "But, Doris, I swear to you, I did not kill your brother."

"Then why do the police think you did?" Doris asked, and though there was fierceness in her gaze, I had the feeling that maybe she didn't really think I was guilty, but she wasn't sure. Maybe she wanted me to convince her of my innocence. "The cops say the evidence they got against the killer is very strong."

"The evidence they have against Quinn doesn't really prove that she killed Henri," Icarus said.

"Henri neighbor say you was banging on his door," Doris said. "Say you was cussing and demanding that Henri open the door. Is that true?"

Wary, I braved a quick look at Icarus, but he was focused on Doris, and I wasn't sure what to say. Yes, it was true that I'd been banging on the yellow door of the little blue house, but I hadn't known that Henri lived there. I'd gone to the house looking for Icarus.

"Yes," I admitted, finally. "But—"

"What did you go there for?" Doris asked, her red-rimmed eyes blazing. "If you don't go to kill him?"

"I wanted to get the video," I said, suddenly remembering the reason for this fiasco my life had become because of Henri and his unholy alliance. "The deal was, if I paid your brother, he would give me the video and he couldn't show it to the whole world. But after Henri let me in, we argued. And then ..."

"And then ...?" Doris prompted, her gaze intent.

"Henri hit me," I said. "He knocked me unconscious. So, I don't remember everything that happened."

"Then maybe you don't remember killing him," Doris suggested, leaning back in her chair, eyes shrewd.

"Quinn didn't kill Henri," Icarus said. "She was unconscious when whoever did kill Henri stabbed him in the chest."

"How do we know she was unconscious?" Doris asked, staring at Icarus. "Because she says my brother knocked her out?"

"Because I found her," Icarus said.

Jolted by his confession, I looked at him, wondering if he would regret admitting that he, too, had been at the scene of the crime. I had neglected to tell the police, not wanting to get Icarus in trouble, but I had a feeling Doris would pass this information on to Detective François.

"You found her?" Doris asked and then slid skeptical eyes my way before quickly returning her gaze to Icarus, asking him, "You went to Henri's house the day he was killed?"

"I went to confront him," Icarus said. "I suspected he was the blackmailer, and I was hoping I'd get him to confess. But, the first time I went, Henri wasn't there. Later, I went back to Henri's place, and that's when I found Quinn, unconscious on the floor in the living room."

"None of this is right," Doris wailed. "I know my brother did wrong, but he didn't have to die. Jail, yes. He deserve to go to jail, but did somebody have to kill him?"

"That's what Icarus and I want to find out," I said, encouraged by Doris's use of the word "somebody", a word she wouldn't have used if she was convinced that I had killed Henri. "And we will, I promise."

Scoffing, Doris said, "You just want to save yourself. You just want to find somebody else who could have done it so you won't go to jail."

Deflated, I tried not to be discouraged by the fact that I'd obviously misread her. "Doris, I want to find the real killer because your brother won't get any justice if the wrong person goes to jail for killing him."

"Quinn is the wrong person," Icarus reiterated.

"Then find the right person," Doris said, her eyes solemn again and her tone resigned, almost defeated. "Find who really killed Henri."

Ten minutes later, Icarus drove away from Doris's tiny house, steering casually and confidently along the winding road flanked by palm trees. The dilapidated, disenfranchised neighborhood was washed in an inky darkness, punctuated every now and again by a sickly porch light or a flickering neon sign in the window of a roadside shack.

"Doris said that Henri's alliance was Stazia, Nick, and Sam," I said, glancing at his profile in the dark. "I know Stazia, but who are Nick and Sam?"

"Nick and Sam both work at the Heliconia," Icarus said, turning onto the main road leading back toward the Heliconia Hotel. "They do fantasies, too."

"Do you think Nick killed Henri?" I asked, staring at the dark road, illuminated by the headlights of Icarus's Jeep. "Or maybe Sam? One of them might have argued with Henri and killed him."

"Need to have a talk with both of them," Icarus said.

"What would we say?" I asked. "If one of them did kill Henri, they're not going to admit that to us."

"Maybe we can trick them," Icarus said. "Maybe I could tell Nick that Sam said he's the killer. And then, I could tell Sam that Nick said he was the killer. Cops use those kinds of tactics, sometimes."

"But you're not a cop, Icarus," I said. "What you want to do sounds dangerous. And what if it doesn't work?"

"Well, I have to try," Icarus said.

"We have to try," I corrected.

"Better if I talk to them alone," he said.

"Why don't you want me to go with you?" I asked, my blood pressure rising.

"Because a cornered animal will always attack," Icarus said and then turned off the highway and onto the private road that meandered toward the hotel's front façade.

Shaking my head, I asked, "What do you mean?"

"Neither one of these guys is going to like being confronted," Icarus said. "And if one of them did kill Henri, then things could get physical. And I'm not going to let anything bad happen to you."

DAY TEN

Chapter Twenty-Five

"Are you sure that Icarus even talked to Nick and Sam?" Lisa asked, suspicion evident in her tone.

"He said he did, and I believe him," I said, pacing around the coffee table between the couches, trying to maintain my resolve to keep an open mind about Icarus and give him the benefit of the doubt. I didn't want Lisa's doubt to infect me.

Last night, after Icarus took me back to the Heliconia, we made out in the car for a while, but eventually, he left to go find either Nick or Sam. He had some ideas of where they might be, places they usually hung out, bars and clubs that locals frequented and where tourists weren't always welcomed.

This morning, Icarus stopped by to tell me he'd been able to track down Nick and Sam last night. Both of them denied any involvement in a deal to blackmail one of the guests. "Not surprised they lied," Icarus had said. I wasn't surprised by their denial either.

After Icarus left to go to work, I called Lisa to give her the latest on the continuing saga of the nightmare my life had become, telling her about my interrogation and arrest, the visit to Doris's, and what we'd learned from Henri's sister.

"You know what I think you should do," Lisa said.

Her phrase made my stomach twist. The last time she'd given me her opinion, she'd had the crazy idea for me to get over my anxiety by flying to St. Mateo, checking into the Heliconia Hotel and embarking on a quest to have an extraordinary amount of sex.

I'd taken Lisa's advice and look what happened.

Immediately, I chastened myself. Couldn't blame Lisa for this mess I was in. Wasn't my best friend's fault that I'd been blackmailed. Wasn't anyone's fault. As Doris had told me, *Didn't matter to Henri who the lady gone be. All that matter is she rich and got the money to pay him.*

Lisa said, "I think you need to call Nick and Sam yourself."

"You think so?"

"Quinn, your freedom is at stake," Lisa said. "You can't go to jail for something you didn't do. You have to get to the bottom of this bullshit. Take control of the situation, stop letting Icarus make all the damn decisions."

"I don't even know how to get in touch with Nick and Sam," I said, hoping Lisa and I could brainstorm some way to make her idea, which I was starting to like, work. "I mean, maybe I could request them for a fantasy, or something."

"I'm sure you can do that," Lisa said.

"Or, maybe," I said, as the idea suddenly occurred to me.

"What?" Lisa asked.

"I can ask one of the maids," I said. "Just like I did when I wanted to get in touch with Joshua."

"You'll do this favor for me?" I asked. "You'll give this note to Nick for me?"

Nodding, the maid said, "And you'll give me three hundred dollars?"

"Right," I said, thankful for the mercenary attitude I'd once judged. "Three hundred."

Moments later, we made the exchange. I put three crisp one-hundred-dollar bills and an aqua envelope—complimentary hotel stationery—in her hands, and then she hurried off to do my bidding.

Closing the door behind her, I walked to one of the couches and sat down, hoping my words would convince Nick to talk to me. *I want to meet in private. Text me and let me know.* I'd also left my cell phone number.

What I hadn't done, and wasn't sure I would do, was tell Icarus that I planned to talk to Nick. Lisa had told me not to, but I didn't know if I should keep things from him. Icarus was on my side, committed to helping me clear my name, but ...

I had to be sure that I could trust him. If Nick agreed to meet with me, and if he corroborated Icarus's story, then I would feel a lot better about trusting Icarus. But, what if Nick didn't corroborate Icarus's story? I wasn't sure how I would feel about that.

Two hours later, a text came through that nearly brought me to my knees. Staring at the words on my cell phone, I wasn't sure if I was disappointed or terrified, or maybe both. My heart pounding, I read the response again:

ok lets meet 2nite. 11p. bar at hotel beach

Slowly, I sank down onto the couch. I wasn't exactly eager to meet Nick at a beachside bar at night, but I couldn't pass up the chance to talk with him. Despite Icarus's warning that "cornered animals attack" and his worries about my safety, I had to try to find out what Nick knew about Henri's alliance and the blackmail plot.

Around ten o'clock, my nerves were shot, and my stomach was doing back flips.

I was no longer convinced that meeting Nick on the beach at eleven was a good idea. But I had to go through with it. Before I lost my nerve, I shoved my feet into a pair of wedge heels, grabbed my purse, and left my suite.

Twenty minutes later, nervous and jittery, I was sitting at the hotel's beachside bar, at the far end, away from a dozen or so raucous couples —female guests and their fantasy dates flirting and displaying too much affection. I'd just taken a second sip of my seltzer and lime when I felt a tap on my shoulder. Startled, I glanced back, gasped, and nearly fell off the stool.

"Ms. Miller?" asked the guy standing in front of me—a guy I recognized. "I'm Nick Presso. How are you tonight?"

At that moment, I was flabbergasted, staring at Nick Presso. He was one of the gods from the waterfall fantasy. *Hermes*, if I was remembering correctly.

After taking the stool next to me, Nick ordered a shot of Hennessey—compliments of me—and when the bartender sat the glass on a napkin in front of him, he took more than a moment to savor the cognac. While Nick sipped leisurely, as though we actually were friends meeting for a drink, I took deep breaths, trying to remember the questions I wanted to ask him.

"So, why'd you want to meet with me?" he asked and then took a slow sip of his drink, giving me a smoldering stare over the rim of the glass. "You changed your mind about the foursome?"

"I'll get to the point," I said, ignoring his sly sarcasm.

"Please do," he encouraged, his expression all business, no longer teasing.

"I'm sure you heard about what happened to Henri," I started and then cleared my throat as I glanced away from his piercing glare. "And I—"

"I'll tell you what I told Icarus when he talked to me," Nick said, putting his empty glass on the bar.

"So, Icarus talked to you?" I asked, cautioning myself to make sure, but joyous relief was already spreading through my limbs.

Nodding, Nick signaled the bartender for another drink, which I was sure would end up on my tab. "He got in my face, asking me about some bullshit plan to blackmail you that Henri had come up with."

"So, you didn't help Henri blackmail me?" I asked, wondering if I'd be able to see through any lies he might be telling me. "You weren't in the alliance that Henri put together?"

"I don't know about no damn alliance," Nick said, taking a quick swig of his second drink. "I'll tell you like I told Icarus—I didn't try to blackmail you. And I didn't kill Henri, either, which I'm sure was your next question."

I stared at him, trying to read his sullen expression, looking for deception. But, all I saw was the flippant, bored attitude of the guy from the waterfall fantasy, who didn't look as appealing with his clothes on, covering his biceps and the eight-pack.

"I heard you killed him," Nick said, his teasing smirk back.

"That's not true," I said.

"Heard the cops got a lot of evidence against you," he went on, as though he wanted to bait me into something, maybe some response that would expose me as a liar.

"The evidence is not as damaging as the cops seem to think it is," I said, trying to stamp out the desperate panic rising within me. "But, unfortunately, it is enough to raise doubts about me. That's why I need to find the real killer."

"The real killer," Nick said, holding his glass of cognac at eye level, examining it. "If it's not you, then I wonder who it could be."

"Do you know?" I asked, my pulse jumping. "Do you have any idea who might have—"

"Like I told Icarus, you might want to have a chat with Sam."

"Sam?" My heart pounded. "Why do you say that?"

"If anybody was working with Henri to blackmail you," Nick said. "It would have been Sam."

"Are you saying you think Sam killed Henri?"

Nick finished his second drink and then put the glass on the bar. "That's what I heard."

"What?" I whispered, staring at him, my heart slamming. "Do you have any proof?

"I don't have proof," Nick said. "But I know somebody who does."

I felt something break free and take off within me. "Who is it?"

"I need to talk to this person first," he said. "They didn't tell me to go repeating what I'd been told."

"I won't say that you told me," I promise, feeling as though something important was slipping away from me.

Nick shook his head. "The person might not want to get involved."

"Please, tell me," I implored. "I am facing a murder charge for something I didn't do, something I could never have done. If there is someone who has proof that Sam killed Henri then, please, you have to tell me. Who is the person who told you?"

With a sigh, Nick said, "It was—"

What sounded like a herd of angry elephants split the tense air between us, the abrupt sound startling the bartender and almost knocking me off my stool.

"What the hell?"

"Sorry. My phone." Nick frowned and then pulled his cell phone from his pocket. Silencing the elephants, he stared at the display screen. "Hold on, I gotta check this text."

Frustrated, I nodded and took a sip of my water, trying not to scream. Did I believe Nick? Not sure. Yes and no. His claim about not being part of the alliance was doubtful. I had a feeling he was telling the truth about not being the killer. Couldn't explain it, but I couldn't imagine him plunging a knife in Henri's chest. He was well-built, but I sensed a lack of self-confidence. He didn't appear aggressive and volatile enough to take a life.

Then again, he'd been eager to rat out Sam. Maybe too eager. Had that been because he didn't want Sam to get away with killing Henri? Or had he been hoping to keep the suspicion away from himself?

I wasn't ready to speculate and make any conclusions just yet. First, I wanted to update Lisa. My best friend had demanded I call her immediately after I met with Nick. I didn't want to engage in any deductive reasoning without her perspective, insight, and input.

"Listen, um, I gotta go," Nick said, still glancing at his phone as he slid off the barstool.

"What? You have to go where?" I sputtered, panicking. "Wait a minute, you didn't tell me—"

"Stazia Zacheo," he said "She's the one who told me that Sam killed Henri."

"Nick, wait," I said, sliding off my stool, eager to follow him. "When did you talk to Stazia? Where is she? Icarus tried to find her, but he said she wasn't home."

"If Icarus really wanted to find Stazia, he could have," he said and turned from me, walking away from the bar, slipping between the frisky couples, and disappearing from my line of sight.

Troubled, I stared at the sea of lust crowding the bar. Nick's words carried a disturbing insinuation, an implication of insincerity in Icarus's intent to locate the fake maid. Equally hard was trying to ignore my suspicions of Icarus, which had been revived somewhat, by Nick's claim. Why wouldn't Icarus want to find Stazia Zacheo? Was he trying to protect her? Or, maybe warn her?

After closing out my tab, I headed back to my suite. Probably wasn't a good idea to overanalyze what Nick had said, I decided. Maybe it had been opinion and conjecture, not solid fact. Icarus had promised to continue looking for Stazia Zacheo, and I wanted to believe he'd been telling the truth. If Nick had been honest with me, then finding Stazia was more important than ever. She had to tell the police what she knew about Henri's murder, how Sam had killed Henri, so the murder charge against me could be dropped.

DAY ELEVEN

Chapter Twenty-Six

"I'm so glad you're here," I said, closing the door after Icarus showed up at my suite around three o'clock. All morning, I'd been texting him, nagging him about his work schedule for the day and reminding him to make sure he stopped by to see me before he headed home. "I need to tell you something."

"What is it?" Icarus asked, taking a seat on one of the tufted divans.

"We need to set up a meeting with Octavia," I began, taking a seat on the opposite couch. "And the police need to be there also."

"Why do we need a meeting with my cousin and the cops?" Icarus asked, leaning forward.

"Because Sam killed Henri," I announced, feeling a bit triumphant, like I used to whenever I would win high-profile cases, a giddy sensation I hadn't felt in the last six months. "We need to tell Octavia and the police, so they can drop the murder charges."

"Sam killed Henri?" Icarus looked bewildered. "How do you know this?"

"Nick told me."

"Nick told you that Sam killed Henri?" Icarus gaped at me. "When did he tell you that?"

"When I talked to him."

"You did what?"

"I met with Nick," I repeated, a bit more adamant in response to Icarus's tone, which was irritatingly admonishing, like an angry managing partner scolding a disgraced litigator.

"Why did you do that?" Jumping to his feet, Icarus stared at me. "When did you talk to him?"

"Last night," I snipped, feeling defensive. "We met up at the hotel bar across from the beach."

"Why the hell would you go talk to him when I told you ..." Icarus trailed off, and seconds later, his eyes narrowed. "You still don't trust me, do you? You didn't believe me when I told you that I talked to Nick."

"It's not that I didn't believe you," I said, wincing at my lies.

"It's just that you still think I had something to do with black-mailing you," Icarus said, shaking his head. "And I guess I can't blame you. That video Joshua recorded for you shows me going into the locker room at Golden Lizard Beach, opening locker seventeen, and taking out the beach bag that you and I put the money in. So, I know it looks like I went to steal the money. And it doesn't help that I lied to you about having to work because I didn't want to tell you about my plan to force Henri to confess."

Sighing, I pinched my bottom lip between my teeth and then released it, saying, "Icarus, I do want to trust you."

Crossing his arms, he said, "But, I'm not making it easy, right?"

"No, not really," I admitted.

"Still, Quinn, you know I didn't take the money," Icarus said, pacing around the couch. "Whoever Henri sent to pick up the cash got to the locker room before I did. That person switched the newspaper-wrapped money bundles for the newspaper-wrapped paperback books then put the beach bag back in the locker and left. The video showed you who took the money. And I don't know why Joshua didn't follow that person. He just stayed there until I showed up and—"

"Wait a minute," I cut him off. "That wasn't on the video!"

Icarus stopped pacing and frowned at me. "What wasn't on the video?"

"The person who took the money out of the beach bag and replaced it with books was *not* on that video."

"They have to be on the video," Icarus insisted. "Whoever that person was, Joshua had to have recorded them."

"But, he didn't," I said, confused, filled with wariness and doubt. "The video only shows you removing the beach bag from locker seventeen. That's the only reason why I thought you were blackmailing me. That's why I went to Henri's house looking for you."

"Wait, wait." Icarus stopped me. "If the video doesn't show who really took that money from—"

"Then we need to talk to Joshua," I said, thinking a bit more like the Quinn Miller who had gone undefeated in her first two years of cases. "We need to ask him if he saw someone else open locker seventeen."

"If he was videoing the whole time, from the moment you showed up until the moment he followed me to Henri's place," Icarus said. "Then he must have video of whoever Henri sent to pick up the money."

"We also need the original footage from his phone," I said, energized by the idea of recapturing my intelligent discernment. "He might not be willing to hand it over, but Octavia can file a motion to compel Joshua to produce the cell phone, if need be. First, however, she'd probably need to have him designated as a fact witness."

"Are you sure you need Octavia?" Icarus said, his tone jocular, his gaze amused. "How do you know what motion she should file?"

Sheepish, I shrugged. "Oh, um, well, I don't think I told you this, but I'm a lawyer."

"Really?" Icarus asked, sounding a bit impressed.

"Complex commercial litigation," I said. "I know nothing about criminal defense, so I definitely need your cousin's help. And, anyway, you know what they say about a lawyer who tries to represent herself."

"No, what do they say?"

"She has a fool for a client."

Icarus laughed and then returned to the couch, sitting next to me. "Well, you're definitely not a fool, Quinn Miller. And you're not a murderer, either," he said, adamant. "We're going to prove that."

"Quinn, don't take this the wrong way," Lisa said. "But, you have got to stop thinking with your hoo-ha."

"What?" I pulled the cell phone from my ear to stare at it and then pressed the speaker button so I could talk and pace at the same time. "What are you talking about? I am not thinking with my ... lady bits."

Icarus was gone and I was talking to Lisa, giving her the customary update of the nightmare my life had become and soliciting her advice and, occasionally, arousing her consternation and indignation.

"I don't believe for one minute that story Icarus gave you about someone else showing up at the changing room, before he did, to switch the real money with paperback books," Lisa said. "Why would Henri tell the person to do that?"

"I don't know," I said. "But, you're right, his story is—"

"It's bullshit," Lisa exclaimed. "If it was true, then it would have been on that video Joshua recorded for you. If it was true, Joshua would have followed that person, and he wouldn't have recorded Icarus taking the bag out of the locker because he wouldn't have been there."

"Maybe I should ask Icarus to show me the beach bag with the newspaper-wrapped books inside of it," I suggested. "Wouldn't that prove that he was telling the truth?"

"Icarus is not stupid," she said. "I'm sure he can produce the bag with the books in it. He's already got a damn good excuse for all his lies, trust me. But don't trust him. I believe he is smart and manipulative and he's probably not going to slip up. So, you have to go with your gut, not your hoo-ha."

"I know, I know," I said.

"Do you really?" Lisa asked. "Do you know what happens to people who get convicted of murder on St. Mateo? Do you know it's an automatic life sentence? Do you know how horrible the prisons are in paradise? You're not going to have any spectacular views of palm trees or white sand beaches or—"

"Lisa, I get it, okay," I said, annoyed. "But, I'm not going to prison for a murder I didn't commit. My attorney thinks we need to find a better suspect."

"What if the better suspect is Icarus?"

"Icarus is not a killer."

"How do you know?" Lisa challenged.

"Because," I started and then quickly faltered, irritated because I couldn't think of a definitive dispute to Lisa's accusations.

"Quinn, forget about the mind-blowing sex for a moment and consider this," Lisa said. "You can't really prove anything that Icarus has told you."

"What do you mean?"

"Let's start with the first blackmail note," Lisa said. "The one instructing you to check out the text message on your phone."

Shrugging, focusing on my irritation and not my growing wariness, I plopped down on the couch. "What about it?"

"The maid told you that Icarus wanted her to deliver the note for him," Lisa said.

"That was a mix-up," I said, reminding Lisa that two maids had come to my room that day. One had the blackmail demand. The other maid, the one who'd told me Icarus had asked her to deliver the note, actually did have the letter that Icarus had written.

"The tale of the two maids and the mix-up with the notes is a story Icarus told you," Lisa said. "A story I'm sure you didn't validate. Did you ask the first maid about the second maid that came to your room that day with another note for you?"

"Well, no, but—"

"And let's talk about the second maid for a moment," Lisa suggested. "Icarus told you the second maid was some girl named Stacy who had been fired from the hotel for stealing."

"Her name is Stazia," I said. "She's the girl Icarus saw on the hotel video cameras and recognized."

"Another story you probably didn't check out," Lisa said. "How do you know if Icarus went to security and looked at the surveillance tapes?"

Disgruntled by Lisa's unrelenting suspicion, I said nothing, but I supposed there was nothing to say. Except Lisa was right. Which annoyed the hell out of me because I didn't want to have all these doubts about Icarus.

"Look, I know you want to trust Icarus," Lisa said. "And for your sake, I hope he's not a lying murderer."

"Why do you still think Icarus killed Henri?" I asked. "Nick said Stazia told him that Sam killed Henri."

"How do you know Nick was telling the truth? Will Stazia say Sam killed Henri if the cops ask her?" Lisa asked. "Or, will she implicate someone else?"

"You think Stazia might tell the cops that Icarus killed Henri?"

"I think you need to be very careful around Icarus," Lisa said. "He just might be that better suspect you're looking for."

DAY TWELVE

Chapter Twenty-Seven

"I talked to Octavia about setting up a meeting with the cops," Icarus said when he stopped by that night, around ten o'clock, after finishing his shift.

"Thanks for doing that."

"Octavia asked me why you wanted this meeting," Icarus walked to the couch and dropped down on the far left side. "But, I told her I didn't know because ..."

"Because what? Why didn't you tell her I found out that Sam killed Henri?" I asked, joining him on the couch, sitting on the opposite side.

"Because Tavie would have asked me how do you know that? And what was I supposed to tell her? That Nick said that Stazia said ...?" Icarus shook his head. "That's not exactly proof."

"We don't have to prove it," I countered. "Octavia said we needed to find a new suspect, a better suspect. There's no better suspect than Sam. He was in Henri's alliance, helping Henri blackmail me. Obviously, they argued over money, and Sam killed Henri."

"Maybe," Icarus conceded, though he didn't sound entirely convinced.

"Look, I found a better suspect," I said. "And I wanted the cops at the meeting so they can be told to start investigating this better suspect I found for them."

"Well, the meeting is set for tomorrow at ten a.m.," Icarus said, rubbing his eyes.

"Good. I'll be right back. I want to update my calendar," I said, jumping up from the couch and hurrying into the bedroom. Sitting on the edge of the bed, I grabbed my cell phone from the night table. I didn't think for one minute I would forget the time and location of the meeting, but calendaring it made me feel more in control, and I relished any opportunity to enjoy the comfort of my old routines. While I entered the details of the meeting into my phone, I pondered Nick's claim about Icarus' ability to find Stazia if he'd really wanted to, and my stomach dropped. I figured I should ask Icarus what Nick had meant, but I was hesitant to reignite the suspicions I was trying hard to forget about.

Five minutes later, I returned to the living room and sat on the couch. Pushing past my reluctance, I cleared my throat, and asked, "Have you been able to find Stazia?"

"Still looking," Icarus said. "That girl does not want to be found."

"You sure about that?"

"What do you mean?"

Sighing, I said, "When I talked to Nick, he seemed to think that you wouldn't have a problem locating Stazia, if you really wanted to."

"Oh, really?" Icarus stared at me. "And did he tell you why I wouldn't have a problem finding her?"

"He didn't exactly elaborate," I admitted. "But, why would he say that if—"

"Nick Presso is not a guy you can trust," Icarus said. "He probably lied when he claimed he wasn't working with Henri to blackmail you. And this story about Stazia telling him that Sam killed Henri is probably bullshit, too."

"I have to believe that Nick was being honest with me," I said. "I have to believe that Stazia will be found and she will tell the cops that Sam killed Henri."

"Yeah, I guess you do," Icarus said, sighing as he walked around me and toward a desk in the far back corner of the living room.

Puzzled by his melancholy, I turned. "Look, I know that both Nick's and Stazia's claims have to be proven, and maybe Nick did lie to me, but don't you think his claims are worth investigating? I mean, Tavie said find a better suspect, so I did, and I thought you'd be happy about that, but ..."

"If Nick was telling the truth, and if there's a way to prove Stazia's accusations, then that will be the best news," Icarus said, facing me. "It's just ..."

"Just what?" I walked to him. "Are you okay?"

"Not really." He shook his head.

Taking his hands, I stepped closer and looked up at him. "What's the matter?"

"When I was at Octavia's," he said, looking down, "she gave me some bad news."

My heart started to kick. "Bad news about what?"

"About you," he said, staring at me with sympathy and tenderness in his bleak gaze. "About the case."

"What did she tell you?" I asked, barely able to push the question past the cotton in my mouth.

"Today, Octavia found out ..."

"Found out what?" I demanded, grabbing the front of his jacket, curling my fingers around the lapel. "Icarus, tell me!"

"The cops found fingerprints on the knife that was used to kill Henri," he said.

Staring at him, I began to tremble, to feel as though my body was frozen solid and yet engulfed in flames at the same time.

"The prints on the knife matched the prints they took from you when you were arrested," he said. "But Octavia said that doesn't mean ..."

Icarus continued to talk, but I didn't hear another word he said; I couldn't, not with the roaring in my head. Nauseated by the panic and fear shooting through my bloodstream like some kind of poisonous toxin, I clutched my stomach, close to retching. I wanted to run to the bathroom, but my legs were mush. I couldn't move. Couldn't think. Couldn't speak. Couldn't believe what was happening to me or understand why or how?

In an instant, I had reverted back to the panicked, near-hysterical, irrational version of myself. Sobbing, I collapsed against Icarus, clutching his shirt and wailing as his arms closed around me.

DAY THIRTEEN

Chapter Twenty-Eight

"So this guy, Nicholas," Detective Richland François began. "What's the last name again?"

"Presso," Octavia supplied, her tone brisk and confident. "Nicholas Presso. As I told you when we spoke yesterday, Mr. Presso is an employee at the Heliconia Hotel and a close associate of the deceased, Henri Monteils. My client, Ms. Miller, believes that Mr. Presso has pertinent and relevant information about the death of Henri Monteils."

"Well, if this information is so pertinent and relevant," the detective quipped, "then why isn't he here to tell me? Did you tell him about this meeting?"

"Um, well, no, I didn't," I said, trying not to wring my hands, trying not to lose hope as I glanced at Icarus, who stood out of the way, near a wall of bookshelves at the back of the office.

"Why didn't you tell him about this meeting?" The detective asked, making no effort to mask his frustration and annoyance. "If you truly believe he has pertinent and relevant information about Henri Monteils' death, then don't you think he should be here to tell me?"

I wanted to kick myself. Why had I let Nick Presso walk away without getting some sort of commitment from him to tell the police about Stazia Zacheo's claims about Sam killing Henri? I should have done things differently. I *would* have done things differently if I had been thinking straight. I couldn't afford to make stupid mistakes, not when my freedom could depend on Nick Presso telling Det. Francois everything he knew about Henri's murder.

"Tell me more about this pertinent and relevant information about Henri Monteils' death that Nick Presso supposedly possessed," Detective Francois suggested.

After a quick, deep breath, I said, "Nick, Mr. Presso, knows who killed Henri Monteils."

"And how do you know that, Ms. Miller?" the detective asked.

"Because he told me." I glanced at Octavia, wondering if my answer was okay. She tilted her head to the right slightly, a nonverbal clue, and I recalled what she'd told me before the detective arrived. If the detective asked me a question I shouldn't answer, Octavia promised to interrupt. She wouldn't let me incriminate myself or accidentally give the detective ammunition to use against me later.

"Nicholas Presso told you that he knows who killed Henri Monteils?"

"Nick said a former Heliconia employee told him that Sam Collins, a man who currently works at the Heliconia, had killed Henri," I said. "The ex-employee is a woman named Stazia Zacheo."

"Ms. Miller, what Nicholas Presso told you is pretty much akin to hearsay." The detective pinned me with a withering gaze. "And even if Mr. Presso told me himself, again, I couldn't take his word. I would need Stazia Zacheo to come to the station and have a talk with me."

"I know that," I said. "But we haven't been able to find Stazia."

"Well, when you find her," the detective said, standing, "then call me. Until then—"

"Are you going to investigate Sam Collins?" I asked, sitting on the edge of my seat, sensing the detective was about to leave.

"Ms. Miller, there's no reason for me to investigate Sam Collins," Detective François said. "I'm not going to waste my time chasing some false lead that can't be validated or—"

"It won't be a waste of time," I insisted. "If you'll just—"

"If Nick Presso or Stazia Zacheo have something to tell the police," Detective François said, "tell them to come down to the station."

"Did you know that Henri wasn't working alone?" I asked, desperate. "Did you know he had partners? Hercules, I mean Sam Collins, was one of Henri's partners and so was—"

"I think we've taken up enough of the detective's time," Octavia said, shooting me a warning glance—translation: Shut up. Now—as she stood and moved from behind her desk. "We'll certainly let you know, Detective, when we get in touch with Mr. Presso or Ms. Zacheo, so—"

"Actually, I have a few minutes," the detective took his seat again. "What were you saying, Ms. Miller?"

Octavia said, "I am going to advise my client not to—"

"Sam and Stazia Zacheo were working with Henri to blackmail me," I rushed out, pretending I didn't see the warning, a glare this time, that Octavia launched at me like a missile, even though she was in my line of sight, standing to the right of the detective's chair. I knew she wanted me to cease and desist talking, forthwith. But I was desperate to convince the detective to focus on Sam Collins, who had a more dangerous motive and a better opportunity to kill Henri.

The meeting had been a bust, but I was determined to salvage what little I could from this opportunity I had been given to talk to Detective François. There was no way I could let him leave without giving him details about Henri's alliance.

"Stazia Zacheo and Sam Collins were blackmailing you, too?" Detective François's eyes narrowed. "Is that so?"

"Quinn," Octavia said.

"They had some kind of alliance," I went on. "But I think it broke apart because they probably argued about the money, and then—"

"Quinn, you need to stop talking at once," said Octavia, the rebuke in her tone making me falter, lose my train of thought, and recognize, as the cloud of panic cleared, that the detective was amused.

Nodding, I looked at my feet, feeling stupid for my outburst, for not listening to Octavia, and for actually thinking the detective would be willing to take anything I said seriously.

"You shouldn't have done that," Octavia said, scowling at me after the detective had left. "When I tell you to stay quiet, you need to stay quiet."

"Quinn was just doing what you told her to do," Icarus said, moving away from his unobtrusive spot near the bookshelf and taking the chair the detective had vacated. "You said she needed to give the police another suspect."

"I didn't mean that literally," Octavia said, returning to her huge, leather chair. "I didn't want Quinn to tell the cops our strategy. The police don't need to know that we're investigating other possible suspects."

"But how will they find Henri's killer if they don't know that there are other suspects they need to look for?" I asked.

"We don't need to be concerned with whether or not the cops find out who really killed Henri Monteils," Octavia said. "Our focus, our only goal, is to get the murder charge against you dropped. To do that, we need another suspect. And we need solid, irrefutable evidence that the other suspect had motive, means, and opportunity. Then I draft a motion to dismiss all charges against you and make some very logical convincing arguments before the court. Faced with undeniable facts, the judge will agree, and you'll be off the hook, free to move on and live your life."

"You're right," I said, nodding. "I'm sorry."

"Listen, I know the attorney in you probably wants to assert herself," Octavia said, "but you have to trust me."

Contrite, I nodded, wondering what Octavia would think if she knew the attorney in me couldn't be trusted anymore.

"Promise you'll let me do my job from now on, okay?" she said and then added a smile. "You're paying me a lot to do it. You should want to get your money's worth."

Shaking my head, I said, "Lawyers make the worst clients, right?"

"Sometimes," Octavia conceded. "But not always."

"Sorry I wasted your time," I said. "I should have been better prepared for the meeting, I should have—"

"It's okay," Octavia assure me. "It wasn't a complete bust. Despite what he said, the detective will be looking into Stazio Zacheo and Sam Collins."

"Well, that's good news," I said, hopeful, but when I glanced at Icarus, he seemed only slightly convinced.

"But, wait, there's more," announced Octavia, moving to the topic of my fingerprints on the murder weapon, which wasn't exactly a smoking gun. The police hadn't found *fingerprints*, Octavia explained, they'd found a fingerprint. And it wasn't one of my fingers; it was a thumbprint, actually. The left thumbprint, which was odd, Octavia believed, since I was right-handed.

"The thumbprint was found on the blade of the knife," Octavia had said. "It wasn't on the handle, which is where you would usually find prints. That would indicate that you'd wrapped your hand around the handle and plunged the knife into Henri's chest."

This news got my hopes up but not too high. The police believed I'd tried to wipe my prints off the knife and had accidentally gotten my thumbprint on the blade somehow. They considered the thumbprint a lucky break and concrete evidence to support their belief that I'd killed Henri.

"The thumbprint is odd," Icarus said. "Quinn was unconscious when Henri was murdered, so why didn't the killer just wrap her entire hand around the knife? He, or she, could have given the cops damaging evidence against Quinn."

"Maybe the killer was more concerned with cleaning the knife than trying to set me up," I speculated. "But he, or she, didn't get all the prints off. I think the killer accidentally left my print on the knife."

Octavia sighed. "Well, I'm going to argue that you picked up the knife to defend yourself against Henri's assault, if the case goes to trail."

"The case is not going to trial," said Icarus with more conviction than I felt at the moment. "We're going to find the real killer. Quinn is not going to jail for a crime she didn't commit."

Chapter Twenty-Nine

"I wish I had asked Nick to come to the meeting," I mused out loud, pacing around the couch, biting my lip and wringing my hands. "I don't understand why I didn't. I have his cell number."

"You were probably just focused on telling the detective about Sam Collins," Icarus said. "Not that it did any good."

"You think I should call Nick?" I asked, irritated by my indecisiveness.

Icarus walked to the couch and sat. "And say what?"

"I want to ask him if he would be willing to go down to the police station and talk to Detective François."

"I don't think so," Icarus said.

"You don't think what?" I asked, the attorney in me thinking of how I would object to his answer if I'd been questioning him during a deposition. Vague, maybe. Non-responsive, possibly. "You don't think I should call Nick? Or, you don't think Nick would go to the cops and tell them what he knows about Henri's murder?"

"Both."

"I want to call Nick," I said. "I have to find out if he would be willing to give a statement to the police."

"And what if Nick refuses?" Icarus asked. "What if he doesn't want to get involved?"

"Octavia can designate him as a fact witness," I said, involuntarily formulating a potential legal strategy despite my promise to let Octavia handle my defense. "Then, she can depose him."

Looking at his watch, Icarus said, "It's almost noon. My shift starts at one o'clock. I get off at nine, but I'll find out what Nick's schedule is, and I'll try to talk to him. I can ask him about giving the cops a statement. What about that?"

"I guess that could work," I said. "I still wish I had asked Nick to come to the meeting. I could kick myself."

"Don't beat yourself up, okay?"

After giving me a quick kiss, Icarus left. I'd barely closed the door before I was calling Lisa. I got her voice mail. *Shit!* Frustrated and annoyed, I left a message telling her to call me, ASAP. Tossing the phone on the couch, I started to pace. Nervous and apprehensive, my mind swirled with regret. Why hadn't I asked Nick Presso to come to the meeting? Normally, I would have made sure Nick was present, available to recount his claim about Sam killing Stazia. If Nick had been at the meeting this morning, the detective might not have believed him, but he probably would have investigated his claims, I thought, taking another slow lap around the tufted divans. Sam Collins was a much better suspect than I was, and some way, somehow, I had to get the police to take a long hard look at him as the possible murderer of Henri. How the hell was I going to manage that?

Grabbing my cell phone, I scrolled through my phone log, found Nick Presso's number, and sent him a text, asking if he had time to talk. Minutes later, my cell phone chimed, signaling an incoming text message. Damn near diving for the phone, I grabbed it, dropped onto the couch and accessed the message, my fingers trembling and heart slamming. *We already talked.*

Fighting discouragement, I responded. *I know but I need you to tell the cops what you told me. Will you talk to the police? Will you tell them what Stazia told you about Sam killing Henri?*

Nick's next message came an excruciating fifteen minutes later. I read the message, my blood pressure spiking exponentially as I read it once more and then again. Staring at the words, one by one, I could hardly believe them.

Can't go 2 the cops. Lied 2 u about sam killing henri. Stazia didn't tell me that. sorry.

Breathing deep, I sent a response. *What do you mean you lied to me? Why did you lie? Are you saying Sam didn't kill Henri?* Minutes that felt like lifetimes later, Nick texted his reply. Reading it, my pounding heart dropped into my stomach, a long, plunging descent that almost made me double over.

icarus told me 2 lie and say sam killed henri. u can't trust Icarus.

"You need to listen to Nick," Lisa said when she returned my call a few hours later. "He doesn't trust Icarus and you shouldn't, either. Can't believe Icarus told Nick to lie to you about Sam killing Henri!"

Exhaling, I stared at the tray ceiling above me. I'd been unsuccessfully attempting to take a nap when Lisa had called, and I hadn't bothered to get out of bed as I updated her on the nightmare that my life had become.

Continuing, Lisa ranted, "No, actually, I can believe it, because Icarus is a lying blackmailing murderer!"

I wasn't sure what to believe, but I remembered Icarus being upset about me talking to Nick. He had been shocked, as though he'd never suspected I would seek Nick out to talk to him.

I couldn't help but wonder when had Icarus told Nick to lie to me? Why would Nick go along with what Icarus wanted him to do? Why would Icarus want me to think Sam had killed Henri if it wasn't true? Did Icarus want to deflect suspicion onto Sam and away from ... himself?

Lisa thought so, but I couldn't bring myself to believe Icarus was that sinister and manipulative. I'd gotten past thinking he was the blackmailer, and I didn't want to revisit those old doubts I'd had about him.

Hours later, about a few minutes to ten o'clock, Icarus stopped by my suite. Sitting next to me on the divan, he looked handsome and weary, and for a moment I wished we were together in a setting of domestic bliss, far away from blackmail and murder and suspicion. Again, even though it was counterproductive, I allowed myself to imagine I was his wife and he was my husband, home from a long, exhausting day at work, happy to see me and the glass of scotch I would have poured for him in anticipation of his arrival. I was more than willing to be a good, faithful, loving, attentive wife, but that was a crazy pipe dream, worse than a fantasy. It was a delusion, and I had to be realistic.

The reality being, I had to talk to Icarus about Nick Presso's text. There was no getting around it, as Lisa had said, and she was right. But would Icarus tell me the truth? If, as Lisa suspected, Icarus was a lying liar who was constantly lying to me, then could I really expect him to be honest?

"Did you get a chance to talk to Nick?" I asked, not ready to bring up Nick's text just yet, still not sure about the best way to confront Icarus. "Is he willing to tell the cops what he knows about Henri's murder?"

"Nick didn't show up to work," Icarus said, slouching against the back of the divan. "And he didn't call to say he wasn't coming, so ..."

The apprehension I'd felt earlier returned, but I resolved to push it away and get on with the business of telling Icarus about Nick's text.

"Icarus," I started and then swallowed. "I need to tell you something. Show you something, actually."

Icarus's confused frown made me hesitant, but I stood, went into the bedroom, got the cell phone, and returned to my spot next to Icarus on the couch. "I got a text from Nick earlier, saying that he was sorry for missing the meeting."

"Yeah, right," Icarus mumbled, shaking his head.

"He said something else, too," I said, my fingers trembling as I accessed Nick's last text to me. "You should look at this."

"Look at what?" Icarus asked, but he took the phone and stared at it.

As Lisa had advised, I watched Icarus's expression, looking for some sign of feigned surprise or fake indignation, but all I saw was sincere confusion and frustration.

"What the fuck is this about?"

"Well, I, um ..." Clearing my throat, I said, "I thought you could tell me. Why would Nick say—"

"I have no idea," Icarus said and then tossed the cell phone on the coffee table and stood. "But, I'm going to find out."

"What do you mean?" I stared up at him, my pulse racing as Icarus headed toward the door. "Wait a minute. Where are you going?"

"I'm going to look for Nick," Icarus said. "And when I find him, I'm going to make him tell me why the hell he sent you that text."

DAY FOURTEEN

Chapter Thirty

"You okay?" Icarus said the following morning, around ten o'clock. When I opened the door and saw him, I hesitated just a bit before stepping to him, allowing him to embrace me. I was reluctant to pull away from him. Holding hands, we walked to the couch and sat.

"Did you talk to Nick about that text he sent me?" I asked, observing him, noting impatience beneath the tired expression.

Icarus nodded. "Yeah, I did."

"What did he say?" I asked, tucking one leg beneath me as I angled my body to face him, so I could stare at him. Earlier, when I'd called Lisa to tell her Icarus had stormed out of my suite last night, hell-bent on demanding answers from Nick about the text he'd sent, she'd warned me again not to trust Icarus.

"Don't just take what he says as the Gospel," Lisa had advised, encouraging me to look for signs of deceit and manipulation. But I didn't want to find any duplicity in his gaze. I didn't want to see shifting eyes that couldn't quite focus directly on me, or fidgeting, or nervous facial tics. I was looking for honesty and sincerity in his words and actions.

"Nick didn't know what the hell I was talking about," Icarus said.

Confused, I said, "I don't understand."

"Nick didn't know anything about that text you showed me," Icarus said. "He remembered texting you, but he never sent a text about me telling him to lie to you."

"And you believed him?"

"He showed me his phone."

"He did?" I asked, more confused than ever. What was going on?

"I saw the texts Nick sent to you," Icarus said. "He didn't send that text about me telling him to lie to you about Sam murdering Henri."

"How can Nick say he didn't send that text?" I shook my head. "That doesn't make sense."

"You still have the text?" Icarus asked. "You didn't delete it, did you?"

"No, I still have it," I said, standing. "Let me get my phone."

After retrieving my phone from the bedroom, I went back into the living area and accessed the text Nick claimed he hadn't sent.

"Can I see it?" Icarus asked. "Just want to check out something."

"What?" I sat next to Icarus, handing him my cell phone.

"Well, now I know why Nick said he didn't send that text," Icarus said, after he'd scrolled for several seconds, thumb moving quickly across the screen. "It didn't come from his phone."

"What do you mean?" I asked, taking my phone from Icarus, staring at the display screen.

"Nick said the last text he sent you was a response to your text about wanting to meet up and talk with him," Icarus said. "The response was we already talked."

"Right," I nodded. "Then I responded back asking him if he would talk to the cops."

"Nick said he decided not to respond to that text."

"Well, if Nick didn't respond to that text, then who did?" I wanted to know. "Because I got a response."

"Take a look at the phone number associated with Nick's text that says, we already talked," Icarus said. "And then look at the number associated with the text saying that Nick lied about Sam killing Henri. The area codes are the same, but the last four digits are completely different."

My heart thudding, I compared the numbers, noting the last four digits of Nick's cell phone, 2364, and the last four digits of the number where the text had come from, 0007.

"So, whose phone ends with 0007?" I asked, irritated because I hadn't thought to check the text log to confirm that Nick had sent the text.

"Let's find out," Icarus said. "I'll call the number and we'll see who picks up."

"Put the phone on speaker," I requested.

Moments later, shrill ringing echoed throughout the living area. "No one is answering," I said, fighting disappointment. "Maybe we can subpoena phone records to find out who the phone belongs to."

"Yeah, I'll ask Tavie—"

An abrupt click interrupted Icarus, and then there was a voice message ...

Hey, it's Henri. Leave a message and I'll call you back.

"Did Henri have a cell phone with the number having the last four digits of 0007?" Icarus asked Doris as she watered three potted Hibiscus plants near the left railing of her small porch.

Standing beneath the awning, Icarus, Doris, and I were shielded from the glare of the mid-morning sun, but not the heat, which had me perspiring even though I was wearing an A-line sundress made of loose, breathable cotton.

Thirty minutes had passed since Icarus and I had heard the voice message from beyond the grave. Hearing Henri's voice, so clear and strong and alive, had unnerved me. Confused, for a split second, I wondered if Henri might actually still be alive, even though I'd seen his lifeless body with the knife in his chest and his blood all over the bed sheets.

Icarus brought me back to reality, wondering who might have Henri's phone. And why would they use it to send a fake text from Nick? Who would want to make me think Icarus had forced Nick to lie to me? None of our questions could be answered until we found out who had Henri's 0007 phone. We decided to start our search with Doris, who had received all of Henri's possessions, everything he'd been wearing, and everything on his person when they'd removed his body from the house.

It seemed unrealistic to think Doris had sent a fake text pretending to be Nick, but we thought she might have sold Henri's phone or perhaps given it away to a friend, or family member.

Icarus didn't have to start his shift until five p.m., so we decided to head to Doris's place, hoping she would be able to help us out.

"A phone with the last four digits 0007? Not that I know of," Doris said, shaking her head. "Not that I can remember, but maybe. Henri had a lot of phones, though. He used to mess around with a lot of different girls, and I think he wanted them all to have different numbers to reach him. That way, if he was staying the night with one of them, he wouldn't have to worry about another girl calling his phone. When he told me that, I said, boy that's a lot of lies to keep straight. What if you're with Jessica, but you accidentally grab the phone that has the number you gave Amy? Henri just laugh, he say, Doris, I know how to handle my shit. But, that wasn't true, was it? Wouldn't have got himself stabbed to death if he could handle his shit."

Silence ensued, and a sudden somberness wafted through the little porch, as though carried by the breeze, settling around us. Doris's mournful, pained expression chilled me, and I felt slightly selfish and uncompassionate. As determined as I was to find out about the 0007 phone and who had sent the text pretending to be Nick, I couldn't forget Doris's grief. She was still mourning her brother, and I felt sorry for her, even though her brother had made my life hell.

Clearing his throat, Icarus said, "But, the cops returned his things to you."

"Yeah, but it wasn't no cell phone in with that stuff," Doris said. "I got a list of what was in the box of stuff the cops gave me. Hold on, let me get it."

Doris sat her green plastic watering can on the concrete floor near the welcome mat and then went inside. Minutes later, she returned with a thin yellow eight-by-eleven-inch piece of paper, the last page of some type of triplicate form, I guessed.

"The cop made me take the stuff out so he could check each item on the list, saying it was returned to me, then he made me sign for everything," Doris said, handing the paper to Icarus. "He say, we do this so you won't claim we stole something or didn't give everything back to you. They kept the bloody shirt, though. Evidence, the cop say."

"No cell phone," Icarus said.

"Let me see," I said, and took the paper from him, scanning it carefully, reading it several times, hoping to find those two words: cell phone. But, no phones were on the list.

"Why you want to know about that phone?" Doris asked, eyes narrowed, as though realizing she should have been more suspicious of us. "Does it got something to do with who killed my brother? You think whoever got that phone killed Henri?"

"Somebody sent Quinn a text from that phone," Icarus said. "We called the phone to see if someone would answer, but we got voice mail. It was Henri saying to leave a message. That's how we know it's Henri's phone that someone used to send the fake text."

"Who was the text from?" Doris asked. "Maybe that person has the phone."

"The text was from Nick Presso, but he claimed he didn't send it."

"Nick probably lied to you," Doris said, derisive. "You can't trust him. He was working with Henri to steal your money."

"I talked to him about that," I said. "Nick claims he wasn't in Henri's alliance."

Scoffing, Doris said, "Another lie."

"Maybe," Icarus said, shrugging. "Listen, Doris, thanks for letting us see the list."

"Wasn't no problem," she said. "Just wish I could have been more help."

"Actually, you can be," I said, faltering just a bit when the doubt clouded her expression. "Whoever has that phone might be the killer, and they might be trying to throw suspicion onto other people. So, I'll give you that phone number, and maybe you could call that number from time to time. If someone answers, see if you can find out who the person is, or if you recognize the voice, and if you do, let us know as soon as possible."

DAY FIFTEEN

Chapter Thirty-One

Around nine the next morning, Icarus showed up with an excited expression.

"What is it?" I asked, after he'd walked in and I closed the door, my pulse jumping as some of his anxiousness seemed to transfer to me.

"I stopped by Tavie's office to tell her about our search for Henri's 0007 cell phone," Icarus said. "Tavie told me she was given a list of all the evidence related to the case the police have, which she showed me."

"Was the 0007 cell phone on the evidence list?" I asked, walking to the divan and taking a seat.

"The cops have two of Henri's cell phones in police custody at the moment." Icarus took a seat on the opposite couch. "Tavie called one of her sources at the police station to ask about the phone numbers associated with those two phones. Neither of the phones has 0007 as the last four digits."

"So Henri had three phones," I said. "Not surprising. Doris said he had multiple phones. Maybe the 0007 phone was stolen before the police showed up at Henri's house."

"That's what Tavie and I think," Icarus said.

"We still have no idea who has the 0007 phone," I grumbled, "And

228

RACHEL WOODS

we have no idea how to find out who has it, except to keep calling the number, hoping someone will answer, which is unlikely."

"The person might answer," Icarus said.

"If the person who killed Henri has the 0007 phone," I said, shaking my head, "then they're not going to be stupid enough to answer it."

"Well, in other news," Icarus said. "Tavie told me that Nick gave a statement to the cops about Henri's alliance and Sam and Stazia's involvement in the blackmail scheme. Apparently, Detective François asked him to come down the station."

"Guess maybe the meeting with the detective wasn't a waste of time, after all," I said.

Nodding, Icarus said, "So, because of Nick's statement, the cops questioned Sam Collins, but he refused to talk without a lawyer. Tavie said they didn't have any evidence against him, so they couldn't keep him."

"Not surprised," I said, trying to fight my disappointment. "There's just no proof that Sam killed Henri."

"There's proof," Icarus insisted. "And we're going to find it."

"Yeah," I said, rubbing the back of my neck, not as convinced as Icarus sounded.

"Well, not that this is really a good thing," he started, his wry smile suggesting a subject change. "But, I was put on probation," he said.

"Why? What did you do?"

"I entered into an improper relationship with one of the hotel guests," he said. "Which is a direct violation of the employee rules."

"An improper relationship with me, you mean," I said, upset for him, although I realized we shouldn't have been so brazen and cavalier with our affections. "How did the hotel management find out about us?"

"Security footage," he said and then shrugged. "Employee gossip."

"So we can't see each other anymore?"

"Not at the Heliconia," he said. "But, you could visit me at my place."

Wary, I stared at him. "At your place?"

"Only if you want to," he was quick to say. "They can't stop you from going wherever you want to go on the island."

That was true, but the idea of hooking up with Icarus at his house worried me. I might be committing to something I wasn't ready to commit to, not just yet, maybe something I couldn't realistically commit to. Maybe I was just overthinking things. Icarus's house was a more convenient place to hook up, where we wouldn't be spied upon and gossiped about.

"So, technically, you really shouldn't be here right now, should you?" I asked, giving in to the sudden onset of friskiness I felt, although to call it sudden would be dishonest. I was always horny whenever I was around Icarus. Standing, I walked around the coffee table, to the divan where he sat, and settled down on his lap.

"Technically, no," he said, wrapping an arm around my waist. "After I leave, I probably shouldn't come back here, since they're watching me."

"Well, then," I said, winding my arms around his neck and lowering my head to kiss him. "I think we should make the most of your last day in my hotel suite."

DAY SIXTEEN

Chapter Thirty-Two

"One of Stazia's cousins texted me this morning and told me that he'd seen her," Icarus said. "So, I went over to her place. But, when I got there, it looked like she'd left in a hurry and ran out the back door. So, I decided to look around and I found this ..."

Excited, and yet apprehensive, I waited, perched on the edge of the chair in front of Octavia's desk, as Icarus stood and removed something from the front pocket of his jeans.

Despite the hour, around ten a.m., the office was gloomy. Outside the wide picture window behind Octavia's desk, dark gray thunderclouds swirled across the sky and over the ocean, giving paradise a steely, almost dystopian pallor.

Icarus placed the object on the large desk calendar on Octavia's desk.

Frowning, Octavia said, "A cell phone?"

"Think it's a burner," Icarus said, taking his seat.

Staring at the cell phone, I couldn't help but notice the date. I was nearing the end of my escape to paradise, but I wasn't going to be leaving unless the murder charge against me was dropped.

"It was dead," Icarus said. "But, I recognized the model and I bought a charger for it."

"Is it the 0007 cell phone?" I asked, hopeful.

Icarus shook his head. "Wish it was."

"How did you get into Stazia's house?" Octavia grabbed a pen from a coffee mug next to her computer.

"When she didn't open the front door," he said. "I went around to the backyard. The back door was open and so I went inside."

"You shouldn't have done that," I scolded. "Could have been dangerous. Stazia was in Henri's alliance. For all we know, she could be the killer and you just walked into her house, and—"

"Wasn't a big deal," Icarus said, with a casual dismissiveness, as though he thought I was blowing things out of proportion. "In the Double-H, people sometimes leave the back door open because they're going in and out. Wasn't dangerous at all."

Scribbling furiously on her legal pad, Octavia said, "Okay, you find this phone at Stazia's, and you charge it up. Did you look at the call log, or—"

"There was no activity on the call log," Icarus said. "But, there were lots of text messages."

"Messages from Stazia?" Octavia asked, grabbing the phone and pushing buttons on its keypad.

"I don't think so," Icarus said. "Don't think the phone belong to Stazia. I think it was Sam Collins' phone."

"Why do you think it was Sam's phone?" I asked.

"The text messages I saw were between Sam and Henri," Icarus said, answering my question.

"How do you know it wasn't Henri's burner?" Octavia asked.

"Well, I guess I don't," Icarus admitted.

"So, right now all we know for sure is that it's a burner with text messages between Sam Collins and Henri Monteils," Octavia said, placing the phone on her desk. "And you found it at Stazia's."

"So, maybe Stazia took the burner from Henri," I speculated. "Or, maybe she took the burner from Sam."

"Where exactly did you find the burner, Ish?" Octavia asked, leaning back in her chair. "I mean, where in the house?"

"It was under the table in the kitchen," Icarus said. "Reason I looked is because one of the chairs was turned over on the floor, which I thought was strange. When I picked the chair up, I saw the phone."

"Earlier, you said it seemed like Stazia had left the house in a hurry," Octavia leaned forward, placing her elbows on the desk. "Was that because you saw the overturned chair?"

"Because of that," he said. "And because her bedroom was a mess. The dresser drawers were pulled out and there were clothes all on the floor. Now that I think about it, I guess it seemed like maybe she'd been looking for something."

"Maybe it wasn't Stazia who'd been looking for something," I said, wary. Icarus's description of Stazia's bedroom made me think the place had been tossed. "Maybe somebody was in her house searching for something."

"Maybe Sam Collins," Octavia suggested, and then tapped the pen against her bottom lip. "Maybe Sam went to Stazia's house to look for something, and he either found it, or he didn't, and when he left, maybe he accidentally dropped the burner phone."

Icarus nodded. "Maybe. I don't know."

"Okay, let's focus on what we do know," Octavia said. "I'm going to have my assistant print out the text messages, but give us the gist, Ish."

Exhaling, Icarus said, "All of them were basically Sam threatening Henri."

"What?" My heart nearly leaped out of my mouth.

"Sam threatening Henri how?" Octavia asked.

"Sam texted things like, *'henri, don't f with me'*," Icarus said. "And actually threatening to kill Henri, like one text said, *'don't play with me, I will fuck you up, they won't find your body'*."

"We need to show the messages on this burner to the police," I said. "They prove that I didn't kill Henri."

"Not so fast," Octavia cautioned, holding up a hand.

"What do you mean, not so fast?" Icarus demanded. "We're not moving fast enough. We should already be at the police station."

"First of all, we're talking about text messages on a burner phone," Octavia said. "There is no way to definitively trace the owner of that phone or who bought it. Second, I'm sure we wouldn't be able to prove that the 'Sam' who sent threatening texts to 'Henri' is actually Sam

Collins. And third, Ish, not that I don't trust you, but we only have your word that you found that phone under Stazia's kitchen table, which the cops will point out."

I shifted in my chair, discomforted by how much Octavia's third point reminded me of my own suspicions of Icarus. I was still trying to put those suspicions behind me, once and for all, but in the back of my mind, I still had doubts.

"So what the hell are we supposed to do?" Icarus asked. "Sit around and let Sam get away with murder while Quinn goes to trial and maybe gets convicted of a crime she didn't commit?"

"No, that's not what we do," said Octavia, in her firm, yet logical tone. "We have to find proof that Sam Collins sent the threatening texts to Henri Monteils."

"Well, I might know how to do that," Icarus said.

From the determined set of his strong jaw, I had a feeling I knew what he was planning. "You're going to talk to Sam, aren't you?"

"You think that's a good idea, Ish?" Octavia asked, skeptical. "I doubt he'll tell you the truth."

"I want to be there when you question him," I insisted, eager to tag along because, honestly, I didn't want Icarus to return with another story about how he hadn't been able to get any information.

"Fine." He stood and held out his hand to me. "C'mon, we're going to look for him now."

For what seemed like weeks, Icarus and I crisscrossed the island in his battered Jeep, relentless in our pursuit to find Sam Collins and question him about the threatening texts on the burner phone. The morning storm clouds eventually dissipated, rolling away to allow for another gorgeous day in paradise, but I hardly noticed as Icarus sped along roads that snaked around the mountainous terrain.

Our first stop was Sam's apartment, a crumbling duplex surrounded by overgrown hibiscus bushes, but Icarus's persistent knocks on the pale green door had gone unanswered.

"He may not be home," Icarus said, climbing back into the Jeep, "but he's somewhere. We'll find him."

Icarus knew some of the places where Sam liked to hang out, and he vowed to check each place.

Dizzy and disheartened, I clutched the armrest. Icarus grew increasingly frustrated as it seemed that time and again Sam wasn't at any of his usual haunts. None of his family, friends, or acquaintances seemed to know where he was, but most agreed to give Icarus a call if they saw Sam. Others told him they would tell Sam that Icarus was looking for him.

Finally, around four in the afternoon, Icarus made an abrupt, wild turn off the highway, eliciting a chorus of angry, trumpeting car horns. He steered the Jeep into the crushed oyster parking lot in front of a local bar on the east side. A faded and chipped hand-painted sign announced it as Nelly's Bar. I doubted it was mentioned in any of the St. Mateo guidebooks. A sad, seedy place, it seemed to be constructed of various materials, corrugated siding, plywood, and even a few panels of unfinished sheetrock.

Inside was worse. Dank and dim, the sun struggled to penetrate the layers of filmy grime on the windows, and it reeked of cheap booze, stringent aftershave, and strong piss.

"There's that son of a bitch," Icarus said, staring toward the bar, which was about fifteen feet from the doorway. Sitting on a stool, with his back to us, was a large, muscular guy, casually dressed in jeans and a T-shirt. I couldn't see what he was drinking, but he was alone.

"Go sit over there," Icarus said, pointing to a small, rectangular table in the far right corner.

"I want to be with you when you talk to him," I insisted, reminding him.

"We'll talk to him at the table."

Slightly irritated, I nodded and went to secure the table. Not that I had any competition for it. Besides Sam, the only other patrons were two guys at a table on the opposite side of the room. Despite the squalor of the place, the table was clean, and as I took a seat, I had no illusions of ordering a drink, but I really wanted one. I was tense, jittery, apprehensive, and not exactly holding out hope that this impromptu meeting with Sam would make a difference.

Octavia was right to question the effectiveness of this idea about confronting Sam. Would he tell us the truth? Absolutely not. So why bother talking to Sam? Why not come up with some other way to prove Sam had sent the threatening texts to Henri?

Glancing up, my heart thudded, and I almost changed my mind about that drink. Icarus and Sam were walking toward the table, both of them frowning, though Icarus seemed determined while Sam was disgruntled.

Icarus and Sam took their seats. I stared at Sam. Months ago, when I was still the shrewd, hotshot litigator, I would always scrutinize the opposition's witnesses, looking for flaws to exploit. As Icarus questioned Sam, I searched his face for signs of deceit, little telltale tics, and a shifty gaze, hoping for the discernment I used to depend on.

Icarus wasted no time in confronting Sam about the threatening text messages. Not surprisingly, Sam denied all knowledge and involvement and quickly became belligerent and aggressive.

"First you come to me with some bullshit about me blackmailing that bitch," Sam said, cutting his eyes toward me, giving me a baleful glare before focusing on Icarus again. "Now, you want to accuse me of killing Henri, who was like my brother? You come to me with shit about me stabbing Henri, something I would never do!"

"I think it's something you absolutely did," Icarus said, his voice rising, causing the bartender to glance over for a moment before going back to polishing glasses. "And it had to do with the blackmail money. You and Henri must have argued about it. Maybe he didn't give you a big enough cut. Maybe he didn't think you deserved any of the money."

"I told you I wasn't helping Henri blackmail nobody."

"And I told you I don't believe you," Icarus said.

"Fuck you," Sam spat. "Anyway, I heard the cops already arrested who killed Henri. If it was me, I'd be in jail, but I'm not."

"You're not in jail, yet," Icarus told him. "But I'm gonna find proof that you killed Henri."

"Oh, what, you're a cop, now?" Sam scoffed. "Look, if I killed

Henri, why didn't the cops arrest me when they told me to come to the station to answer questions? Because they couldn't. They ain't got no proof that I killed Henri, I don't care what Nick told them. Nick lied to you and to the cops."

"Why would Nick lie and tell the cops that Stazia said you killed Henri?" Icarus asked.

"I don't know," Sam said, dismissive. "What I do know is that Stazia didn't tell Nick that I killed Henri. That bitch knows better than to do something stupid like that. She knows I'll ..."

"You'll what? Kill her?" Icarus demanded, leaning forward. "Like you killed Henri because he didn't give you your cut of the blackmail money?"

"You ain't got no proof I killed Henri," Sam said, laughing as he got up to leave, staring at me. "Don't I know you?"

"What?" I shook my head, trembling, praying that my worst fears were not about to come true. "No, I don't think we've met."

"Yeah, we met." Sam leered, nodding as he gave me a smug smile. "You're the one we were supposed to give it to by the waterfalls."

Peripherally, I knew Icarus was staring at me, and though I wasn't looking directly at him, I could feel the questioning skepticism in his eyes.

"What the hell are you talking about?" Icarus demanded.

"She knows what I'm talking about," Sam said. "She remembers. She was supposed to take all three of us—me, Henri, and Nick—but, the bitch got scared."

My body went rigid as anger and disgust paralyzed me. Glaring at him, I wanted to scratch his eyes out and rip his balls off.

"You were acting like a dumb virgin that day, but I bet you a real nasty freak. I bet you would have loved being screwed by three guys at the same time," he said, leering at me. "I would have enjoyed myself, too. I bet you got a real tight, wet—"

Standing, Icarus said, "Get out of here before I—"

With a scoff and a sting of curses, Sam gave us the finger, turned, and walked away.

Chapter Thirty-Three

"Can we talk about the meeting with Sam now?" I asked, following Icarus into his little yellow house, baffled by his dour mood, which I'd picked up on as soon as we left Nelly's Bar. Tense, fractured silence surrounded us as Icarus navigated the roads he knew so well. Icarus refused to be coaxed into a conversation, though there was much to discuss, and I gave up trying to talk to him. The silence followed us into the house, swirling around us like some polarizing specter.

Mumbling something I couldn't make out, Icarus walked out of the living room, into the kitchen, and through a door that appeared to open to the back of the house. Curious, and worried, I followed. In the backyard, Icarus sat on a large palm tree whose trunk had grown horizontally to the ground. With his back to me, I noticed his head was down and his shoulders seemed slumped.

Cautiously, tentatively, I walked across the grass to the palm tree, stopping about five feet away, close enough for him to hear me when I said, "Icarus, what's the matter?"

For a moment, he didn't move, and though I was discouraged, I was determined not to be ignored.

"Icarus ..."

Squaring his shoulders, he stood, and faced me. "You ready to go back to the hotel?" he asked, his tone flat, slightly distracted.

"Go back to the hotel?" Confused, shocked, I stared at him, trying to see past the lifelessness in his gaze, searching for some hint of his true feelings, which I knew he was suppressing. Why did he seem to be closing himself off from me?

"It's almost eight," he said. "I thought you might want to get back."

Frustrated by his apathy, which I suspected he was using as a defense mechanism against his feelings for me, I said, "I don't want to go back to the hotel. I want to ..."

"You want to what, Quinn?" he asked, a slight spark in his gaze, the first sign of life I'd seen so far, but I wasn't sure what emotions fueled it.

"I want to know what's wrong," I said. "You haven't spoken to me since we left the bar. Are you upset about something? Did I do something, or—"

"Tell me about the waterfall fantasy," Icarus said with a solemn finality.

Confused by his request, I stared at him. "What?"

"Tell me about the waterfall fantasy you had with Sam, Nick, and Henri." His whiskey-colored gaze was blank as he stared at me, almost apathetic, but then I realized he wasn't really looking at me. He was focused on something just to the right of me. My heart plummeted into my gut. Why did he seem as though he couldn't stand the sight of me? Or, was I imagining the barely disguised disgust in his gaze?

Perplexed, I shook my head. "There's nothing to tell."

"Sam said—"

"Sam said I acted like a scared little virgin," I reminded him. "I don't agree with that assessment. I wasn't afraid, I just didn't want to have an orgy with three guys. The hotel created that ridiculous fantasy for me, but there was no way I was going to go through with it."

"Why not?" Icarus asked, a dangerous edge in his voice. "Didn't you come to the Heliconia to be screwed into oblivion by as many guys as possible?"

His speculation of my reasons for visiting the Heliconia was demeaning and made me angry, but mostly, his scathing judgment hurt.

"It may be difficult," I started, "but I'll try to explain why I came to the Heliconia."

"I think it's obvious why you came to the Heliconia," he said, though there was no sarcasm in his tone.

"No, it's not obvious," I said, tears in my voice. "I know what people think about women who come to the Heliconia. That we're lonely, horny women who can't get a man so we have to pay to have dirty sex all day and all night with as many different men, and maybe even women, as possible."

"And that's not why you came to the Heliconia?" Icarus said, a healthy dose of skepticism in his voice.

"I came to the Heliconia to get my mojo back," I blurted out, unable to stop the tears from flowing.

"To get your mojo back?" His doubt turned to bewilderment. "What do you mean?"

Letting out a long, weary, sad exhale, I swiped at my cheeks, letting my gaze wander to a wall of sea grape trees lined in a row at the rear of the yard.

"Six months ago, around November of last year, I started having really terrible nightmares, which was strange, because I've never really suffered from bad dreams ... " Hesitant, I exhaled, reluctant to open up to Icarus. I was afraid to be honest and vulnerable about an issue I previously hadn't believed was a valid issue but more of a nuisance, something to be tolerated until I could get my mind right and get over it.

Now, in this moment, realization dawned, and I knew the anxiety I'd been suffering could not be ignored, or wished away. My anxiety had to be examined, and most importantly, it had to be understood— my sanity and emotional well-being demanded an understanding of what had caused the anxiety."

"What were the dreams about?"

"Usually, um, I'm standing in a courtroom, giving my closing argument, and it's going great," I said. "I know I'm winning over the jury, which is one of my specialties. I know how to pick a jury that will give me the verdict I want. I know this jury is going to render a verdict on behalf of my client, but ..."

"But what?"

"But ... I don't know," I said, not sure why I was so disconcerted and flustered all of a sudden. "I mean, the worst part of the dream happens when I turn around to go back to the defense table and I see a woman at the back of the courtroom ..."

"Do you know the woman?"

"I think so," I hedged and then admitted, "Yeah, I do know her, which is why it's very disturbing when she shoots me."

"So, you started having anxiety dreams about being killed by someone you know?"

"She doesn't kill me," I said. "She never kills me, even though she shoots me in the heart. I don't die, and I know this because the dream will change to me in a hospital bed reading a newspaper and the head-line says something like 'Lawyer Survives Shot to the Heart.'"

"And you don't know why you started having the dreams?"

"No, I don't," I said, though I wasn't convinced that was true. "I've tried to figure it out, but all I know is that the dreams started because of the anxiety, and the anxiety robbed me of my ability to make sound, strategic decisions for my clients, and not being able to do that led to me losing three cases."

"So, the dreams started before you lost the three cases?" Icarus asked.

Nodding, I said, "In November."

"What was going on in your life in November?" he asked. "Were you under a lot of stress?"

"Actually, it's funny, because November was pretty great for me," I said, remembering. "I won a huge case. My career was on the rise. I was close to making partner."

"But winning a huge case is a good thing," Icarus said. "Why would you start having anxiety dreams after winning a case?"

A good question, one I didn't know the answer to, but I should have. "The anxiety dreams don't matter. What matters is ..."

"What matters is?" Icarus prompted.

"What matters is my career," I said. "I worked so hard for so long to get to a point where I was respected as a competent litigator, and it wasn't easy considering my background."

"Your background?"

"I come from a family of lawyers," I said. "My grandfather started a firm fifty years ago, and it's highly respected and veneered and extremely lucrative. When I went to law school, everyone thought it would be so easy for me because I could step out of law school and into my grandfather's firm."

Icarus remained quiet, listening, and when I glanced at him, in the dusk around us, I couldn't discern his expression.

"I had to prove that I was a damn good attorney, and I was doing that. I had done that," I said. "And then that damn anxiety comes along and ruins my life, and why? I don't understand it, but maybe I don't have to. What I have to do is get over it."

"And you thought coming to the Heliconia would help you get over the anxiety?"

"Truthfully, deep down, I don't think I really thought coming to the Heliconia would do any good," I admitted. "But, I was desperate. I was grasping at straws. I was looking for any way I could to be who I used to be, the shrewd, intelligent litigator. That's who I am. That's what the stupid anxiety stole from me and I want my old self back."

"Are you sure you want your old self back?"

Confused, I wiped my damp cheeks. "What do you mean?"

"You said the anxiety dreams started in November when you won your case," Icarus said. "Back then, you were a brilliant, successful lawyer, right? So, maybe the anxiety dreams didn't stop you from being brilliant and successful. Maybe the dreams are a sign of something else."

"Something else like what?"

"Fantasy is not going to cure your anxiety," Icarus said, a gentleness in his gruff baritone. "I think you need to figure out why you started having anxiety after you won that big case."

DAY SEVENTEEN

Chapter Thirty-Four

Following a light breakfast, I took a long shower, dried off, and dropped the towel on the floor. Naked, I walked into the bedroom and stretched out across the bed, thinking about my confession to Icarus last night. Over and over, I analyzed what I'd told him, my reasons for coming to St. Mateo. I'd spent an equal amount of time pondering his suggestion to me—*figure out why you starting having anxiety after you won that big case.*

Mallette v. Du Vert Pharmaceuticals had been my biggest case, to date, and centered around a plaintiff named Clayton Mallette, who accused the pharmaceutical giant of performing illegal experiments on his deceased spouse. Bessie Mallette had passed away during a drug trial sponsored by Du Vert. Her death had been a tragedy, yes, but not negligence. Certainly, as Mallette claimed, her death had not been the result of Du Vert's "intentional construction of monstrous beings."

On the witness stand, Mallette was dodgy and, at times, incoherent. Against my shrewd, methodical cross-examination, he appeared psychotic and out of touch with reality as he tried to convince the jury that Du Vert was manufacturing "zombies," which they planned to "unleash on the world" in an attempt to "control the population." Faced with my blitzkrieg of logic and rational evidence to the contrary of Mallette's outlandish claims, the shifty-eyed widower was seen as a sad, grief-stricken man unable to cope with his wife's death. The jury felt sorry for him, but they didn't believe him and found Du Vert not negligent or liable in the death of Bessie Mallette.

I was celebrated and congratulated for the big win, for my outstanding success, on behalf of an important, influential client. Except, thinking back, I didn't feel very victorious, for some reason. After so many months, I realized—

"Where's the cell phone, bitch?"

The deep, derisive voice sent several mind-jolting sensations through me, one hotter than fire, the other colder than ice, and both rendering me paralyzed and speechless. Panic and horror raced through my veins as I sat up, staring at the man who stood at the foot of the bed, sneering at me.

Sam Collins.

"What are you doing in here?" I could barely whisper as I drew my legs toward my chest, desperate to cover myself, mortified and terrified by the idea that he'd been watching me. "How did you get in my room?"

"The maid let me in," he said, smug. "She's a friend of mine. I told her I'd left something in your room so she opened the door for me."

"Get the hell out of here," I told him, grabbing one of the large pillow shams to cover my body.

"Oh, you don't want me to see you naked?" His laugh was scornful. "Bitch, I already seen everything."

Humiliated, and disgusted by his flippant vulgarity, I held the sham in front of me and said, "Get out of here! I'm calling security, and I'm having both you and whoever let you into my room fired!"

"Relax, okay," he said. "All I want is the phone."

"What phone?" Naked and exposed, I was frozen, afraid to move.

"The phone Icarus has with those messages from me," he said. "The messages where I'm threatening Henri."

"Why do you want the phone?" I asked, wondering if I could jump out of bed and run out of the door, and yet knowing that he would most likely catch me, slam me to the ground, and do God only knew what to me. "So you can erase all those threatening messages you sent to Henri?"

"That phone belongs to me," he said. "And I want it back. Now, if you give it to me, then I won't call the cops and tell them that Icarus stole it."

"Icarus didn't steal your phone," I said, wishing I had my phone so I could enable the recording app. "He found it at Stazia's house. You must have accidentally left it there when the two of you met to plot how you would steal the blackmail money from Henri and then kill him."

"Bitch, you crazy." He sneered, walking to the dresser across from the bed and opening the top drawer. "I told you, I didn't kill Henri. You think if I killed Henri I'd still be on this island? And I didn't leave my phone at Stazia's. That bitch stole it and then gave it to Icarus."

My heart nearly imploded. "Why would Stazia give Icarus your phone?"

"Why you think?" Sam asked, a sly taunt in his tone. "It wasn't me and Stazia plotting to kill Henri. It was Stazia and Icarus."

"That's not true." I shook my head as he rooted through the drawer he'd opened, slinging my bras over his shoulder. "What the hell are you looking for? That phone is not in any of those drawers!"

Laughing softly, he nodded and opened more drawers, flinging my clothes left and right, searching for the burner phone he seemed to believe was hidden in my suite. "Did you know they used to be together? Icarus and Stazia? They were friends with benefits. A lot of benefits."

Disturbed, I looked away.

"Figured Icarus hadn't told you about his former fuck buddy. Although, I'm not sure they really ever stopped hooking up. Stazia probably told Icarus about Henri's idea to blackmail one of you dirty rich skanks," he said, taking a moment to glower at me. His look of disgust was almost tangible, like a slap. Despite his employment, I sensed he had only resentment, scorn, and maybe hatred for the women whose fantasies he made come true.

"I think Icarus went to steal the blackmail money from Henri," he said, sending several pairs of my underwear sailing toward me to land on the bed. For a moment, I thought he might be distracted enough to give me an opportunity to escape, but when I glanced at him, I saw that he was staring back at me though the mirror, keeping an eye on me. "Then Henri caught him, and they argued, fought, and Icarus stabbed Henri. Then, Stazia steals my phone and sees the messages I sent Henri—"

"The messages where you threatened to kill Henri," I reminded him.

"Wasn't really gonna kill Henri," Sam sulked. "I was just trying to let him know not to fuck with me. Trying to scare him."

"Why would you need to scare Henri?" I asked, trying to focus on getting more info from him. "I thought the two of you were close."

"Yeah, well, money is interesting," Sam said. "It can make a person forget who their real friends are."

"Is that why you killed Henri?" I probed, feeling slightly like my old self, slyly coaxing a witness into impeaching themselves. "Because he was going to take all the blackmail money? He wasn't going to give you your cut of the cash like he'd promised?"

"I didn't say that," Sam said. "I'll tell you this, though. Stazia's ass is mine when I find that bitch. Bad enough the bitch steals my phone, but then, she reads my messages and sees the threats I sent Henri, which I wasn't gonna follow through on. But, she tries to use the messages to her advantage."

"What do you mean?"

"Bitch tries to blackmail me," Sam said, shaking his head, astonished. "She tells me if I don't give her the money Henri blackmailed out of you, she's going to show the cops the threatening messages I sent Henri. Bitch lost her mind. First of all, I ain't got the blackmail money. I don't know where it is. Henri must have hid it before he got his sneaky, shady ass killed. I tell that bitch Stazia I'm looking for the damn money myself. She calls me a liar, says Henri told me to go pick up the money from the drop location, so I must have it. But, that ain't true. Matter of fact, some bullshit is happening because Henri told me that he was gonna have Stazia pick up the money from the drop location."

"So, Henri lied to both of you?" I stared at him, my heart pounding.

"Sonofabitch."

My head spinning, I asked, "So, who did Henri really tell to pick up the money from the drop location?"

"Fuck if I know," Sam growled, advancing toward the bed. "Can't worry about that. I need my phone. If Icarus gives my phone to the cops, it's gonna look like I could have killed Henri, but I ain't gonna let that happen."

"I don't have the burner phone," I told him. "Now get the hell out of here!"

Heart slamming, I stared at him as he came closer to the bed, a strange look on his face, a mix of disgust and desire.

"What I don't understand is, why did you come to this hotel?" Sam shook his head.

"What?" I asked, confused by his disjoined incongruity.

"You're a damn good-looking bitch," he said. "I can't believe that you ain't never had nobody screw you right."

As Sam came closer to the bed, my heart nearly exploded, and I tried to scoot back as far as I could, but there was nowhere for me to go. I was pressed against the tufted headboard with only a pillow sham to protect me from what I suspected would be Sam's attempt to assault me.

The only potential weapons at my disposal were just out of reach. On the night table to my right, there was a silver clock and a conch shell paperweight. On the table to the left of the bed was a lamp. The bedroom accessories were heavy enough to stun and disarm so I could get away, but I was lying in the middle of the king-sized bed. If I tried to go left or right, Sam would most likely get there before me.

"Can't believe you gotta pay somebody to bang you," Sam said, still sneering and smug.

"Go to hell!"

"Bitch!" he grunted, and before I could react, Sam was on the bed and then leaping toward me, grabbing me, trying to pin me down. Screaming, I kicked my leg out, but he slammed a fist against my ankle. Undeterred, and despite the pain, I kicked again, connected with his shoulder, and then flipped over, scrambling toward the bed table, determined to grab the conch shell paperweight, and—

Abruptly, my body flipped violently, and I saw the tray ceiling and then Sam's hulking form over me, his hand swinging toward my face, crashing against my cheek. Lights popped and pinged behind my eyes as the pain, localized at first, quickly spread, throbbing toward my eye, across my nose, and down my jaw. Dazed, I was barely able to lift my arms to fight him.

Pinning my hands over my head, he thrust a knee between my thighs, forcing them open, the rough denim of his jeans scratching my skin.

"No, don't! Stop it!" I screamed through gritted teeth, and when he removed his hand from my left wrist, I slapped and scratched at his face, but he bobbed and weaved his head, avoiding my blows as he started to unzip his pants. "Get away from me!"

"You know you want it, bitch," he said, his voice a low growl as he reached into his boxers and exposed himself. "You should have let me have it by the waterfalls. Now, I'm gonna give it to you good, baby. I'm gonna enjoy putting all twelve of these inches into you."

Shocked and terrified, I struggled to fight, but I felt defeated and deflated. Feeling the head of his penis near my opening, I screamed out my protest. Trying to summon the courage to fight him, I resumed my assault, whacking my fist against his chin and his jaw and his shoulder.

"It's okay if you fight me, baby," he said and then smiled. "We can have our own little rape fantasy. The hotel offers that, you know. Some of you nasty sluts like to be knocked around while you're being—"

A piercing, high-pitched scream cut through the air, and then a horrified voice said, "What are you doing? Get away from her!"

Grunting his rage, Sam rolled off me. Confused and trembling, I struggled to sit up. Eyes wide with shock, a maid stood in the bedroom doorway. Lumbering toward the frightened housekeeper, Sam yelled, "Get out the way!"

Frozen, the panicked young maid shook her head, but she was slow to obey his orders. Sam made her pay for her shell-shocked hesitation. Grabbing her by the throat, he slugged her and then shoved her toward the wardrobe near the door. Crying out, I crawled toward the edge of the bed as Sam took off, running from the bedroom. I swung my legs over the side of the bed and stood. Wobbly, I grabbed the robe I'd draped over a chair at the dressing table this morning, put it on, and stumbled to the maid. Slumped against the wall, she was stunned and moaning, her lip split and bleeding.

"It's okay," I said, tying the sash around the robe and then kneeling next to her. "I'm going to call security. You're going to be okay, all right?"

Trembling, the maid stared at me, still confused. Standing, I ran toward the desk in the corner, grabbed the phone and punched the zero button. "Hello, this is Quinn Miller in suite two-oh-four," I rushed out, my voice high and trembling. "I need security to come to my room immediately! A man just tried to rape me, and he assaulted one of the maids. Please come right now!"

Chapter Thirty-Five

"Quinn, are you okay?" Icarus grabbed me into his arms, pulled me into the living area of his small, yellow house, and closed the door. "Did that son of a bitch hurt you?"

"No, he didn't," I assured him, staring into his eyes, caught up in the comfort and protection I couldn't find anywhere except in his arms. "He tried to, but he didn't."

Sighing, Icarus said, "If that bastard had—"

"But, he didn't, okay," I said, not wanting to think about Sam's attack.

It was a few minutes after nine. I was exhausted, but still jittery and jumpy from Sam's attack and from being questioned first by the senior hotel management and then by the hotel security team and finally by the St. Mateo police, who were more suspicious than sympathetic.

Detective François, who showed up to take my statement, asked me if Sam's attack had something to do with the fact that I'd accused Sam of working with Henri to blackmail me. The detective thought I'd confronted Sam, with no viable evidence to back up my claims, and Sam had retaliated because he wanted me to stop spreading rumors and lies about him.

Once the police left, I called Icarus, who'd been texting me for the past four hours. I hadn't been able to respond because I'd been going through the St. Matean Inquisition. Icarus found out Sam had broken into my suite and attacked me, and he had invited me to his house because I'd been temporary displaced at the hotel. My suite was, officially, still considered a crime scene and would be for the next day or so. The hotel didn't have another suite available, so they'd offered to provide a suite for me at their sister property, the Hibiscus, but I told them I'd made other arrangements.

After Sam's vicious attack, I didn't want to spend the night alone. I was still on edge, still rattled from the things Sam had told me, disturbing things I didn't want to accept or believe—things I couldn't ignore.

Icarus walked me to the couch, and we sat down next to each other. Reluctant to leave his embrace, I leaned against him, tucking my legs beneath me.

"Thank God, the maid came to clean your room when she did," he said, kissing my forehead.

"I am thankful to her," I said. "I just wish Sam hadn't hit her."

"Were you in the room when Sam broke in?" Icarus asked. "Or did you walk in and catch him?"

"I was there," I said.

"What did he want?" Icarus asked. "What did he say to you?"

"Sam admitted that the burner phone you found at Stazia's house was his," I said. "He said Stazia stole it from him and saw the threatening messages to Henri, and she tried to blackmail him."

"Why am I not surprised?" Icarus exhaled, rubbing his jaw. "Blackmail was what the alliance was all about."

"Sam insisted that he was just trying to scare Henri," I said. "He wasn't really going to kill him."

"We need to tell Tavie about this," Icarus said. "And Detective François, too."

I thought about Sam's accusations against Icarus. I wasn't really in the mood to discuss any of Sam's wild, baseless claims, but I couldn't ignore what he'd told me, or pretend it didn't matter, or that my doubts about Icarus hadn't been reignited.

"I need to ask you something," I said, snuggling against him.

"What?" He tightened his arms around me.

I hesitated, not knowing how to speak the questions I needed to know the answers to.

"Quinn ..." Icarus prompted.

"Before Sam attacked me," I began, a slight tremor in my voice. "He said some things to me."

"What do you mean?" Icarus asked. "What things did he say to you?"

"He said that, um ..." I cleared my throat, and then said, "He said ... nothing. Forget I even brought it up."

"I can't forget it because I don't think you would have mentioned it if it wasn't important."

"But, it's not important," I insisted. "Just stupid lies I didn't believe, that I would never—"

"But those stupid lies bothered you, didn't they?" Icarus asked. "Because now you're wondering if maybe those stupid lies are really true?"

"No, I don't—"

"What did Sam say about me?" Icarus asked, his voice rising.

"He was trying to implicate you, saying you could have killed Henri," I rushed out. "He said you wanted the blackmail money."

"That's bullshit!" Icarus said, staring in disbelief. "Tell me you didn't believe him."

Trembling, I looked away, not knowing what to say, or what I believed, or—

"Quinn!" Icarus jumped up from the couch, glaring at me. "You cannot believe that I killed Henri for that blackmail money."

"I don't want to believe that!" I told him. "But, I ..."

"But, you do? Even though it doesn't make sense?" He shook his head, his expression solemn. "If I really wanted the blackmail money, I could have gotten it before Henri got his dirty hands on it. After I had you deposit the money into my account, I could have flown to the Cayman Islands, withdrawn the cash, and then taken off with it. You never would have seen me again."

"I don't believe you killed anyone," I said. "But when Sam told me those things, I started to have doubts because he said you and Stazia—"

"Me and Stazia what? Did Sam tell you we were scheming to kill Henri and take the blackmail money?" Icarus asked, sitting next to me. "Since I found out Stazia delivered that damn blackmail letter to you, I have been trying to find her and make her tell us—"

"Sam said you and Stazia used to be together." I stared at him. "Is that true?"

Icarus stared at me, saying nothing.

"He said the two of you used to hook up," I said. "You were some kind of friends with benefits."

Sighing, Icarus rubbed his jaw and looked away.

My stomach twisted. "So, it is true?"

"We hooked up once," Icarus said. "It was a long time ago. We weren't friends with benefits. And I wasn't working with her to steal the blackmail money from Henri. And I didn't kill Henri."

"I know that," I said.

"No, I don't think you really do," Icarus said, taking my hands in his and leaning toward me. "I know you still have doubts. How could you not, with Sam Collins trying to make you think you can't trust me, telling you that I'm lying to you, trying to make you think I black-mailed you? I am going to show you that you can trust me."

Leaning forward, I pressed my lips against his, and when he embraced me again, I allowed him to comfort me and protect me, even though I wasn't sure I was entirely safe in Icarus's arms.

DAY EIGHTEEN

Chapter Thirty-Six

"I need to talk to Icarus," Doris said. "I know he ain't here because I don't see his Jeep, but you know where he went?"

"Doris, hi," I said, stepping out on the porch, closing the front door behind me. Despite the overhead awning, it was damp and steamy, the atmosphere humid from an early morning thundershower. The concrete steps were still slick, and water had collected in puddles where the porch floor was uneven. "Are you okay?"

"Yeah, I guess," she said and shrugged, but her frown told a different story—as did the greenish-purplish bruise near her right eye.

"Did you hurt yourself?"

"Ran into a fist," she said, her wry smile wavering. "Stazia's."

"Oh my God," I said. "Stazia hit you? Why? Wait, when did you see her?"

"Early this morning, I caught Stazia in Henri's house, sneaking around, looking for something," Doris said. "One of his neighbors called me and said somebody breaking into your brother's house. So, I rush over there and find Stazia. I confronted her, asked her what are you doing in my brother's house? She attacked me and even snatched Henri's medallion from my neck and hit me with it."

I winced when Doris pointed to a nasty scratch above her left eye.

"She took the medallion when she left," Doris said. "Probably try to pawn it but I don't think it's real gold."

Sighing, I said, "Doris, Icarus is at work. Why do you need to talk to him?"

"I need to ask him something very important." She folded her arms and shook her head, nostrils flaring, as though she was still struggling not to cry. "I want to ask Icarus if he killed my brother."

"Why would you think Icarus killed Henri?" I asked, curious, a bit worried.

"That's what Sam Collins say."

"When did you talk to Sam?"

"Yesterday. Last night."

"Did Sam tell you what he was doing yesterday afternoon?" I asked. "Did he tell you he broke into my hotel room and tried to rape me?"

"What?" Doris looked shocked, but skeptical.

"He broke in to look for a burner phone that Icarus found at Stazia's place," I said. "The phone had some threatening messages on it that Sam sent to your brother on the day Henri died. Messages where Sam threatens to kill Henri."

"You think Sam killed Henri?" Doris looked aghast, disbelieving. "That can't be right. Sam and Henri was like brothers."

I felt a slight vibration against my hip. Removing my cell phone, I glanced at the screen, noting the small envelope icon—a text message.

"You had told me you was going to find who really killed Henri since you claim you didn't do it. But, ain't heard nothing from you, don't know whether you found nothing out about who really killed my brother," she said. "So, I decided, if you want something done, you gotta do it yourself. So I say, I'm going to tell the cops what I been thinking about who might have killed my brother."

"And what have you been thinking?"

"I been thinking about Stazia," Doris said. "I think she was looking for that blackmail money in Henri's house this morning."

As Doris explained why she now suspected Stazia of killing her brother, I accessed the text. As I stared at the message, my heart slammed.

my name is Stazia. u dont know me but i need u 2 meet me. i want 2 tell u the truth.

With shaking fingers, I typed my reply: *the truth about what?*

Nervous and apprehensive, as Doris went on and I waited for the reply from Stazia, I checked the text log, wondering if Stazia had texted from the 0007 phone. When my suspicions were confirmed and I saw the last four digits, 0007, I nearly leaped out of my skin.

Minutes later, my phone vibrated, signaling an incoming text.

i can prove Icarus killed Henri. meet me at the spa bungalow @ 3. i am very serious. my life is in danger and i need someone 2 trust. i know u been looking for me. i have been hiding from Icarus. please meet me 2day.

"Doris, listen," I stopped her. "I've got a work situation I have to take care of right now, I'm sorry."

After Doris left, I went back into the house, anxious to call Icarus about the text from Stazia. Pacing Icarus's small living room, I willed him to answer but got voice mail. Instead of screaming my frustration, I left him a message to call me immediately.

Dropping down on the couch, I tried to calm down, but I couldn't. Stazia had texted me from the 0007 phone. Which meant she had also sent the fake messages from Nick Presso, trying to trick me into thinking Icarus had forced him to lie about Sam killing Henri. The elusive Island girl must have realized her text from Nick hadn't worked, so maybe she thought I would believe a claim straight from her.

Icarus responded twenty minutes later with a text. He would be tied up chauffeuring all afternoon but would end his shift at four o'clock, an hour after the time Stazia had requested to meet.

"Can you get off any earlier?" I asked, after he answered my call.

"Unfortunately, no," Icarus said. "Text Stazia back and tell her you can meet at four thirty."

"What if she doesn't want to do that?"

"Quinn, I don't want you to meet her alone," Icarus said. "I don't know what the hell she's up to, but I'm sure she's desperate and scared, and that's a dangerous combination."

"You think she might try to hurt me?" I asked, thinking of Doris's bruise.

"She might try to take you hostage," Icarus said. "If she killed Henri, and I think she did, then she probably wants to get off the island and she might try to force you to help her."

After promising Icarus I would text Stazia to request a new meeting time so I could wait for him to get off work, I ended the call with every intention of keeping my promise. My emotions were all over the place, and I couldn't think rationally. Panicked, I knew Stazia would leave if I didn't show up at the requested time. I didn't think I could risk letting Stazia slip away again. There was nothing logical about meeting her alone, but since logic had abandoned me six months ago, I decided I would meet the mysterious Island girl by myself.

Chapter Thirty-Seven

"Stazia ..." I called out, twisting the knob of the large bamboo door and pushing it open. "Stazia are you in here? It's, um ... it's Quinn Miller. You sent me a text asking me to meet you at three o'clock and I'm here. Stazia, are you here?"

What the hell was I doing? Why had I come there? Why had I been so quick to meet with Stazia? I couldn't even be sure that the text really was from her. I shouldn't be here, I knew. I was trespassing on the hotel's property, meeting a former employee who'd been fired but somehow was able to get onto the property and unlock doors. I shouldn't have come here. I should have texted Stazia and requested a later meeting time. I should have waited for Icarus to go with me to the spa bungalow. I should have gone straight to Octavia's office and showed her the message, but ...

i can prove Icarus killed Henri.

i want 2 tell u the truth.

Staring at the text, reading the words one by one, something had come over me, and I wanted, more than anything, to question the elusive, mysterious woman. I wanted to interrogate her, like the old Quinn would, and find out what she really knew about Henri's murder.

Unlike Icarus, I didn't think Stazia had killed Henri. Definitely, she'd been lying when she'd claimed Icarus had killed Henri. I had a feeling Stazia knew who might have murdered Henri. Sam Collins had said neither he nor Stazia had been sent to pick up the blackmail money, but apparently Henri had lied to both of them. He'd told Sam that Stazia had picked up the money, and he'd told Stazia Sam had been sent to the money drop. I doubted Henri had picked up the money himself. He'd sent someone to the Golden Lizard Beach locker room. Who? And could that person have killed him?

"Stazia ..." I said, knowing I should turn around and get the hell out of the spa bungalow. But I couldn't leave. I had to find out the truth Stazia wanted to tell me.

From the brochure Liberada had given me about the spa's services, I knew the bungalow would be deserted in the afternoon. Most of the treatments were done in the early morning or in the late afternoon. The staff of massage therapists and estheticians was given a "siesta" of sorts before beginning their second shift.

I walked into the bungalow, feeling as though I was losing my mind. Definitely, I was not thinking clearly because if I was I wouldn't be here. I was making all the wrong decisions today, but I couldn't seem to stop myself.

Beyond the rainforest, the sun had been hot and bright, but the spa bungalow buildings were nestled between the thick, waxy branches of banana, bamboo, elephant leaves and dozens of other flowering bushes and shrubs, and surrounded by branches and climbing vines. The terrarium-like atmosphere blocked the sunlight and the rooms were cool and shadowy, somewhat mysterious, allowing an almost mystic eeriness to swirl through the air.

I hadn't been back to the bungalow since the day I'd arrived on the island, when Icarus had led me down the path through the rainforest, claiming he had to make sure the spa's doors had been locked.

Wary and yet excited, I had no idea what type of adventure awaited me. Even now, the intensity of the memories was potent, transporting me back in time to the moment when Icarus and I first made love.

Exhaling, I told myself to snap out of it. Now was not the time for reminiscing. Now was the time for truth. Hopefully. If Stazia actually planned to tell me the truth, which I was starting to doubt. I was also starting to doubt she was here or that she would even show up.

Leaving the small reception area, I headed down the hallway and ended up in the first room, which was slightly bigger and featured the long panels of whispery gauze I remembered. The room seemed darker and there appeared to be more panels.

A sudden, strange whirring noise made my hair stand on end and gave me goose bumps. I moved around and among the gauzy panels, trying to identify the sound, but a moment later, the whirring stopped and I froze.

Standing still, I concentrated on listening, but I could barely hear over my pounding heart. Letting out a shaky breath, I took a step. A muted click, and again I froze. What was that? Had the bungalow door opened?

"Stazia?" I turned. Gauze panels seemed to swing toward me. Startled, I pushed them aside, trying to see through the fabric. I shuddered, realizing Henri must have been in the bungalow, watching and secretly recording Icarus and me as we made love.

In the second room, a faint, spicy smell of incense lingered. Stazia wasn't in the room. There was a massage table, and around the perimeter of the room, bamboo shelves and cabinets housed towels, candles, stacks of stones in various sizes, and dozens of oils and lotions in various bottles and jars.

"Stazia?" I sighed, annoyed, not sure if I should search the last room or just accept that I'd been made a fool of, again, and—

Something brushed my back, and I jumped just as I remembered the gauzy panels; however, there were no gauzy panels in this room, the second room. The gauze panels were in the first room. Heart slamming, I spun around. There was nothing behind me, which made the panic increase. I *had* felt something on my back, hadn't I? Maybe. Or maybe not. Maybe I was just jumpy and irritated, pissed because it was becoming more and more obvious that Stazia wasn't going to show up to tell me the truth about Icarus.

Facing the hallway I had just walked through, I peered into the dim, shadowy passageway. I could see into the first room a bit, where the gauze panels swayed slightly, the fabric disturbed by the hints of breeze seeping through slivers of space in the walls. Exhaling a slow breath, I stared down the dim hall, mesmerized by the gauzy panels, trying to discern if someone else was in the spa bungalow.

"Stazia," I called out just in case she *had* arrived and was making her way through the gauzy gauntlet, looking for me. "Stazia?" No reply. With heightened apprehension, I turned and headed toward the hallway that would lead to the last room.

The third room was the largest, used exclusively for guests who wanted some type of sexual spa fantasy. Walking through the hallway, I thought about my own experience in the third room, where Icarus and I had made love for—

A whispery scurrying gave me a jolt of panic and fear so potent that my legs went rubbery, and I almost lost my balance. Pressing a hand against the bamboo wall to steady myself, I glanced behind me and then looked ahead, my pulse jumping. Farther along the hall, closer to the entryway into the third room, a window let in an unusual burst of bright sunshine in the shape of a square on the opposite wall. As I passed the window, I turned my head toward it for a second and then looked ahead, continuing down the hall.

The after-image of a face in the window flashed in my mind, and I froze, stopping dead in my tracks, confused and panicked. *A face in the window?* Trembling, I turned slowly and took a step forward, walking back to the window. Determined to overcome my hysteria, which I knew was just my mind playing tricks on me, I faced the window. Squinting from the bright sunshine slanting through broad leathery green leaves, I stared at the cloudy glass pane and—

A face, transparent and shadowy, like a flickering specter, stared back at me. Terrified, I gasped at the wide eyes and opened mouth. I was about to scream when I realized I knew the face in the window.

It was my own ghostly reflection.

Shocked and embarrassed, I spun away from the window, shaking my head as I hurried down the long, narrow hall and into the third room.

The room where Icarus and I had first made love brought back a torrent of memories, and yet the room wasn't the same. There was something different about the large, airy space, I realized, as I stepped toward the king-sized bed. Trembling and confused, I frowned and forced myself to take another step, trying to process what I saw.

Dizzy and nauseated, I stared at the body sprawled in the middle of the bed. A large knife jutted from the center of the chest while white sheets, stained with pools and splatters and splotches of blood, were twisted around muscular limbs.

A scream rose in my throat, but when I opened my mouth, only strangled gasps escaped as I walked even closer to the bed. I recognized the lifeless face.

It was Sam Collins.

"Oh my God," I whispered, holding a shaking hand against my lips.

Horrified, I took a step back, my mind racing, struggling to figure out what was happening even as something was telling me to leave, to turn around and run as fast and as far away as possible. I didn't understand why Sam Collins was lying on the bed in the third room of the bungalow with a knife in his chest.

I coughed and cleared my throat as a vague sound filtered through the haze in my mind, something like a strange crackling noise.

Glass shattered, and before I could jump, there was a series of tinkling pops. Panicked, my breath coming in short bursts, I turned from Sam's dead body and stared toward the hallway leading back to the second room.

"Oh no ..." I sputtered, coughing again as the cloud of smoke in the hallway drifted into the third room. Smoke? I didn't understand. Why was there smoke in the hallway? I took several steps forward, but then jumped back when more glass shattered and the strange crackling sounds grew louder.

My heart pounding, I tried to peer through the smoke. There was a sudden flash of orange at the entrance into the second room. Gasping, I skittered back, still staring down the smoke-filled hallway, my stomach twisting as I saw more flashes of orange and realized what they were.

Fire.

Coughing harder, I backed away from the entryway and spun in a circle, looking for an exit, some way to escape, but there were no windows in the third room. Only bamboo walls and a thatched roof. I had to get out of the bungalow. Now. Before the walls caught fire and the flames spread to the roof, consuming me.

The smoke in the hallway terrified me. In seconds, it seemed to have grown more voluminous and potent, and I was wheezing, trying to breathe. I could not stay in the third room. Several minutes more and the entire space might be swirling with smoke. I'd read somewhere that most people who died in fires expired from smoke inhalation. The smoke got into their lungs, burning them from the inside out.

Assailed by another fit of coughing, I tried not to scream and cry as I made tentative steps toward the hall. Pulling the hem of my tank top over my nose, I headed down the hall, hesitant at first and then breaking into a jog as smoke and heat surrounded me, stinging my eyes and burning my throat.

From the hallway, I ran into the second room. The heat was intense, and as I squinted, I had to force myself not to scream. The second room was on fire. Flames crackled and snarled as they devoured the bamboo walls surrounding me. The smoke wasn't as thick, and I was able to make my way to the hallway leading to the first room. Blindly, I half-walked, half-ran, through a wall of smoke that seemed heavy and oppressive and determined to choke me to death.

I couldn't die like this! *Please, God, no*, I prayed, hacking and coughing, struggling to breathe as I pushed through the hallway and then entered the first room. Gasping, I stumbled back into the hall, watching in horror as flames leaped and danced around the room. The gauzy curtain panels were no match for the fiery conflagration. Fire raced up the filmy gauze, leaving behind smoldering charred fabric.

The flames roared and rose. Flames joined other flames, creating small infernos that twirled and swirled. The fire had a life of its own and was spreading. Smoke grew thicker, cloudier and dark, like brimstone straight from the bowels of hell.

Coughing and gagging, I tried to peer through the roaring flames, tried to figure out a path I could take to get to the hallway that led to the reception area. All around me, the gauze looked like swirling, burning ribbons of fabric, but the walls of the room were not completely engulfed. If I stayed low and kept to the perimeter, then maybe I could make it to the hallway. Maybe. I wasn't sure. I was hacking and gagging and could hardly see, but I had to try to escape. I couldn't just stay there.

A thunderous mountain of burning straw and bamboo crashed to the floor in the middle of the room. Screaming, I hurried along the side of the wall, staring up at the sky. Sun shone through the section of roof that had fallen while thick clouds and plumes of smoke escaped though the opening, allowing me to breathe just a bit easier. I continued around the perimeter, avoiding the fiery gauze as much as possible, wincing and crying out when sparks flew and landed on my hands and arms.

Undaunted, I ran though the hallway as fiery flames leaped toward me and cloying smoke burned my eyes and throat. It seemed as though the fire had personified into some kind of flaming spirit, sent to destroy me.

The fire and smoke hadn't made it to the reception area—yet. Gulping and gagging, I ran to the door, grabbed the knob, and—

Screaming in pain, I yanked my hand back from the white-hot knob. Hysterical, I stared at my shaking hand, wincing and crying when I saw the glistening red blisters. Sobbing, my hand throbbing, I dropped to my knees. Something swung forward in front of me, and when I sat back on my heels, I realized the swinging object had been my purse, the small cross-body purse I'd looped around my neck before I left Icarus's little yellow house.

My phone! It was in my purse. Wincing, I used my left hand to unzip the purse and pull out my phone. I forced myself to concentrate. Behind me, the smoke and fire were on their way, but I looked away, focusing on the display screen of my cell phone. Trembling, I started to enter my four-digit password, but I dropped the phone, and it skittered across the room beneath a chair.

Cursing and screaming, I did a diving crawl toward the chair and then flattened my body, reaching beneath the chair with my left arm. Feeling across the dusty floor, I located the phone, grabbed it, and then rose to my knees.

Beyond the smoke-filled hall, there was a cacophony of breaking and shattering and crashing, but I forced myself to ignore it as I entered my password on the phone's display screen. Sweat broke out on my face, and I blinked rapidly, trying to keep the sweat from my eyes as I accessed the keypad and dialed the number.

Whimpering in shock and fear, I listened to the ringing, praying that—

Pain exploded at the back of my skull, spreading like poison as the phone fell from my hand. Confused and terrified, I felt bile rising in my throat. I fell forward, blackness engulfing me as thoughts fled and consciousness slipped away.

DAY TWENTY-ONE

Chapter Thirty-Eight

"Can you tell me what happened, Ms. Miller?" Detective Richland François asked.

Sitting up in the narrow hospital bed, propped up against the pillows, I stared at the detective. Standing at the foot of my bed, he gave me his familiar skeptical gaze, a mix of doubt and cynicism.

Hesitating, I looked down at my hands—the right one bandaged and the left one marred with a few burn scars from the fire I'd survived three days ago, thanks to Icarus, who was standing by the door with his arms crossed and a grim expression on his handsome face.

The story of Icarus's heroism had been recounted to me more than once by several different nurses, all of them impressed by his bravery, and by his looks, no doubt. As the nurses told it, Icarus had found me unconscious in the bungalow, after rushing into the burning building, risking his own life, and had rescued me from the inferno. Once at the hospital, I'd been treated for moderate smoke inhalation, a pretty nasty burn on my right hand, and various cuts, gashes, and superficial burns on my arms and legs. Those weren't my only injuries. Initially, the doctors had assumed the lack of oxygen had caused me to lose consciousness, but upon further examination, they discovered I had suffered some type of trauma to the back of the head. It was concluded I'd been struck with a blunt object and knocked out.

Earlier this morning, I'd called Lisa to update her. There were tears when we talked about the fire and how it had nearly taken my life—if not for Icarus. Lisa was grateful for his bravery, but she claimed she still didn't trust Icarus, though I noted a lack of vehemence in her suspicion of him.

"Why were you at the spa bungalow when it was closed?"

Glancing at Octavia, I looked for some sign from her, a nonverbal cue, as to whether or not I should answer the question, but she looked as curious as the detective, and there may have been some suspicion in her gaze. Standing behind her, near the door to my hospital room, was Icarus, giving me a shrewd look.

"We spoke to the hotel staff, and they told us the spa's hours," the detective said. "They weren't open during the time the fire broke out. They also told us that the spa would have been locked, so how did you get in?"

"I don't know," I said, deciding on a course of action that I might not be able to make work, but I had to try. I had to stall until I could talk to Octavia and Icarus alone.

"You don't know why you went to the spa?"

"No, I don't," I said. "What I mean is, I don't know because I don't remember."

"You don't remember?"

Determined not to falter under the detective's withering gaze, I shook my head. "I don't remember. The doctors told me that I've been in and out of consciousness, which is why they wanted me to stay in the hospital, so they could monitor me, and today is the first day that I've been able to stay awake for longer than an hour. And, all morning, since I woke up, I've been trying to remember why I went to the bungalow, but I can't. The only thing I can think is that I booked an appointment and got the time wrong."

"You didn't have an appointment at the spa that day," the detective said. "We checked with the hotel."

"Well, then, maybe ..." I shook my head. "I don't know. I wish I did."

"And, let me guess," Detective François said. "You don't know anything about Sam Collins' murder?"

"What?" I said, trying to sound surprised, trying to forget the images of Sam's lifeless body and the bloody sheets and the knife in his chest. "Sam Collins is dead? Why would I know about that?"

"My client is not answering any questions about the murder of Sam Collins," Octavia told the detective.

"Ms. Miller, when I initially tried to get your statement, three days ago, your doctors wouldn't let me talk to you," the detective said. "As you said, you were in and out of consciousness, so they advised me to come back when you were more lucid and able to answer questions. Not once did they mention anything about you losing your memory."

"The doctors may not be aware that Ms. Miller is having difficulty recalling the events of the incident in question," Octavia said. "Which is why I think you should take her statement at a later date. I can tell the doctors about her memory issues, and they can run more tests. When Ms. Miller is able to provide you with more details, I will let you know."

Shrugging, the detective said, "Ms. Miller, the problem with your memory is that you have forgotten how to tell the truth."

Pretending to be offended, I said, "I'm not lying. I don't—"

"Detective, let's allow the doctors to determine whether or not Ms. Miller's memory has been impaired by the tragic ordeal she barely survived," said Octavia, with a stinging rebuke that seemed to have chastened the skeptical lawman. "In the meantime, have you made any progress in finding out who started the fire and assaulted Ms. Miller?"

As he headed out of the room, the detective mumbled his reply, which was something about the investigation into the fire being ongoing.

Once the detective was gone, Octavia frowned at me.

"What?" I asked, wary, glancing at Icarus for support, but he seemed just as frustrated as his cousin.

"Okay, what's the real story?" Octavia asked. "I want the truth."

Icarus moved from his spot by the door, where he'd been rooted, and walked to the foot of the bed. "The truth is that Quinn went to the spa to meet Stazia."

"What?" Octavia's head whipped toward Icarus and then back to me, her frown turning to a scowl. "Is that true?"

Contrite, and slightly irritated, I said, "Yes, but—"

"Quinn, why would you go to meet her alone?" Octavia asked. "That was a very dangerous thing to do, and as it was, you could have been killed."

"She wasn't supposed to go alone," Icarus said, giving me a pointed stare. "I was supposed to go with her, but she didn't wait for me."

I glared at Icarus. "I was worried that Stazia would leave if I didn't show up at the time when she wanted to meet me."

"Neither of you should have been meeting Stazia without telling me about your plans," Octavia admonished. "You need to always keep me abreast of everything you're doing as you search for the better suspect."

"Speaking of the better suspect," I said. "I just remembered something Sam Collins told me."

After telling Octavia and Icarus about Henri's lies to both Stazia and Sam, Icarus said, "We need to find out who Henri sent to the money drop."

Nodding, Octavia said, "That person could be the killer."

"We don't have all the details," Octavia said, "but I think we can agree there was probably an argument about the blackmail money and Henri was stabbed."

"We don't need the details," Icarus said. "We just need to know who picked up the money for Henri."

"Which means we need to talk to Joshua," I said, feeling decidedly more like the old Quinn than I had in a long time. "He had to have seen who Henri sent to the money drop."

DAY TWENTY-TWO

Chapter Thirty-Nine

"Tavie, are you serious?" Icarus asked. "Are you sure?"

"I'm absolutely sure," Octavia said. "My friend, Kale, who works at Channel 3 is a video editor, and he is two hundred percent sure that the video Joshua filmed of that blackmail money drop in the locker room at Golden Lizard Beach was edited."

Astonished, I shook my head, trying to absorb the significance of what Octavia was telling us, though eight in the morning might have been too early for startling revelations of profound consequence. Even after two cups of coffee, I was a bit groggy, possibly from the pain meds I'd been given to temper the throbbing in my right hand.

I'd been released from the hospital yesterday around seven in the evening. Icarus took off early to pick me up, and we went back to his place.

After a casual, yet romantic, dinner in the backyard at a bistro table beneath a large pergola festooned with outside string lights, Icarus grabbed a bottle of wine, and we climbed into a hammock strung between two palm trees. As the balmy island breeze caressed our skin, we talked and laughed about silly things of no consequence, staying far away from any topics that were even remotely related to blackmail or murder or the fire that had put me in the hospital for three days.

Later, we made love, but it felt tense and combative. It seemed as though we both were trying to dictate, control, overwhelm, and subdue the other. It was powerfully satisfying, but it left me feeling unsettled.

I wasn't sure what was happening between us. Were we two people falling in love? Or merely lovers, whose lust for each other was all-consuming, like a raging fire? I wasn't sure, but I knew fires didn't burn forever. Even the most destructive blaze would eventually either die out on its own, or be put out by some outside element.

Watching him sleep, I couldn't help but wonder if I was sleeping with the enemy.

But it was a new day, and after an abrupt early morning summons to Octavia's office to discuss something monumentally important, my apprehensions from last night disappeared.

"Yesterday, when I first looked at the video," Octavia said, "it seemed strange. I asked Kale to take a look, and immediately, he says this video has been edited. Portions of the video had been removed, is specifically what he thinks."

"Did he say which portion?" Icarus asked.

Nodding, Octavia said, "The part between when Quinn leaves the locker room and Icarus arrives at the locker room and removes the beach bag. I'll show you guys. See if you can detect it."

A few moments later, Icarus and I were standing behind Octavia's desk, peering at her computer screen as Joshua's video played. Octavia had to play it twice, but eventually, both Icarus and I were able to discern an imperceptible moment where the video seemed to skip.

"That little blip you saw," Octavia said, glancing over her shoulder up at us, "is where the video was edited. Kale says it could be one of several things. Either a portion of the video was removed or erased and then spliced back together to appear as though it was one continuous shot. Or, the video was paused, or stopped, and then started again, and the two separate videos were edited to appear to be one continuous shot."

"So, what did Joshua not want me to see?" I asked, confused and disturbed.

"Obviously, he didn't want you to see who picked up the blackmail money," Icarus said, heading around to the front of Octavia's desk, facing her.

Octavia asked, "Ish, you think Joshua was working with Henri?"

"I didn't tell Joshua that he would be filming a money pickup," I said, remembering our conversation. "I just offered him money and told him what I wanted him to video."

"Did he ask you why you wanted him to make a video of you putting a beach bag into a locker at Golden Lizard Beach?" Octavia asked. "Did he ask you why you wanted him to film the person who would take the beach bag out of the locker and then follow that person?"

"He didn't ask," I said. "He seemed half-curious, half-suspicious. I thought he would question me, but he didn't."

"I think Joshua knew about Henri's blackmail scheme," Icarus said. "That's why he removed portions of the video. He had to take out the part where whoever Henri told to pick up the money showed up at the locker room. I'll bet you that if I hadn't gone there to get the money so I could use it to force Henri to confess, Joshua would have given you some bullshit story about how he wasn't able to get any video because something happened to his phone."

"I think Quinn is right," Octavia said. "I don't think Joshua knew he was filming an extortion money drop. But, I think he got curious, so he took a look. And while he was looking in the locker, he paused the video."

"But, how would Joshua have gotten into the locker?" Icarus asked. "If he opened that locker, it was because he knew the combination Henri told Quinn to use, which means he was working with Henri. He might have stopped filming to remove the money himself."

"Or, maybe he stopped the video because he saw Sam or Nick or Stazia," I suggested. "He knows them, right? So, if he sees me put the beach bag in the locker, and then he sees one of his coworkers take the beach bag out of the locker, he might have wondered what was going on."

Nodding, Octavia said, "Joshua might have stopped filming the video to ask."

"We can't keep speculating and guessing. We need to find out for sure," Icarus said. "I'm getting off around eight tonight. And then we're going to have a little talk with Joshua."

Chapter Forty

"Did you edit the video you filmed for me at the Golden Lizard Beach locker room?" I demanded as soon as the phone was answered.

I'd been trying to reach Joshua for days, it seemed—though, actually, it had only been hours—and I wasn't in the mood for pleasantries and greetings, not when I was fuming and frustrated, realizing he'd made a damn fool of me.

It was a little after five o'clock, and I'd had too much time, since Icarus dropped me off and went to work, to kick myself because I'd never suspected that Joshua had tampered with the video. It made perfect sense. Even Lisa agreed despite the fact that Joshua's creative editing took quite a bit of suspicion away from Icarus. Walking aimlessly from room to room, nervous and agitated and pissed and frustrated, I'd updated my best friend on the latest bombshell. It was obvious that Joshua hadn't wanted me to see the person who'd actually picked up the blackmail money. Question was, why? Had Joshua been working with Henri all along?

"What are you talking about?" Joshua asked. "I gave you the video that I filmed."

"Did you tamper with the video?" I asked. "You didn't give it to me immediately after you filmed it, remember? You sent me a text saying your phone died, and—"

"It did die," he insisted, his voice rising several octaves. "Because of all that video I'd filmed, it ran the phone battery down. I couldn't give you the video until I charged my phone and—"

"Maybe you couldn't give me the video until you removed the portions that showed the person who came to get the bag out of the locker."

"Icarus is the person who took the bag out of the locker," Joshua said. "Didn't you see him on the video? Icarus opened the locker and—"

"Icarus wasn't the first person who went to the locker and opened it," I said, jumping up from the couch. "Someone got there before he did, and I want you to tell me who it was."

Silence ensued and then stretched. For a moment, I wondered if Joshua had ended the call, but then I heard what sounded like a sigh.

"Joshua?" I sat down again. "Are you still—"

"You wanna know who got to the locker before Icarus did?" he asked, but something in his tone made his question sound like a taunt. "I'll tell you. But that information is not for free."

"What?" Shocked, I stood up. "Oh my God, are you trying to extort money from me?"

"Don't act like you don't have the money."

His apathetic, mercenary attitude was discouraging and hard to believe. The information he wanted money for could possibly help the police catch a coldblooded murderer. The person who took the money from the locker before Icarus got there just might be the person who'd killed Henri and Sam. Joshua could be protecting the murderer's identify just to make a few bucks.

"How much will the information cost me?" I asked.

"Twenty-five thousand," Joshua said. "Bring it to me tonight and I'll tell you what you want to know."

Chapter Forty-One

"I am sorry about calling Joshua," I said. "I should have waited until you got off work."

It was a few minutes after eight o'clock and the sun had already set, leaving behind wispy streaks of pink and creamy orange against a lavender sky. Icarus and I were headed to Joshua's apartment, traveling toward the northern end of the island. The trip was taking us on a circuitous route along winding coastal roads with mountainous tropical forest on one side and beach vegetation that sloped to pristine white beaches on the other.

"When Octavia told me that Joshua edited that video, I just couldn't believe it," I said. "I got impatient and I had to know if it was true."

"I probably would have done the same thing," Icarus said. "Actually, I did do the same thing when I didn't tell you that I found out that Henri had blackmailed you."

"How did you find out?" I asked, not sure if I wanted to know. "You never told me."

Icarus was quiet, and then he said, "You remember what Sam told you about me and Stazia working together to steal the blackmail money from Henri?"

Flooded with disillusionment and disbelief, I stared at Icarus's profile, feeling as though someone had just opened the door of the Jeep and pushed me out.

"So ... you *were* working with Stazia?" I asked, struggling to breathe.

"No, I wasn't working with Stazia," Icarus said, sounding more weary than insulted by my question.

"But, you just said—"

"Henri came to me and asked me if I wanted to go in on this idea he had," Icarus said. "It was over a year ago. He had come up with this bullshit plan to blackmail one of the guests. He tried to tell me how easy it would be. He said that he could make a secret sex tape of one of his fantasies and then threaten to release it if the woman didn't give him a bunch of money. I told him it was a stupid idea and his ass would end up in jail, but ..."

"He found someone who didn't think his idea was so stupid," I said, my heart rate slowly returning to normal. "He found two people, actually. Sam and Stazia."

"Anyway, when you accused me of blackmailing you," Icarus said, "and when you showed me the sex tape of us and said the blackmailer was threatening to show it to everyone, that conversation I had with Henri about his stupid idea came back to me. And I knew Henri was the blackmailer. I knew that sonofabitch had gone through with that stupid plan."

"It was like his sister told us," I said, leaning back against the seat, remembering Doris's chilling words. "Henri didn't care who he was going to blackmail. All the woman had to be was rich. But there was nothing really special about me."

Saying nothing, Icarus made a sharp turn, downshifting as the road dived into a steep curving descent.

"So, anyway ..." I started. "I've been thinking about what you told me when I told you my reasons for coming to the hotel."

"You said you were anxious and trying to deal with your nightmares."

"Nightmares that started after I won a huge case," I said. "And you told me to figure out why a win would give me nightmares."

"And did you figure it out?" Icarus asked.

"I'm not really sure," I said. "But, I remember not feeling very good about the win. The company I was representing is shady, and I think they may have manipulated evidence and bribed experts and government officials. I think they were guilty, and still I defended them. When I was working up the case, I knew something wasn't right, but I went ahead and presented the evidence to that jury. I defended them, but I didn't believe they were telling the truth. I was so caught up in making partner that I turned a blind eye."

Icarus said nothing, and I worried his opinion of me was changing. Maybe he thought if I was capable of defending a guilty client, then I was capable of murder.

Fifteen minutes later, Icarus was navigating the twisting streets of Boleslau, the seaside neighborhood Joshua called home. It was a lively part of St. Mateo, and it seemed as though we were heading into the middle of a street party with the sounds of hard-driving reggae music, raucous laughter, and conversations in which people shouted across the street at each other. The gravel shoulders were littered with roadside vendors hawking various and sundry wares, everything from jewelry and scarves and bootleg DVDs to roasted goat and stewed plantains.

Seedy sexiness seemed to be the way of life on the narrow palm-lined roads of the north side.

Icarus parked the Jeep in the parking lot of an abandoned convenience store. After we got out, he took my hand, and we crossed over cracked concrete to the shoulder and then crossed to the opposite side of the road. The air was electric and the atmosphere infused with the smells of smoke, roasting meat, fruit, animals, and sweat. The sea breeze was a waft of salty air blowing away a bit of the humidity that floated through the indigo twilight.

As we walked past huge barrel BBQ pits with rows of quartered chickens and large coolers of beer, I decided that Boleslau was bacchanal and yet mercenary. The street vendors seemed to want attention just long enough to determine if I might be interested in what they were selling. As I shook my head at their offers, their eyes flickered past me. I was discarded as they looked for the next potential customer.

Still holding my hand, Icarus led me down a side street, and then several minutes later, we arrived at a large, two-story duplex. Skirting the front driveway, we went around the side of the house, taking a paved stone path through thick palm fronds that led to a two-car garage behind the duplex.

"That's where Joshua lives," Icarus said "The garage was converted into an apartment."

We walked to the back of the garage and then turned a corner, making our way through a narrow space between the side of the garage and a chest-high chain link fence.

At the door, Icarus knocked. "Joshua? Open the door. It's Icarus. Quinn Miller is with me, too. Open up."

Moments passed during which my heart raced, as faint sounds of reggae and laughter floated in the air, and a balmy breeze wafted across my skin.

"Joshua," Icarus said and then knocked more forcefully. "Open the door."

"Maybe you should tell him I have the money he wants," I whispered, jumping slightly when I heard a faint rustling and then relaxing a bit, realizing it was a lizard, scurrying along the top of the chain fence.

"But you don't have the money," he reminded me.

"Yeah, but he doesn't know that," I said. "Maybe it'll make him open the door."

"I don't think he's here," Icarus said, knocking again and then grabbing the doorknob. "I think maybe—"

The door opened a crack, and Icarus cursed as he took a step back.

"How did you open the door?" I asked, my heart racing faster. "Was it unlocked?"

"I don't know." Icarus shook his head. "I guess so ..."

"Should we go in?" I asked, wary.

"I'll go in," he said. "You stay here."

Deciding not to protest, I nodded reluctantly, folding my arms. Hesitant, Icarus pushed the door open a bit wider and then poked his head inside, calling Joshua's name before he went into the garage apartment.

Disgruntled about having to wait outside, I bit my bottom lip and—

Abruptly, Icarus stepped outside the door. His apprehensive expression made my pulse skyrocket, and I knew something was wrong. "What is it?" I asked.

"Go back to the Jeep and then call the police," he instructed.

"Why?" I demanded, my heart pounding. "What's going on?"

"Quinn, just go call the cops," Icarus said, fear and frustration in his tone.

Slipping past him, determined to find out what the hell was happening, I pushed the door open and stepped inside the garage apartment. "Oh my God," I whispered, pressing trembling hands against my mouth as my eyes darted back and forth. Blood seemed to be everywhere. There were splatters all over the sparse furnishings. Splotches stained the walls. Smears on the floor. But the most horrific sight was the trail of bloody spots that traveled from the door to the center of the room, leading to Joshua, who was sprawled on his back with a large knife jutting up from his abdomen.

Terrified and confused, I turned to Icarus, unsure of what to think, barely aware of his arms encircling me as he guided me out of the door, away from the hellish scene.

Chapter Forty-Two

"Was Joshua Christophe conscious when the two of you got here?" Detective Richland François asked.

A few hours had passed since Icarus and I discovered Joshua in his apartment, nearly stabbed to death. Upon seeing the bloody mess he'd been left in, I'd automatically assumed Joshua was dead, and summarily, I became hysterical, my mind unable to process the realization that Joshua was the third person I had seen stabbed with a knife.

After Icarus managed to calm me down and keep me from completely unraveling, he'd determined Joshua was still alive. His pulse was faint, but he was still breathing. Icarus called an ambulance, and fifteen minutes later, the paramedics arrived. Immediately, they began attending to Joshua, and despite his attempt to extort money from me, I prayed he would make it.

Soon after, Detective François and several other police showed up. Presently, the detective, Icarus, and I were standing near the kitchen area while the deputies collected evidence.

"No," Icarus said. "He was barely breathing when we found him."

"How did you two find him?" the detective asked, his gaze shrewd. "What were you doing at his apartment?"

"We came to talk to him," I answered.

Detective François asked, "About what?"

"I don't think Quinn should talk to you without her lawyer present," Icarus said.

"I'm not accusing Ms. Miller of anything," the detective protested, clearly irritated. "I just want to know what the hell happened here."

"We told you what happened," I said, thankful Icarus had stopped me from making the mistake of talking to the police without Octavia's guidance. "We found Joshua in his apartment and he'd been stabbed. That's all we know."

Detective François gave me a skeptical look. I could tell he thought I knew something about how that knife had found its way into Joshua's stomach and was about to voice his suspicions, but he was interrupted by the deputy he'd instructed to take a look in the bathroom.

"There was more blood in the sink, sir," the attentive deputy said. "Looked like someone had washed their hands and then wiped the sink, but they left behind some smears."

Nodding, the detective said, "The crime scene techs should be able to get specimens to test."

"Found this, too, sir," the deputy said, handing the detective a small plastic bag. "It was wedged behind the toilet. Got a few blood smears on it."

As the detective took the plastic bag, I stole a look at the contents. Seemed to be some kind of flat, gold-colored hockey puck, but something about it seemed familiar to me, though I wasn't sure why.

Frowning, the detective peered at the gold hockey puck for a moment and then looked at me. "This pendant wouldn't happen to belong to you, would it, Ms. Miller?"

"Pendant?" I asked, and shook my head.

"That belongs to Henri," Icarus said.

I glanced at him and then back at the gold hockey puck the detective held up in front of me. At once, I knew Icarus was right. What I'd mistakenly thought was a golden disk was actually the cheesy wanna-be-rapper medallion Henri had been wearing during our ill-fated waterfall fantasy. The medallion Stazia had stolen from Doris.

"This belonged to Henri Monteils?" The detective gave Icarus his piercing, shrewd stare. "You sure?"

"Henri always wore that stupid-looking thing," Icarus said. "I don't even think it was real gold."

"Any idea how it ended up behind the toilet in Joshua Christophe's apartment?" the detective asked us, his tone suggesting he might suspect I'd snatched it from Henri's lifeless, bloodied corpse and then placed it in Joshua's bathroom in some desperate attempt to deflect suspicion from myself.

"No idea at all," Icarus said.

Shaking my head, I said, "I don't know, either."

"Well, Ms. Miller, hopefully, we won't find your fingerprints on that pendant," the detective said, and something in his tone made me think he was being sincere. "I would like to get official statements from the two of you about this incident. Call your lawyer, Ms. Miller, and come down to the station tomorrow morning."

Chapter Forty-Three

Staring out of the window that faced Icarus's backyard, I felt slightly forlorn.

My last day on St. Mateo should have ended a few days ago. But I hadn't been able to leave the island because of the charge against me, and I wouldn't be going anywhere until the situation with Henri's murder was resolved. Or solved, rather.

So far, I was still the only suspect the police had, but I knew I wasn't the best suspect. The person who killed Henri was on the island somewhere, probably laying low, waiting for me to be tried and convicted, allowing them to get away with murder. I couldn't let that happen. I had to clear my name. But finding a better suspect wasn't going to get me off the hook. I had to find the actual killer.

But how? My attempts, to date, hadn't helped my case. I was convinced one of Henri's so-called alliance members had killed him, probably over some dispute with the extortion payment. Problem was, one of the alliance members had suffered the same fate as the alliance founder.

Sam Collins was dead and thus off the suspect list.

Although, in the strategy meeting yesterday, Octavia had suggested that just because Sam was dead didn't mean he hadn't killed Henri.

"There was definitely no honor among those thieves," Octavia had said.

Icarus had agreed. "Maybe Sam and Stazia plotted to kill Henri and steal the money."

"But then Sam wanted to keep all the money for himself," I'd said, warming up to the theory. "So, Stazia killed him."

It was an interesting theory, but how the hell could we possibly prove it.

"And we're sure Joshua didn't kill Henri?" I'd asked. "He could have stolen the money from the locker and then, somehow, Henri might have found out and confronted him."

"I don't think so," Octavia said. "I told the police about the video Joshua filmed for you."

"But, Icarus is on that video," I said. "What if the police—"

"Tavie told the cops they would see me on the video," Icarus said. "And she told them what I was doing there that day."

"Did the police believe you?" I asked Octavia.

"Maybe, maybe not," she said and then shrugged. "But I agree with Ish. I don't think Joshua was working with Henri or that he killed anyone."

"Well, once Joshua is out of ICU, he'll be able to tell the police who stabbed him," I said. Though considering the long road to recovery Joshua was facing, I wasn't exactly relying on him to provide us with another suspect to focus on.

"Did you tell Quinn about Henri's pendant?" Icarus asked.

"Almost forgot. Glad you reminded me." Octavia focused on me. "The pendant the cops found at Joshua's apartment was identified by Doris as belonging to Henri. There were fingerprints on it but not Quinn's."

Octavia said the prints were a match for Stazia Zacheo, and the cops wanted to question her. They'd said nothing about her as a possible suspect, though I was starting to think the elusive island girl was a heartless killer.

"The interesting thing about the pendant?" Octavia shook her head in amazement. "It was a secret audiovisual recording device."

"There was a camera in the pendant?" I was beyond flabbergasted.

"That's how he recorded us," Icarus said.

"The police believe the videos Henri secretly made were down-loaded onto a laptop they found when they searched his house," Octavia said. "It appears you might not have been his only blackmail victim, Quinn."

Sighing, I stood and walked to the picture window in Icarus's bedroom.

Since Sam's attack, I'd been staying with Icarus, and now that my checkout date at the Heliconia had come and gone, I didn't have any place else to go. Except, of course, to another hotel, which was what Lisa wanted me to do, but I didn't want to check into the Hibiscus or one of the other luxury resorts on the island.

I liked staying with Icarus. Lisa called it "playing house" and had warned me I'd end up disappointed, but I enjoyed falling asleep in his arms and waking up to the smell of breakfast and coffee. Still, I wasn't sure if Icarus and I were in a relationship. Did we even want to be in a relationship? Could we make a relationship work? We hadn't exactly had one of those "meet cute" moments. Our introduction to each other had been ignited by lust, a combustible passion. But, passion wouldn't sustain us. We had to get to know each other. We had to learn, and then attempt to understand, each other's goals, perceptions, hopes, wishes, prayers, and dreams.

On the heels of desire, blackmail and murder had distracted us from finding out more about each other. Getting to know each other would be suspended until either Henri's real killer was caught or the charge against me was dropped, or both.

And there was still my anxiety. The dreams had stopped, but I'd been trying to figure out why they'd started and had come to startling conclusions ...

My anxiety had begun after I'd won a huge case. The victory should have had me walking on cloud nine, but instead it had become an alba-tross around my neck, weighing me down. Lisa had said the anxiety was most likely the result of some hidden fear, and she'd been right. Winning a case for a crooked, dishonest client left me with the fear of losing my soul, ignoring my conscience and abandoning my principles. I wanted to make partner so badly, driven to prove I didn't need the support of my dad or the safety net of my grandfather's firm to be successful. I forgot myself, forgot the kind of person I was raised to be. Not just astute and clever but compassionate, caring, honorable, and, most of all, ethical.

I came to St. Mateo to get my so-called mojo back and to become, once again, the superstar litigator. I'd been duped into believing I was only valuable if I was winning cases, securing favorable verdicts on behalf of powerful companies. I'd been convinced I was nothing if I wasn't who the firm expected me to be.

Now, the last thing I wanted to be was a woman so hell-bent on career success she would willingly give up her morals, her sense of what was right, good, honest, and fair.

Well, I was no longer willing, or maybe even able, to sacrifice my morals and ethics for professional gain. The best weapons in my arsenal would no longer, and never again, be used to defend shady, crooked conglomerates.

First, and foremost, my weapons would be used to make sure I didn't end up in jail. And then ... well, I wasn't sure, but they would be used in more altruistic, sympathetic, and philanthropic endeavors. Maybe I'd go to work for my dad, after all. Or, maybe—

"What are you thinking about?"

Turning from the window, my heart fluttered as Icarus walked out of the bathroom, wearing only a towel wrapped around his waist.

"Oh, nothing really," I said. "So, are you headed to work?"

"Later," he said. "This morning, I'm meeting with a home inspector."

"A home inspector?"

"It's related to the loan I'm trying to get to renovate my aunt's house," Icarus said. "The bank wants the inspector to write up an assessment of the potential repair items and associated costs before they make a decision about the loan."

Walking to him, I slipped my arms around his waist and then stood on my toes to give him a kiss. "Well, I hope it goes okay."

"You wanna come?"

Delightfully surprised, I nodded. "Yeah, I'd like to see your aunt's house."

After the loan officer left, Icarus showed me around the property his aunt had willed to him, a sprawling estate called Esperança House.

"Esperança means 'hope' in Portuguese," Icarus had explained. "That was my aunt's name. Hope. Her husband, Mr. O'Reilly, named the estate for her."

As Icarus gave me a tour of the grounds, I noticed lots of wear and tear, and some outright neglect, but the bones of the house were excellent. At one time, it had been a glorious showplace. At more than 20,000 square feet, with three stories, and ten bedroom suites, it could easily be made over into a luxury boutique hotel.

Large double doors opened into an expansive foyer with a double curving stairway leading to the second floor. Behind the stairway, a wall of pocket doors opened to reveal a wide hallway leading to a large great room, a ballroom, a huge kitchen with a hearth, a library, a study, an office, and a den.

The mansion sat nestled among five acres of lush, tropical rainforest and had its own private beach.

"Your aunt's house is so perfect," I told Icarus over dinner at sunset, another romantic meal in his backyard beneath the string lights. "The bank has got to give you the loan. It would be such a great investment. And good for the east side economy, too."

"That's what I'm really excited about," Icarus said, his whiskey-colored gaze dancing with his hopes and dreams. "The east side has a lot to offer, and people in this area deserve the chance to show everyone that we can be just as enterprising and financially stable as the west and south sides of St. Mateo. But, I have to be realistic."

"What do you mean?" I asked, pouring the last of the wine into our glasses.

"Well, part of the bank's reluctance is because the house is close to the Double-H," Icarus said, sighing as he grabbed his wine glass. "So, I feel like I have to work three times as hard to convince them that a hotel so close to an area that most tourists have been told is scary and sketchy could be profitable."

"I think you can convince the bank," I said and then finished my wine.

"Let's hope you're right," he said, pulling me closer to him and then dropping his head to kiss me. Instantly intoxicated by his mouth, the wine on his lips, and his tongue swirling slowly around mine, I wrapped my arms around his neck and moved onto his lap.

Quickly, our kisses led us into the bedroom. Icarus lit a candle and when a soft, sepia-toned glow spread across the room, he placed the candle on the bureau near the doorway.

Small, but cozy with tropical furnishings, the bedroom was dominated by a queen-sized bed with four posts draped in gauzy mosquito netting. Across from the bed was a large picture window, opened slightly, allowing a sultry breeze to slip into the room, like the incense of an incantation, casting a spell over us.

Turning to me, Icarus pulled me into his arms and kissed me. I parted my lips, and as soon as I felt his tongue slip into my mouth and swirl slowly, I lost control. Standing on my toes, I wrapped my arms around him and whipped my tongue around his, thrusting it into his mouth as I rubbed against the hard throbbing below his navel, grinding slowly at first but then faster as the lust took hold, guiding me.

Icarus broke the kiss and pulled away just long enough to help me out of my sundress and panties. With frenzied movements, I helped him get naked and then he picked me up and carried me to the bed. Writhing against the cool duvet, I was aching for him, desperate to be filled, but he wanted to make me wait. With his tongue and fingers, he taunted and teased me until I decided to take the lead. Coaxing him onto his back, I straddled him and then guided him inside. Moaning from the exquisite feel of that hard thickness separating me, I clamped my knees against his hips and started to move up and down.

Smiling at me, Icarus put his hands behind his head and watched as I gave him a show.

Feeling sexy and sinful, I touched my breasts, twirling my fingers around the nipples. Staring at Icarus, I could tell he was starting to squirm, and inside me, I felt him jerk forcefully. Relishing in his unabashed desire for me, I trailed my hands down from my breasts to my waist and then lower to touch myself.

Circling my hip as I slid up and down, I moved in sensual undulations, the fingers of one hand dancing around my clit while I grabbed my breast with the other hand, pulling the nipple as the sensations intensified. I moved faster, imagining that I was giving Icarus the best damn lap dance of his life. Rocking with a force that was almost feral, I leaned forward and clutched his broad shoulders, desperate to explode.

Crazed with lust, I moved from a straddle to squat, my rhythm frantic as Icarus thrust upward into me as I bounced up and down on him, groaning and panting.

The eruption came abruptly before I was fully prepared. The force of it was so violent and yet so blissful. In the clutches of rapture, I trembled and shook and thrashed wildly as the pleasure grabbed me, refusing to let me go.

As my thrashing subsided, I felt myself being rolled over onto my back against the warm, damp sheets, and then Icarus was inside me again, thrusting with such vehemence that his velocity stoked the dying embers and I was wet and ready in an instant, rocking my hips against his, matching him thrust for thrust until I caught his frantic rhythm and we moved together. Whispering his name, I arched my back, and with one leg hooked over his shoulder and the other leg stretched out toward the edge of the bed, I pumped with relentless vigor, feeling the stirrings of the release that was coming. The pleasure intensified as we moved faster, desperate and seething, both of us anxious to erupt. Once again, I felt rabid with lust, addicted to the feeling of Icarus inside me, huge and pulsating, driving me insane.

With a primal cry of desire, Icarus bucked violently as he came. His tumultuous spasm sent an eruption through my body that shook me until I was limp and dazed. Icarus was still twitching inside me, causing slight aftershocks of pleasure, and as I moved my hips slowly to take advantage of the subsiding feelings, I became aware of Icarus's mouth on mine.

He kissed me, slow and sensual, as he whispered words against my swollen lips, words that, as I realized what they were and, more importantly, what they meant, filled me with emotions that were too profound to acknowledge and yet impossible to ignore.

Chapter Forty-Four

"She sent me a text about the blackmail money."

Confused, still somewhat half-asleep, I rolled over on my back and stared up at the ceiling, listening. At first, I thought I was dreaming about Icarus, dreaming he slipped out of bed to make a phone call, but as I turned my head to the left, I saw him standing in the middle of the room, a gray silhouette in the darkness.

What was he doing? Who the hell was he calling at—what the hell time was it? I lifted my head to glance at the clock on the bed table. 1:07 a.m.?

Pushing my head from beneath the cover, I looked over to the right. An inky outline of Icarus's tall, muscular form standing in front of the dresser, his back to me, a cell phone pressed against his ear was all I could see.

"We're going to meet at my aunt's house in twenty minutes."

Rolling over on my back, slowly, I pressed my head against the pillow and inched down until the duvet covered my nose. I turned my head to the left, the covers still obscuring most of my face. If Icarus looked over toward me, I could quickly close my eyes, and maybe he'd think I was asleep.

What the hell was I doing? Hiding halfway under the bed sheets, spying on Icarus? As if I was still suspicious of him? As if I still had doubts about his feelings for me? When we'd made love, Icarus had told me he was falling in love with me, and how was I repaying his sentiments? By resurrecting and revisiting those doubts I still couldn't seem to bury.

Icarus turned and stared toward the bed. "Quinn? You awake? Quinn ..."

Panicked, I lowered my head, squeezing my eyes shut, praying he didn't see me, wondering why I was lying there as though I was guilty of something when I should have been confronting Icarus, demanding to know who the hell he'd been talking to, agreeing to meet at his aunt's house at one o'clock in the morning.

I opened one eye.

Icarus walked to the door and left the bedroom, careful and quiet as he pulled the door closed behind him.

Questions and doubts scrambled in my head, fighting for my attention, and I rose up, letting the bed sheets fall to my waist, looking over toward the door. Without thinking, I pushed the covers away and jumped out of bed.

Heart hammering, I tiptoed to the bedroom door and grabbed the knob. After a moment's hesitation, I opened the door, hoping Icarus wouldn't be standing there, praying I wouldn't have to explain why I'd jumped out of bed to follow him.

The hallway outside the bedroom was clear, but I wasn't relieved. My blood pressure ratcheted to an unsafe level as I stepped outside the bedroom. Rigid, I listened, wondering if Icarus had left the house.

A door opened and then closed. The front door, I was sure. My heart kicked as I dashed down the hall. Hurrying through the living room, I went to the window and lifted one of the slats of the plantation shutters. Glancing between the slats, I stared out into the night, just able to discern Icarus's tall, muscular form in the dark.

As he walked to the Jeep, his stride was quick and purposeful. Icarus opened the driver's door, hopped in, and then slammed it close. Seconds later, the Jeep's engine rumbled, and then the headlights sent a blast of bright illumination between the blinds. Startled, I gasped and lowered the slat just a bit, worried Icarus might have seen me in the window.

As the Jeep backed out of the driveway, all I wanted to know was who the hell had Icarus been talking to? Who was he going to meet at his aunt's house? Who had sent him a text about the blackmail money, and why?

Closing the slats, I took a step back, my heart slamming.

There was only one thing I could do now, only one way to get the answers I needed.

Ten minutes later, I was standing on the porch when the cab pulled into the empty driveway in front of Icarus's little yellow house.

Jogging down the porch steps, I ran to the idling cab, opened the passenger door and got in, immediately thanking the driver for his willingness to come out after midnight.

"It's okay, miss," he said, his island lilt attentive and yet weary. "Where you want to go?"

I gave the cab driver the address to Icarus's aunt's house.

"The Esperança estate?" The driver's voice rose in surprise with a hint of suspicion. "Why you want to go there? Don't nobody stay there."

Opening my cross-body purse, I pulled out a one-hundred-dollar bill and held it up. "Can you take me, or should I call another cab?"

Shifting into drive, the cab driver grabbed the money and said, "I know a shortcut. Get you there in fifteen minutes."

Turning off the main road, heading between the ornate gates, the cab driver headed down a gravel lane cut between a thick tangle of trees.

"You can let me out here," I said, looking toward the double doors of the mansion and taking a deep breath.

The driver steered the cab toward a palm tree, about thirty or so feet from the courtyard, where Icarus's Jeep was parked under the portico. "Here you are, miss."

"Thanks," I said, distracted as I opened the passenger door.

"You sure you gonna be okay?"

"I'll be fine," I said and then tried to give him a smile. "That's my friend's car."

Chapter Forty-Five

Standing in the foyer of Esperança House, I glanced around. It was dark and gloomy, almost creepy. Earlier, when Icarus had given me a tour, I'd been entranced by the house, able to see the promise and potential in the large, cavernous rooms and soaring ceilings, but now ...

I took a few cautious steps out of the foyer and down the main hall, dimly lit by wall sconces, casting eerie shadows. A few more tentative steps and I passed a set of paneled doors to my right. Pushed back into their pockets, the doors were opened, revealing the large great room. Stopping at the entrance, I peeked inside. The room was dark, and unable to really see anything, I continued down the hall, trying to remember the layout of the house. About ten feet ahead, to my left, double doors opened to a library, if I remembered correctly.

The mansion was a maze of hallways, some long and wide, others short and narrow, serving as connections between dozens of rooms. The library doors were open, and after a quick glance inside, I saw that nothing seemed to be stirring, but it was hard to tell. With the only light coming from the sconces, not much illumination traveled into the darkened rooms save for a weak glow that didn't reach the far recesses, nooks, and crannies. The light didn't reach the places where someone might be hiding and watching, waiting to ... to *what*? What was I expecting? I was sneaking around this huge, musty old mansion to find Icarus and whomever he'd come here to meet. There was no need to scare myself for no reason, I thought as I continued down the hall. Nothing was going to jump out at me and—

A door slammed, the sound somewhere behind me.

My heart took off, punching against my chest, and I turned, peering in the direction I came from, trying to detect signs of movement in the dim hallway. What the *hell* was that? Was someone behind me, following me?

Turning, I decided to head back to the foyer. Listening for sounds, I hurried by the library, and then eventually walked past the closed paneled doors of the great room, wondering if—

Wait a minute. Panicked, I turned, facing the paneled doors. They'd been open when I walked past them a few minutes ago, hadn't they? They were, I remembered. Why were the doors closed now? Had someone gone inside the room and closed them?

My pulse jumped and I took a deep breath. I didn't know what the hell to do, but I figured I had two options: Get the hell out of the house, which I absolutely wanted to do; and check out what, if anything, was behind the paneled doors, which I absolutely did not want to do. And yet I had to know.

Before I changed my mind, I pushed the panels back and crossed the threshold. The room was as big as a hotel ballroom with a vaulted ceiling and thick, plush carpeting. A wall of long, wide windows dominated one side of the room, but gauzy curtains blocked the view outside. Feeble light came from the antique sconces on the walls in the hallway. Venturing into the room, I was just barely able to see what looked like the outline of a lamp, sitting on an end table next to a grouping of four large, upholstered divans in the center of the room. Making my way to the lamp, I reached beneath the shade and pulled the cord. Dim, cozy illumination extended just to the middle of the divans, but it was enough for me to see a light switch panel in the corner by the windows.

I glanced over my shoulder and walked across the room, heading toward the light switch. Inches away from the switch, I was starting to regret my decision to investigate the room, starting to think—

A loud bump came from behind me.

Frozen, my heart in my throat, I managed to turn just in time to see the lamp falling to the floor, followed by some unidentifiable form that crashed down on the lamp, shattering it, dousing the light, and shrouding the room in darkness.

Chapter Forty-Six

Fingers trembling, I flipped all six of the light switches at the same time, flooding the great room with several megawatts, and then turned around, my heart pounding.

Standing behind one of the divans, maybe ten feet away, was a tall, well-built guy dressed in jeans and a T-shirt. A tall, muscular guy I recognized, a guy I knew too damn well. His back was to me and sprawled at his feet was a girl in shorts and a tank top. I couldn't see her face, but she had long, dark hair. She wasn't moving; her body was perfectly still, and it was covered in blood.

Splashes of blood on her body seemed to be the same blood on the large knife the tall guy with the muscles was holding as he looked down at the lifeless body.

Creeping closer, I struggled to find my voice, struggled to breathe, struggled to stay on my feet, but I was about pass out. "Icarus ..." I whispered, trying to hear over the roaring in my head.

Icarus turned to face me, clutching the knife and staring at me.

Shocked and terrified, I stared at the knife, wet with blood. My gaze trailed to the body at Icarus's feet and then to the blood stains on the rug and ...

"Quinn?" Icarus looked confused. "What are you doing here?"

Staring at Icarus, I didn't know what to think except that everyone had been right about him. Everyone had tried to warn me. Lisa had warned me. Stazia Zacheo had warned me. Sam Collins had warned me. They had all told me Icarus was the killer, but I didn't want to believe it. I couldn't believe it. But, I had been wrong about Icarus. I had been so damn wrong about him!

Screaming, I rushed out of the room, running as fast as I could, heading to the foyer. Once there, I hurried to the doors, grabbed the knobs, and yanked.

The doors wouldn't open. What the hell was going on? What was happening? Crying, I yanked harder, but the doors wouldn't budge, and I didn't understand why. It didn't make sense. Why wouldn't the doors—

"Quinn!" Icarus's booming baritone carried down the hallway. "Don't run from me! Quinn!"

Panicked, I spun from the doors. The double staircase ascended majestically. I didn't know if I should go upstairs, but I couldn't stay in the foyer. I couldn't just stand there and wait for Icarus to come and stab me to death like he'd stabbed the girl lying dead on the floor in the great room.

Dashing to the stairs, I ran up the steps. Stumbling, nearly tripping, I made it to the second-floor landing.

At the top of the staircase, I sprinted down a wide, expansive hallway until I came to the fork separating the two second-floor wings. I went left. Along the long hallway, which was narrower than the main hall I turned from, there were three closed doors, bedrooms probably, two on the left and one on the right.

My heart thundering, I veered right. Yanking the knob on the first door, I twisted it and then shoved the door open. Slamming the door, I closed myself inside the dark room and slapped a hand along the inside wall near the doorframe, feeling for a switch. My hand closed over a knob. A dimmer, maybe? Frantic, I turned the dimmer to the right. The room brightened and I spun around, trembling, trying to think as I surveyed the bedroom. Large and ornate, it was dominated by a huge, canopied bed. There was a sitting area, two loveseats with a coffee table in the middle, an alcove with floor-to-ceiling bookshelves, a desk, and a set of French doors leading out to a terrace.

Trembling, apprehension slamming through me, I started to unzip my cross-body purse, intent on pulling my cell phone out and calling—

The door burst open, banging against the opposite wall.

Gasping, I jumped and spun around. Icarus staggered into the room, clutching his stomach, blood spilling over his fingers.

"Quinn ..." he whispered, lurching toward me and grimacing. "You have to ... get out ... of here! You ..."

Icarus fell to the floor. Rushing to his side, I dropped to my knees next to him. "Icarus!" Slipping an arm behind his neck, I struggled to pull him up. "What happened?"

"Quinn ..." he whispered, voice hoarse, eyes fluttering.

"Oh my God!" I stared at his face, splattered with blood. "Icarus, what happened to you? Can you hear me?"

Slowly his lids opened, and the whiskey-colored eyes focused on me. "Get out of here."

"What are you talking about?" I asked, confused, trying to swipe the speckles of blood away, smearing them across his cheek. "What happened?"

"Not safe here." His eyes closed, and his Adam's apple jerked as he swallowed.

"Icarus, please, tell me what happened to you!"

"Stabbed me ..."

"What did you—"

And then I noticed the slashes on the front of his T-shirt and the blood soaked into the fabric. Carefully, my hand shaking, I lifted the hem of the T-shirt, wincing as he groaned. Shell-shocked, my stomach lurching, I stared at the bloody gash below his right pec. It was still bleeding, mixing with sweat rolling down the side of his heaving chest.

"Who did this?" I asked, my mind racing. What was going on? I didn't understand anything! Downstairs, in the great room, Icarus had been holding that bloody knife, standing over the dead body of the girl, but now he was lying in my arms, bleeding from a stab wound. What was happening? Nothing made any sense!

"Get out of here," Icarus whispered again, closing his eyes.

"We have to get you out of here," I said, looking over at the bed linens, wondering if I could use them to make a bandage. "I'm going to try to stop the bleeding and then I'm calling an ambulance and—"

"Go ... not safe," Icarus said, eyes wide. "... stabbed me when I tried ..."

"What?" I asked, terrified that he was about to die in my arms. "When you tried to what?"

"Tried to ..." He trailed off and coughed, a thin, wheezing sound that made my heart drop, made me wonder if maybe his lung had been punctured. "I ... to get ... proof."

"What proof?" I ask.

"You didn't kill Henri," he said, grimacing. "Stazia ..."

"What about Stazia?"

Icarus grabbed my shirt, pulling himself closer to me. "Called ... said ... had proof, but ..."

"But, what? Stazia lied to you? Is that who you were talking to?" I asked, my head in shambles. "You came here to meet Stazia and she stabbed you? Tell me who stabbed you! Icarus, did—"

"You have to leave," he whispered. "You have to ..."

"Icarus, who stabbed you?" I pleaded with him, wiping sweat from his forehead. "Did Stazia stab you?"

"Quinn ..." Icarus coughed again, took a breath, and said, "You need ... go! Now!"

"I'm not going to leave you!" I promised him, my panic increasing as his eyes fluttered and started to close. "I'm going to call an ambulance, but you have to stay with me, okay? Don't close your—"

Abruptly, his eyes widened, and Icarus rasped, "Behind you ..."

Chapter Forty-Seven

"Behind me?" Confused, I stared at Icarus, trying to understand. Behind me? What was behind me? What did he mean? What was he trying to—

"The light of the wicked shall be put out ..."

Startled, I froze for a second, recognizing the lyrical St. Matean cadence, trying to recall where I'd heard it before. Just as quickly as my body froze, it thawed, and I whipped my head right, toward the door.

Doris stood just inside the bedroom, breathing deep, her eyes wide with an emotion I couldn't quite identify but which unnerved me. Her tank top, arms, and face were smeared with what looked like dabs of blood. Her hair was unbound and wild, hanging in limp strands around her shoulders.

"Doris? Oh my God!" I stared at her, my heart pounding fiercely. "What are you doing here? What happened to you? Icarus was stabbed! He was tricked into coming here! I think it was Stazia, but I don't know. All I know is, there is a girl in the great room and she's dead! Icarus was stabbed! Doris, we need to call the police! I think the killer is still in this house! We have to get out of here! We have to—"

"When Elijah killed the prophets of Baal, do you think that was murder?" Doris asked, a bizarre, incongruous question, posed rhetori-cally, as though she didn't really expect an answer even though she was staring at me, a piercing gaze that seemed to bore through my soul. "No, it was not. It was God's judgment on those wicked, evil idolaters."

"Icarus needs help! I'm going to find something to stop the bleed-ing." Puzzled by the spark of wildness in her dark gaze, I took a step back and then glanced at Icarus. Seeing his eyes closed, my heart slammed. "Can you call the police? I have a phone if you don't."

"Because the evil and wickedness was so great in Sodom and Gomorrah," Doris said, her voice calm, almost circumspect, "the Lord sent angels to destroy that evil place."

"What the hell are you talking about?" I raged at her. "Icarus might die if we don't—"

"And so he should die," Doris said, a hint of hysteria seeping into her tone. "The Bible say, 'his own iniquities shall take the wicked himself, and he shall be holden with the cords of his sins.'"

"What do you mean, Icarus should die?" I stared at her, feeling as though her hysteria was transferring to me.

"Upon the wicked he shall rain snares, fire and brimstone, and a horrible tempest: this shall be the portion of their cup! That is what the Bible says. The same thing that happened to Henri, and Sam, and Stazia, has to happen to Icarus."

"What do you mean, the same thing that happened to Henri, Sam, and Stazia?" I asked, my pulse racing as chaotic revelations and realiza-tions crowded into my mind. Henri and Sam had been killed. Was Doris saying Icarus should be killed? Stabbed to death? Why would she say that? Why would she think that—

"Icarus is the wicked," Doris said, her voice rising a few octaves, as though gathering strength and gaining momentum for some powerful oration. "And a wicked man is loathsome and cometh to shame. The wicked is driven away in his wickedness. The way of the wicked is an abomination to the Lord!"

"Oh my God," I whispered, as the revelations and realizations unified, exposing a horrific truth I didn't want to face, a truth I couldn't deny as Doris made several drunken-like side steps toward the love seats in the sitting area, a position directly diagonal from where Icarus and I were on the floor near the bed.

The truth was in Doris's right hand.

A large, blood-smeared kitchen knife.

Chapter Forty-Eight

"Henri was raised by a good, God-fearing woman who taught him right, but he let the devil trick him and take his mind," Doris said and then lurched forward a few steps, clutching the knife and swaying on her feet, as though she was moments from collapsing. "The Bible say, 'Enter not into the path of the wicked, and go not in the way of evil men! For they sleep not, except they have done mischief; and their sleep is taken away, unless they cause some to fall! For they eat the bread of wickedness and drink the wine of violence! The way of the wicked is as darkness: they know not at what they stumble.'"

Trembling, I stared at Doris, paralyzed by her words and the righteous condemnation in her tone, feeling as though she was damning me to the blackest pits of hell.

"Henri stopped going to church. He stopped reading his Bible," Doris went on, remorseful now, hints of sadness and regret in her voice. "He was a good boy until he started working at that evil place! That hotel of sin and wickedness! The Heliconia Hotel. It is an evil place of sinful lust and wanton idolatry, an abomination! The Bible say you must purge the evil from among you!"

My fear turned to terror.

Doris was trapped in the throes of some strange religious mania, caught up in some belief that she had been divinely chosen to rid the island of the evil brought upon it because of the Heliconia Hotel.

What I saw was a woman losing her mind right before my eyes; a woman losing her grip on reality and embracing the psychotic rage propelling her; a woman who had become homicidal and believed herself to be some sort of avenging archangel, destroying sin and wickedness with the slash of her blade.

"Henri tricked me," Doris said, and at once, she seemed lucid, almost serene. "He told me to go and pick up a package for him. He said this package would be at the Golden Lizard Beach, in the locker room. Henri tell me inside the bag there will be five little packages, wrapped in newspaper."

The blackmail money, I realized, shocked to learn Henri had sent his sister to the drop-off location to retrieve the cash.

"Henri had given me a plastic grocery bag and inside was five little packages wrapped in newspaper," Doris went on. "Henri said take the five packages from the grocery bag and put them in the beach bag and then put the packages from the beach bag into the plastic grocery bag. Then he said put the beach bag back in the locker and then bring the grocery bag back to him."

The newspaper bundle switch was what Doris had just recounted. A story I had been suspicious of when Icarus had told me, but he'd been telling the truth.

"All of these instructions seemed very strange to me," Doris said, swinging the knife back and forth at her side, her grip firm. "I said to Henri what is this all about? What is going on? He tell me just do what I say. But, something about it seem wrong. And so, before I took the grocery bag back to Henri, I opened the little newspaper-wrapped packages, and inside of them was filthy lucre! And I knew it was evil riches. The fruits of an evil plan from the devil himself!"

"That's when Henri told you about the plan to blackmail me?" I asked, staring at the knife, thinking that maybe if I could keep her talking, I could somehow distract her and get away.

"They is demons!" Doris ranted, teetering back and forth. "All of them! Henri, Sam, Icarus, and Stazia, they all belong in hell for the evil wicked things they did!"

"So, you killed Henri because he blackmailed me?" I asked and then glanced at Icarus, lying unconscious, slumped against the foot of the bed. The bloodstain on his T-shirt seemed to have expanded. My heart lurched, but I forced myself not to scream. There was no time for hysterics. I had to get help for Icarus. The girl in the great room—Stazia, I was guessing—was already dead, but there was still a chance to save Icarus. But, first, I had to get away from Doris. No, no I couldn't run away. I couldn't leave her alone with Icarus to finish him off. I had to overpower Doris, somehow. I had to make sure she wasn't able to get up and come after me.

"Henri had to die, don't you understand?" Doris scowled at me. "The evil among you have to be purged. Henri was evil. Sam was evil. Stazia was evil. Icarus was evil. They had to be purged. It is not murder to get the sin and evil from among you!"

"What about Joshua?" I asked, glancing toward the terrace, wondering if it might be my only hope. If, somehow, I could lure Doris out onto the terrace, then maybe I could … could what? Push her over the railing? Killing Doris would make me no different from her. And I wasn't a murderer, but …

"Joshua is wicked and evil," Doris said, her features twisting into macabre masks and grimaces as she spoke. "He try to blackmail me. He told me he had a video of me taking that evil money out of the locker, but he say he removed that part of the video because we know each other a long time, he say. But, then he say he want all that evil money or he will show the video of me to the police. But, I tell him I don't have that filthy lucre! I burned that evil money! But, he don't care. He expect me to give him ten thousand dollars. So, I made a fool of him. I call him and say I got your money. Can I come over and give it to you? He said yeah. So, I go to his place and stabbed him because evil must be purged."

"He didn't die, Doris," I said. "He's still alive. The evil wasn't purged."

"The wicked shall be turned into hell," Doris said, but she faltered a bit, as though she wasn't quite so sure. "The flame burned up the wicked! That's what Sam Collins found out. I sent that evil greedy Sam Collins a text. I made him think I was Stazia. The text say I have the money. Meet me at the hotel spa and we can split it. And that fool, he come to the spa, and he got what he deserved!"

"You killed Sam Collins," I said.

"The wicked shall be turned into hell," Doris repeated, as though maybe she was reminding herself. "That is what the Bible say, and it had to happen!"

Stabbing Sam Collins hadn't been murder; in Doris' warped mind, it had been the judgment he deserved, divine judgment for his sins.

"You sent me a text pretending to be Stazia, too, didn't you?" I asked, my mind churning. "The same day you sent Sam a text, you sent me a text."

"But, you never suspected me, did you?" Doris smiled. "I was with you when you got that text. You lied and said it was something from work, but I knew it was the text I had scheduled to be sent to you at that time."

Crazy like a fox, I thought, realizing her psychotic ingenuity.

"I was gonna make it look like you had killed Sam Collins," Doris said, and shrugged. "But, then I figured I would kill two demons with one stone, so I set the fire."

"But you didn't kill me," I said. "Icarus saved me."

Glaring at me, Doris said, "But he ain't gonna save you this time. He's probably already in hell where he belongs."

Terrified, I took deep breath.

"I tricked Stazia, too," Doris said, smug. "She's an evil, greedy Jezebel. The dogs will eat her flesh. All I had to do was send her a text. I made her think I was Icarus. I texted her I know where the money is hidden. Meet me at my aunt's old place. And, she text back immediately I am on my way."

As Doris swayed back and forth, my terror turned to disgust and anger. I felt the need to extract my own vengeance—against Doris.

"And so she come here," Doris said. "She sees me and she is surprised. Doris, she say, what are you doing here? She is no fool, though. She know her time is come and so she tried to fight me. She almost got away, but the wicked shall be turned into hell."

"You stabbed Stazia," I said, dazed by her twisted confession, trying to force myself to come up with some sort of plan, some way to prevail against her.

"And then I trick Icarus," Doris said, smiling slightly. "I make him think I'm Stazia because I know he been looking for her. So I send him a text, telling him to meet me at his aunt's house."

Staring at Doris, I entertained ideas of lunging at her, wrenching the knife away, and stabbing it into her chest, just like she'd stabbed her brother, Sam, Stazia, and Icarus. She was nothing but a cold-blooded, heartless sociopath, twisting her religious beliefs to justify her own homicides.

"The Bible say the robbery of the wicked shall destroy them! And they had a plan to rob you. Don't you see why they had to be destroyed?"

"Doris, please listen to me," I started, deciding to take a page from her psychotic playbook—I would have to trick her. " I think—"

"But, I can tell you don't understand what I had to do," Doris said. "How could you? You are the wicked, too. You are just as filthy and sinful as Henri and the rest of them! I saw what you did with Icarus in the spa."

"You're right, Doris," I said, pretending I agreed with her, trying to save my life. "That was a mistake. And, I do regret it. I never should have done it, and if I could go back—"

"You're a wicked Jezebel!"

"I made some terrible choices," I said, trying to breathe, trying not to cry. "I shouldn't have done those horrible things with Icarus."

"Liar!" Doris growled the words through gritted teeth, an angry crease between her brows. "You wanted to do those evil, lustful things!

"No, Doris, I—"

"I could tell you liked it!" Doris said, eyes wide, glistening with rage. "On the video—"

"But, I didn't like it," I said, stumbling over my words, my heart thundering. "I hate what I did, I never—"

"Evil must be purged!" Doris stalked toward me. Face twisted with rage, she charged me, the tip of the blade leading the way.

Screaming, I leaped onto the bed, my gaze focused on the wall of

French doors about fifteen feet from the bed, thinking I could crawl across the thick duvet and then sprint to the French doors and ... and then what the heck would I do? Go out on the terrace and leap over the railing to the ground below? Fall to my damn death?

Still struggling to come up with a plan of escape, I was halfway across the bed when Doris vaulted over the footboard and lunged at me, landing on top of me.

Doris was petite but strong. She had no trouble pinning my arm over my head and holding it against the bed as she tried her best to make ribbons of my face with the knife.

Adrenaline flooded me, infusing me with strength, and I fought for my life.

Grunting and screaming curses, Doris raised the knife and slashed it down toward my face. Quickly, instinctively, I moved my head and saw Icarus at the foot of the bed as the knife stabbed into the mattress, inches from my ear.

"Dirty, evil bitch!" Doris grunted, yanking the knife and ripping the comforter as the blade sliced through the padded fabric. She plunged the knife down again, and I jerked my head, avoiding certain death as I resumed slapping and hitting her face, desperate to get away.

Doris yanked the knife, but it wouldn't budge. She cursed and yanked it again, but the blade seemed to have gotten stuck between the thick cotton mattress padding. Taking advantage of her distraction as she wrestled to dislodge the knife, I balled my hand into a fist and slugged her as hard as I could.

Crying out, more in shocked rage than in pain, it seemed, Doris abandoned the knife and clamped her hands around my throat. Gagging, unable to breathe let alone scream, I tried to pry her hands from my neck as my body jerked and twisted. Knees drawn toward my chest, I slapped my feet up and down on the mattress, not sure what to do or how to get Doris's hands from around my neck.

Punching and scratching her hands and arms wasn't working. Her hold was like a steel trap, and as she glared at me, her eyes narrowed to thin slits, I knew she was not letting go until she'd squeezed all the breath from my body. But, I would be damned if I let her kill me.

I slugged her again, my knuckles slamming into her left eye. Immediately, a blood vessel burst, streaking her pupil with thick red lines. Screaming, she released my throat and cupped her eye with her hand. I hit her again, as hard as I could, ignoring the pain as my fist jammed into her jaw. The strike was forceful enough to send her toppling off me. Freed from her, I sat up, my eyes on the door, and—

Doris backhanded me, a stinging blow that set off a ringing in my head. Dislodging the knife, she scrambled on top of me, straddling me as she raised the knife. "You wicked—"

"Freeze! No one move! Everyone stay exactly where you are! Do not move!"

Chaos erupted as more than a dozen cops swarmed the room, converging upon us as they took up tactical positions around the bed, weapons drawn, loaded, and locked on me and Doris.

Above me, clutching the knife, Doris looked like a rabid animal—nostrils flaring, eyes crazed, and teeth bared as she growled, "The wicked shall be turned into hell!"

"Drop the knife, Doris!" one of the cops bellowed. "Now! Drop it!"

"You stupid wicked fool!" Doris spit the words back at the cop as she glared at me, lowering the knife in her shaking hand until it hovered inches from my eye, wobbling slightly.

Frozen, I stared at the tip of the blade, trembling, my heart and pulse racing to levels that couldn't possibly be safe and would give me a heart attack or a stroke, possibly both. On a night where nothing made sense, and nothing was what it seemed and nothing could be believed, this moment was the accumulation of all the rage, panic, shock, disbelief, and abject horror I'd experienced. Dizzy and nauseated, I wasn't sure if I would ever recover from this bizarre nightmare.

Seconds later, 1 recognized Detective François's voice as he said, "Doris, put the knife down! Don't make me shoot you! Throw the knife on the floor, and then put your hands on top of your head!"

"You don't understand!" Doris said, glaring at me. "Evil must be purged!"

"Throw the knife down, and put your hands on your head!" Detective François ordered. "I am not going to tell you again!"

With a lightning-quick flick of her wrist, Doris brought the knife to my throat. Pressing the blade against my neck, she said, "The wicked shall be turned—"

The gunshot was like a detonation, reverberating like a powerful shockwave. Dazed and terrified, I screamed as Doris's body fell toward me.

DAY TWENTY-THREE

Chapter Forty-Nine

"How are you feeling?" I asked Icarus as I sat in the chair next to his hospital bed.

"Could be better," Icarus said. "But not as worse as I could be, I guess."

The doctors expected Icarus to make a full recovery, but he'd lost a lot of blood and probably wouldn't be released from the hospital just yet. Two days had flown by in a blur since the nightmarish experience at the Esperança House, when Doris had tried to kill me. Once the police arrived—thanks to the cab driver, who had been suspicious of me and had called the cops because he'd thought I was "up to no good"—things happened in a quick, dizzying succession.

After falling on top of me from a gunshot wound to the shoulder, Doris had immediately rolled off the bed and onto the floor, where cops swarmed her. As they cuffed Doris and explained her rights, she continued to rant and rave about purging evil and sending the wicked to hell.

An ambulance was called, and when it arrived ten minutes later, Icarus had been transported to the hospital. Stazia Zacheo—the dead woman on the floor in the great room—had been zipped up in a black body bag and taken to the morgue.

With Doris being led away, I was attended to by paramedics while being interrogated by Detective François. Grateful to be alive, I'd given my story, telling him everything from the time I'd arrived at the Esperança House to the moment when Doris fell on top of me.

It took nearly three hours, what with the detective interjecting questions, but eventually, he was made aware of how Doris had admitted to killing her brother and the members of his alliance because she believed she was supposed to purge evil and send wicked people to hell.

Icarus had given a statement yesterday, telling Detective François he'd been tricked into coming to the Esperança House when Doris sent him a text, pretending to be Stazia, claiming to have proof of my innocence. Proof she would give him, for a price. When Icarus arrived, he'd found Stazia crawling down the hallway, bleeding from several deep stab wounds to the chest and neck. Hoping to save Stazia's life, Icarus had picked her up and brought her into the great room. Placing her on the floor, he'd removed the knife and was about to turn on a lamp when light flooded the room. Turning, still holding the knife, he'd seen me.

I'd seen him and had taken off, confused and horrified, assuming I'd been a fool and he'd been the killer all along. Icarus had followed me but encountered Doris. He'd been surprised to see her and even more flabbergasted when she knocked him over the head and then stabbed him.

"I'm just glad that every time I open my eyes," Icarus said, "I see you sitting at my bedside."

"I'm just so thankful that you're in this hospital bed and not ..." Feeling tears welling, I remembered how close Icarus had come to death.

Taking my hand, Icarus said, "I'm okay now."

I squeezed Icarus's hand, and he gave me a comforting glance. I smiled back, hoping to reassure him I was okay, but nothing could comfort me when I thought of Icarus's stab wound. I was still panicked and traumatized by what had happened to him.

Clearing my throat, I said, "I know, but you could have—"

"But, I didn't," he said and then gave me a mischievous grin. "I wasn't about to die and miss my chance to be with you."

"Silly," I said, teasing as I bent my head to give him a quick peck.

"Good news!" Octavia announced as she entered the hospital room, smiling as she walked to the foot of the hospital bed. "Great news, actually."

"What is it?" Icarus asked, carefully sitting up.

Curious, hopeful and wary, I stared at Octavia, my heart pounding.

"So, I just got back from a meeting with Detective François," Octavia said. "Doris did the old 'villain's soliloquy' yesterday, going on and on about how she'd killed her brother, Sam, Stazia and how she'd stabbed Joshua and Icarus because they were wicked and evil and deserved to die, and how she was executing the Lord's righteous judgment."

"I doubt very seriously that the Lord told her to kill three people," Icarus deadpanned.

"I'm sure she was upset that she didn't kill me," I said, remembering what Doris had called me, a wicked Jezebel.

"Profoundly upset," said Octavia. "But, the point of the meeting was to inform me that there is a video recording of Doris killing her brother."

"What?" I stared at Octavia, unable to register any other emotion except extreme shock.

"How?" Icarus asked.

"Remember the ugly fake gold medallion Henri always wore?" Octavia started. "Well, he was always recording every damn second of his miserable life, it seemed. The medallion worked like a digital camera. It had a SIM card that stored the videos he recorded. So, at the end of each day, Henri would remove the SIM card, place it into his laptop, and download his recordings for that day. Then he'd erase the SIM card and put it back into the medallion."

Astonished, I shook my head though I had a feeling I knew where the story was going.

"The day Henri was killed," Octavia said, "he was recording his life. But, of course, because he was killed, he didn't get a chance to download the recordings to his laptop."

"But, wait," said Icarus. "How did the medallion end up at Joshua's place?"

"Doris told me that Stazia beat her up and took the medallion," I said.

"Joshua is doing a bit better and has been able to talk to the cops," Octavia said. "He confirmed that Stazia asked him to keep the medallion for her, but she didn't tell him why. It's possible Stazia knew about the recording device, but we'll never know for sure."

"No, we won't," I said, sobered by the memory of Stazia's body zipped up in that black bag.

Octavia said, "Joshua also admitted to tampering with the video he filmed for Quinn so he could extort money from Doris."

Icarus shook his head. "Who knew there were so many extortionists working at the Heliconia."

"Well, according to the detective," Octavia said. "The video from the medallion on the day Henri was murdered shows Doris and Henri arguing about the blackmail money. Doris accuses him of tricking her and tells him she burned the 'filthy lucre.' That's when Henri went ballistic and hit Doris. But, Doris isn't having that. She picks up a kitchen knife—the same knife you tried to use to defend yourself with, Quinn—and she stabs Henri. Detective François said the video is crazy. It's from Henri's point of view and, apparently, when you watch it, you feel as though it's happening to you when Doris comes at Henri with that knife."

"Wow," Icarus said and then sighed.

"My sentiments exactly," I said, still reeling from the revelation.

"The great news is," Octavia said, "that the recording Henri was making the day he was killed also showed him trying to assault Quinn. The detective said it clearly shows Henri knocking you out and leaving you on the floor unconscious. In fact, when Doris came over, she argued with her brother about what he'd done to you."

My mind still spinning, I asked, "So, what's next, Octavia?"

"Well, after I talked to the detective, I spoke to the prosecutor."

"And?" Icarus prompted. "What does the evidence against Doris mean in terms of the charge against Quinn?"

My heart skipped, soared, fluttered, and did all sorts of crazy things as I thought about what it would mean to finally have the murder charge dismissed. The black cloud that had loomed over my life for the past weeks would disperse, and I would be able to enjoy, and appreciate and be grateful for, the blue skies and sunshine that would greet me.

"The prosecutors have dropped and dismissed the murder charge against you, Quinn," Octavia said, smiling. "You're a free woman and now you can feel free to move on with your life."

Epilogue

Six Months Later

"Oh, I forgot to tell you," Icarus said, slipping an arm around my waist.

"What's that?" I asked as we strolled along the water's edge of the hidden beach, the beautiful, magical expanse of white sand Icarus had introduced me to the day we first met so many months ago when I was a different person—anxious and illogical, suffering from crazy nightmares.

But, there were no more bad dreams.

And I absolutely, without a shadow of a doubt, was no longer going to be making unethical decisions, trying to be the hotshot litigator, desperate to make partner. The woman in black who always tried to kill me in those strange nightmares hadn't been trying to kill me. I'd been trying to kill the diabolical ambition threatening my soul and my sanity. I had regained confidence in all of my positive attributes, but I had a different purpose now, different dreams and desires.

After the murder charges against me were dropped, Icarus and I spent a month getting to know each other and realized we were falling in love and wanted to explore the possibility of what might develop between us.

Additionally, I wanted to explore potential career opportunities in the Palmchat Islands. With Octavia's help, I'd secured my first client, a local man from St. Felipe who hired me to represent him in a lawsuit against the powerful auction giant, Rutherford's. The case centered on a fancy vivid pink diamond, which my client claimed Rutherford's had stolen from him. I'd filed a suit, claiming the auction house knowingly tried to sell the diamond in contravention of the plaintiff's ownership rights. I'd won the case, and the gem had been returned to my client. It was a victory I could be proud of, one that hadn't given me crazy dreams.

"The Esperança House isn't the only thing my aunt left me. She also left me this," he said, pulling something from one of the pockets on his board shorts, and then displaying it on his palm.

"Oh ..." I squeaked, staring at the large, emerald-cut diamond ring. "It's beautiful."

"She left some explicit instructions with this ring," Icarus said.

"Explicit instructions?" I asked as we stopped near a palm tree.

"She said I couldn't sell it," he said. "And I couldn't pawn it, and I couldn't remove the stone and have the diamond cut into smaller pieces, or anything."

"Why would you want to destroy such a beautiful ring?" I asked, staring at the stone and then at Icarus, intoxicated by the desire and love in his gaze.

"Well, I think she just wanted to make sure I followed the instructions."

"And what were the instructions?" I asked, leaning toward him, my heart fluttering and soaring, as unrestrained joy pooled in my chest.

Slipping an arm around my shoulders, Icarus said, "Her instructions were that the only thing I could do with the ring was give it to the woman that I wanted to spend the rest of my life with ..."

"Those are pretty explicit instructions," I said, my heart slamming.

"She wanted me to find a beautiful, sexy, exciting, intelligent woman—"

"Beautiful, wonderful, sexy ..." Laughing, I asked, "What was the rest of it?"

"Exciting and intelligent," Icarus said, laughing with me. "And I'm happy to say, and you'll be glad to know, that I have found that woman."

"Oh, really?" I asked. "And is she beautiful, wonderful, sexy, exciting, intelligent?"

"She's all that, and so much more," Icarus said, leaning closer to me, his lips inches from mine. "And, you know her?"

"Is that right?" I put my hand on his strong jaw and then kissed him. "Well, she's a very lucky girl."

"And I'll be a lucky guy if she says yes," he said.

"Yes ..." I whispered, an entrancing rapture dancing throughout my body, "to what?"

"Quinn ..." Icarus took my hand, and his whiskey-colored gaze was so intent and potent, I felt my body responding in a way that only his love could accomplish.

Moving into his arms, I said, "Yes ..."

Icarus put the gorgeous diamond ring on my finger and then said, "Will you marry me?"

"Yes ..." I whispered, kissing him.

Note from Rachel

Thanks so much for taking the time to read Temptation Island. I hope you enjoyed it as much as I enjoyed writing it.

Honest reviews by readers are the most powerful way to help others discover my books. Please consider taking one minute to share your thoughts on the book by rating and reviewing it on Amazon. I'd be eternally grateful!

Exclusive Offer from Rachel Woods

Rachel Woods has been entertaining readers with her brand of romantic suspense -- sexy dangerous fiction. Now you can get one of her books for FREE, you just need to go to the link and tell her where to send it: http://eepurl.com/bxtIF9

In addition to the FREE book, you'll also get:

- Access to Rachel's Flash Fiction for FREE, exclusive to her mailing list subscribers.
- Chance to win books and Amazon gift cards in Rachel's monthly giveaways.
- Invitation to join Rachel's advance readers team — Sexy Dangerous Partners.

What are you waiting for? Join today!

Also by Rachel Woods

MURDER IN PARADISE SERIES

Stand-alone romantic mystery novels all set in the fictional Palmchat Islands.

REUNION ISLAND

SPENCER & SIONE SERIES

Gripping romantic suspense series with steamy romance, unpredictable plot twists and devastating consequences of deceit.

FLAWLESS MISTAKE

FLAWLESS DANGER

FLAWLESS BETRAYAL

About the Author

Rachel Woods studied journalism and graduated from the University of Houston where she published articles in the Daily Cougar. She is a legal assistant by day and a freelance writer and blogger with a penchant for melodrama by night. Many of her stories take place on the islands, which she has visited around the world. Rachel resides in Houston, Texas with her three sock monkeys.

For more information:
www.therachelwoods.com
therachelwoodsauthor@gmail.com

About the Publisher

BonzaiMoon Books is a family-run, artisanal publishing company created in the summer of 2014. We publish works of fiction in various genres. Our passion and focus is working with authors who write the books you want to read, and giving those authors the opportunity to have more direct input in the publishing of their work.

To receive special offers, bonus content and news about our latest ebooks, sign up for our mailing list on our website.

For more information:
www.bonzaimoonbooks.com
bonzaimoon@gmail.com

Made in the USA
Lexington, KY
06 January 2018